PATIENCE'S PERFECT WORK

Patience's Perfect Work

R.F. Sanderford

Contents

This book is dedicated to my wonderful
wife, Amanda.

"If not for you, the words would never
have made it from my heart to the page."

Foreword

Although an advocate for the world of words and reading, especially as a book editor, there was one genre that I had intentionally steered away from up to this point in my career—fiction; novels in particular.

Far too often, fiction can serve as an escape route from the realities of life that God calls for us to meet head on, to own, and to resolve. Sometimes I would see a story attempting to bring things full circle, to make certain lessons applicable to real life, but it was rarely done without creating a moral inconsistency or even committing significant spiritual compromise. The truth is, good intentions do not automatically equal good outcomes. In addition, as someone who has worked in both the ministry sector and the halls of Congress, I can say that the label of "Christian" or "faith-based" alone is not enough. True following of Christ must be manifested, not merely named—in everything that someone does, including the realm of written works.

For these reasons, I specialized in nonfiction. And then, this story came along.

After receiving a description, I agreed to review the manuscript. The plot sounded like a "worthy cause." So, I began reading—to see what exactly the story entailed.

And then, tears came.

Now, I am not a default crier by nature. But the Lord has a way of letting us sometimes respond emotionally to certain points of truth through the presence of tears. It is something that the Joseph of the Old Testament did after being reunited with his brothers in Egypt years and years after walking through the heartbreak of familial betrayal. In fact, the way that Joseph cried at one point is referred to in the original Hebrew as a *nathan*, and the word can be traced back to the meaning of "gift."

Tears are a gift. From God, to us—because they cleanse. They testify that something has been touched, released, or connected.

And not only did I have tears: so did the characters in the story. Many. On multiple occasions. And it is not because they were not emotionally mature or not personally stout but rather because they were walking through the process of life, and life comes with tears. A lot of them.

It's called the human experience.

And no one escapes the human experience.

What Ricky does in this story—the tale of a family and of a community, over the course of multiple generations—is relay the human experience . . . and he does one thing that, sadly, many writers forget to do. He shares the one and only solution; the one and only reality that anyone can turn to, if they wish to be fully alive while living out the human experience: the placing of our faith in the Lord Jesus Christ—including a personal relationship with Him—and how that choice impacts and redeems our existence (in spite of all that the human experience offers each one of us).

So, I encourage you to receive from the story any lessons that you might need to, to be open to crying (or laughing) as the twists and turns might lead you to, and to let patience have its perfect work in your own life as you progress through the human experience.

Expectantly,

Emma Hatcher

Editor, Author, and Book Coach
White Arrow Press LLC

One

Brothers

"Flight 417 from Los Angeles, arriving at Gate B," the voice announced throughout the Memphis airport.

"That's Frank's flight!" Opal Calloway said aloud. She was there with her family to welcome her oldest son home from war. She could barely contain the mistiness in her eyes as she hurried through the airport, eagerly searching for his gate.

"This way, Mama," Dan said, taking his mother's hand.

They all stood there, staring out of the series of windows that created a glass wall, as the plane slowly taxied into the gate. It was the spring of 1972, and some of America's finest were making their way home from a war that had no winners and seemingly no end. Sadly, many were returning home to a country that did not care. Society had blurred the lines between right and wrong, good and bad. A good number of those who had taken up arms for God and country, duty and honor, would pay double the price. But that was not the case for Frank Calloway, because the opinions of society meant nothing to a mother. There would be no spitting, no shouts of "baby killer," no pointing of fingers in anger—instead, a loving family awaited him, and it would be a true homecoming.

He had served two tours in Vietnam. The second tour was to take the place of Dan, his younger brother. Only a deep love would move one brother to volunteer to stay in hell one year extra, just to keep the

"

other from seeing such horrors. Patiently, Opal and the rest waited as, one by one, each passenger exited the craft.

Family meant a lot to the Calloway clan. Opal and her late husband, Joel, were third-generation Mississippi farmers. They had raised their sons, Dan and Frank, to carry on the family business with much love and respect for the land and for others.

Sarah Calloway searched every face filing off the plane, looking for the first glimpse of her husband. The crowd gathered and moved in closer, hindering Frank Jr.'s view. So, he held his mother's hand and stared up at her and waited for that expression: the one that would tell him that his daddy was home.

Finally, Frank stepped off the plane. Sarah began to cry and wave her hands. "Frank! Frank!" she shouted; her emotions were contagious as tears began to run down each family member's face. Frank Jr. leapt up and down at his mother's excitement, holding tightly with both hands to his mother's arm. His small head danced and weaved back and forth. He was trying with all his might to catch a glimpse of his father through the mass of bodies shuffling to and fro.

Frank made his way through the crowd to Sarah. He wrapped his arms around his wife and lifted her into the air, both of them weeping with joy as he caressed and kissed her face over and over again. As he let her back down, he stared at her, trying to convince himself that she was real. He softly declared, "I am never leavin' you again."

Frank Jr. wrapped his arms around his father's waist and repeated over and over, "I missed you, Daddy! I missed you!"

Frank lifted him up into his arms and said, "I missed you, too, Buddy! I missed you a whole lot! My goodness, you've gotten big!"

"Yep, I'll be ten in a few months," Frank Jr. declared.

"I know, Son, I know! Did you take care of Mama while I was gone?"

"I sure did—just ask her!" Frank Jr. answered as he pointed toward his mother.

Looking around, all that Frank could see were Calloways smiling and crying.

"My goodness, Sarah—you brought the whole family!" Frank said with a slight quiver in his voice. As he surveyed their faces, a sense of rapture flooded over his heart. His eyes settled on his mother, who had been patiently waiting for her son to call out to her. But, without any words, he walked over to her, leaned over, and mother and son embraced. She hugged him with all of her strength. She was hugging past the man to her child. It's the kind of embrace that only a mother knows. Then, she released him. The slight quiver in Frank's voice from earlier had now morphed into tears. They streamed down his face and gathered on the lapel of his jacket, soaking through just above his heart.

Opal reached up with her kerchief and gently wiped the tears first from her son's cheeks, and then from her own. Being the forever-loving, attentive mother, the first words that she spoke were, "You look thin, Honey."

"Army food will do that to you, Mama," Frank replied with a half-smile. Both knew that food had little to do with Frank's weary appearance.

Out of all the joy that Opal felt for her son's homecoming, there was still a vapor of sadness. She noticed the lines on his face and an extra gray hair here and there. His looks exceeded his twenty-nine years, for combat drains a man's soul. In one sense, he had not changed, yet he was not the same. Opal felt as if she were looking at a beautiful painting, one which had faded over time. The image was still there, but life had left its mark.

Dan walked over and put his arms around Frank, "Welcome home, Brother! I love you. Elizabeth sends her love too. She wanted to meet you here with the rest of us, but Tom's been runnin' a bit of fever, so she kept him home."

"I love you too, Dan. And you tell Elizabeth that's just fine and to just take care of that boy." After a brief pause, he continued, "Better yet, I'll tell her *myself*. I know your better-half well. She's a good lady, and I know she would've been here if she could."

From that point on in the welcome, their words were brief as they both struggled to keep their composure. There were only three years separating the two in age, and they had always been very close. Much had happened over the last several months, and now they hoped to put the hard times behind them.

Frank noticed the little, blonde head peeking out from behind Dan. "Mercy, Dan! Is that Dee?"

"Yep, he just turned six," Dan said, pulling his son from behind him and positioning him in front of Frank. Dee continued to hold his father's hand as Frank smiled and knelt down to Dee's level. "Hey, little man. I guess you probably don't remember me, but I'm your Uncle Frank," he said, offering his hand to shake Dee's.

The boy looked up at his father momentarily and then back at Frank. After a second or two, he slowly let go of his father's hand and stepped into Frank's uniformed chest, past the hand that had been perched in his direction. Dee wrapped his arms around his neck, laying his head on Frank's shoulder and gently patting him on his back.

With his lip quivering once more over the tender moment, Frank embraced his nephew and glanced up at Dan with a forced half-smile. The whole family was moved by Dee's small, unexpected act of compassion. Sometimes, a child's pure heart can see more clearly what is needed for true healing to begin.

The long drive home was mostly quiet—the occasional up and down of the wipers clearing away the mist that was peppering the windshield was the only sound for a while. The excitement of the day had gotten the best of Sarah and the boys, who had been asleep for quite some time.

"I'm sorry I missed Daddy's funeral," Frank's words broke the silence.

"It's okay, Frank," Opal, always a comforter, responded, "Everyone understood. It wasn't your fault. Daddy was so proud of you and what you were doin'. He knew that war came with enough heartache—he wouldn't want you to let this weigh you down. He loved you very much and would be quick to tell you, 'Don't worry, Frankie, we'll see each other again.' The important thing is that you are home now—for good."

"That's right, I am home . . . home again," Frank said, slowly closing his eyes and leaning his head back on the seat of the old station wagon.

Frank and Sarah enjoyed his homecoming after being apart for so long. It was a true blessing to hold each other again; to be together again. That first night, Frank lay there silent, watching Sarah as she slept. He watched as her side slowly rose and fell with every breath. He inched closer to her—close enough to feel a gentle blow with each exhale. He studied her face and the long hair that he had always treasured. It was important to Frank to take it all in. It helped him shake off where he had been and focus on where he was now. He thought about the times behind him and about the times that lay ahead—feeling optimistic about their future. He determined through the early hours of the morning that the nightmares from "over there" would not make their way here to his home . . . to *their* home.

The next week, spring rains began to give way to clear skies, and Dan and Frank were eager to get back to work. So, they went into town to pick up some tractor parts. Kyle's Tractor and Farm Supply was a landmark in Pelo, Mississippi. The Kyle family built the store in 1901, and it was built to stay. Its plank walls and ceilings gave it a distinct appearance. The smell of cedar and hay ever permeated the air. Anything and everything related to farming was to be found at Kyle's. "Jumpin' Jehoshaphat! It's the brothers Calloway," Mr. Kyle bellowed as he moved across the store toward the pair.

George "Bull" Kyle was enormous in size and spirit—six feet, eight inches tall and just shy of 300 pounds. He had earned the nickname *Bull* because, supposedly, in his younger years, he had pulled a full-grown Braford from a mud bog with his bare hands. But some would say it was because of the nonsense that he carried on.

"Frank, it is so good to see you, Son! When'd you get back?"

"A few days ago," Frank replied.

"A few days ago! And Dan already has you out *workin' again?*"

"Yeah, well, it's good to get things back to normal," Frank's response was accompanied by a slight shrug.

The brothers knew the real reason that they found themselves at Kyle's store that day. Frank needed a distraction from what lay ahead. He had been on the other side of the world, knee-deep in fear and death when they laid his father to rest. Today was the day that he would say goodbye. We are forever our parents' children, regardless of age, time or distance. They see us with their hearts, not their eyes. Frank knew this and the pain that would come with seeing his father's grave. The child in him wanted to put it off as long as he could.

"That's true, Frank. What can I do for you boys?"

"We're needin' a PTO clutch for a John Deere 730," Dan replied.

"A PTO clutch for a JD 730? Dan, how long are you gonna hang on to that Johnny Popper? That thing is an antique!" Bull's intonation could make even the most simple statements pop like fireworks.

"Well, Bull, if we all got rid of everythin' because it was old, Jean would have traded you in years ago," Dan said with a grin; his ever-present toothpick protruding from the corner of his mouth, this time pointed at a near forty-five degree angle.

Bull, bursting into husky laughter replied, "Ain't that the truth? I'll have your clutch in about a week, Dan. Speakin' of Mrs. Jean—y'all come by sometime for supper, and I'll have her fry up some of her chicken. Frank, we appreciate your service, son. It's good to have you home. Tell Mrs. Opal that I said hello."

"We'll do it, Bull—and thanks," Frank replied.

On their way home, Dan and Frank passed by the cemetery. It was the third time that the brothers had passed Pelo Cemetery that day. But this time, they stopped. Dan killed the engine, and the two just sat there; silently staring out of the windshield. Several minutes passed, and not a word was spoken. Frank clasped his hands together in his lap and slowly looked down toward the floor of the truck, as if silently saying a prayer for strength. He stayed in this position for only a few seconds and then drew in a deep breath and let it out. He looked over at Dan and gave a gentle nod, affirming his readiness. The two brothers exited the truck and began to walk to the entrance of the cemetery. Frank hated that he had missed his father's funeral, but war is hell for a lot of different reasons.

The brothers had been close to their father, Joel. They seemed to be carbon copies of him, each in their own way. Both shared his fortitude and his strength—strength developed from hard work and hard times. He had taught the Calloway boys that there was never a wrong time to do the right thing. The brothers loved their father deeply.

The feeling was surreal as they walked through the garden of stone. Joel Calloway had been larger than life in the eyes of his sons, so losing him seemed almost an impossibility. It was as if they were visiting the grave of a friend or distant relative, but not their father. Seeing the words made it all too real, "Joel Gray Calloway, beloved father and husband."

The men stood there, quietly looking at the stone and the ground before it. Frank leaned over as if to say something and posted himself up with a hand on each knee. As he did so, the pain of losing his father, which had been deferred many months before, came flooding back. During his two tours in Vietnam, killing and death had become an everyday occurrence for Frank. He had seen it done, and he had done it himself; but today, death's reality laid on Frank's heart like an anvil. He began to cry, trembling with tears like a child with a broken heart. Dan never said a word, for fear of crying himself; he just stood close by with a single hand on Frank's back, trying to provide comfort, yet ready to catch him should he fall. He knew exactly what his brother was feeling. Not one day had passed that Dan didn't think about their father.

Dan and Frank sat on the grass for a while next to their father's grave. Neither spoke, as if waiting patiently to hear their father's voice with a word of instruction or guidance. In the quiet, both relived memories of him from their childhood. Frank recalled the first time that Joel had let him drive the tractor. He was barely big enough to see over the steering wheel. So, his dad sat him in the cab, holding Frank in his lap. "That furrow I left behind was all over the place," Frank remembered within himself, a faraway smile coming to his face for a moment as he did so. Joel had never said a word of discouragement. He just patted him on the back and said, "Good job, Frankie." Dan's thoughts took him to a time from his childhood when Joel saved him from a copperhead. They had been on a camping trip. He remembered how the snake emerged from a spread of ivy that was only inches from his feet. Then, in an instant, his dad scooped him up with one arm and stepped directly on top of the snake's head—all in one lightning-fast motion. "I didn't even know that he was close by—the truth was, he had been there the whole time," Dan thought to himself. After about a half hour between the inward waves of memory and grief, Dan broke the silence, "Frank, Dad doesn't have any flowers." The brothers looked at each other, then surveyed the trees about them. One hosted a handful of early spring blooms. They closed in on the magnolia tree, which seemed to almost be waiting patiently for them. Dan drew his pocket knife, and they fashioned a wreath. Then, they gently laid it on their father's grave.

"Now, that's better," Frank said with a smile.

"Yeah, Dad loved magnolias," Dan replied.

In that moment, it was as if the brothers had received the words from their father that they had been waiting on: "Work together and love one another. You'll make your own memories." And, "When you don't know what to do, just do what you know."

It was September 1977. Dee and Tom Calloway were starting a new year at Pelo Middle School—one that would draw them closer as brothers. At 2:45 in the afternoon, the school bell rang, declaring freedom for the day. Dee rounded the corner of the school gym, look-ing for Tom. There, he found Jody Simms waiting for him.

"Hey, Jody, what's goin' on? Have you seen Tom?" Dee asked.

"Yeah, I've seen him—and that's why I'm here. His mouth has got-ten him into a bad situation," Jody replied.

"What's he done now?"

"You know Jake Stephens?"

"Yeah, I know him. Ain't he in junior high, and what's he got to do with Tom?"

"Well, Mr. Umber, who is Tom's math teacher—"

"Yeah, I know him—he taught me in fourth grade," Dee inter-rupted, his impatience over seemingly meaningless details starting to show through.

"Well," Jody started, his voice fully animated, "he asked Tom to take some papers up to the high school office for him. So, Tom takes the papers, runs out the door, and zips around the corner of the buildin' and down the sidewalk to the office. Jake and a couple of his buddies were standin' there, next to those old, tall shrubs—you know, the ones that the principal caught George Temple and Jan Bobbins kissin' at that one time?"

"Yeah—I know where you're talkin' about. But you still haven't told me where Tom is," Dee uttered with increasing irritation.

"I'm gettin' to that," Jody continued. "Turns out, that's where Jake and his buddies go to smoke and talk about girls and stuff. Well, he saw Tom runnin' down the sidewalk and tripped him as he came by, and Tom hit the ground . . . hard. Not only that, but Mr. Umber's papers flew out of his hands and all over the ground and sidewalk." Jody's hands flailed into the air as he spoke, as if to emphasize the chaos he was describing. "Jake and his buddies just laughed and told Tom that the sidewalk belonged to them and that he'd have to walk around. Tom just popped right up and stepped up onto the side-walk—that's when Jake shoved him down.

"Let me guess—Tom shoved him back."

"Yep, and now they're goin' to fight after school today."

Dee's eyes widened as he heard this part, "Jake is twice Tom's size and probably won't show up alone. Where are they supposed to be fightin'?"

"Behind the lunchroom. What are you goin' to do?"

"I'm goin' to try and even the odds."

"Well, I'm comin' with you!"

Dee's suspicions were confirmed when they found Tom and Jake—along with three of Jake's friends—behind the lunchroom.

"Hold on, Jake! You know this ain't right," Dee said.

"Well, Dee Calloway—you comin' to save Baby Brother?" Jake asked in a sarcastic tone.

"Naw, I'm just here to make sure it's a fair fight," Dee looked Jake square in the eye. It was not the time to let any fear show through.

"Fair?" Jake replied with a smug smile.

"Yeah, I'm pretty sure Tom can take you. Me and Jody are just here to make sure none of your mouth breathers jump on Tom once he starts whoopin' you good," Dee said, turning his glare to Jake's buddies.

"Hey, I don't need any help with your munchkin of a brother," Jake retorted, the thought of having an audience to watch him receive back up suddenly rubbing his pride the wrong way.

"Alright then, but let me ask you one thing. Suppose Tom *does* whoop you, what you goin' tell everybody then? You know, you bein' twice Tom's size and all. I mean . . ." Dee said, pausing momentarily for effect, "you know you *could* whoop Tom—but even if you do, you'll have to whoop him every time he sees you. Sooner or later, you're gonna be the one who gets whooped."

Jake's three friends began to look at each other. Jake himself hesitated, as there was some degree of truth to Dee's words. "Aw, you're just stallin'—tryin' to save Little Brother," Jake replied, his confidence waning.

"You're right, Jake, but you know what that means?"

"What?"

"It means every time you fight Tom, you're goin' to have to fight me."

"And me," Jody interjected.

"Maybe the best thing is for you to let Tom out of this," Dee continued.

"Wait a minute," Tom exclaimed with his brow lowered and his fist clenched, "he started it!"

"Tom!" Dee hissed through clenched teeth, pulling Tom to the side and speaking low enough the others couldn't hear what he had to say, "Do you want this fella to whoop you every day for the next three years?"

"I ain't scared of him!" Tom shot back, looking past Dee at Jake.

Dee placed both hands on Tom's shoulders and gave him a knowing look, "Tom, all I need for you to do is shut your mouth and let me talk. What do you think Pop will say when he finds out you've been fightin'?"

Tom's expression changed—it was the first time that he had thought about that part of the equation. "Well . . . okay."

"So, what's it goin' to be, Jake?" Dee asked loudly, turning once more to look at the aggressor.

Jake had known what the outcome was going to be, but all of Dee's angles had planted just enough doubt to change his mind. "Well, I'm goin' to give the munchkin a pass—this time. I don't want to send him home cryin' to his momma," Jake said, turning to his friends with a smile and a wink, as if he was showing them what a big man he was for letting Tom go. But Dee knew the truth, and so did Jake. Facing Tom was one thing, but dealing with both Calloway brothers was not something that Jake would want to be a part of.

Dee beckoned to Tom, "Come on. It's gettin' late, and Mom's gonna be mad if we don't get home soon."

The next morning, Dee and Tom grabbed their books and started their walk to school. It was a mild day. The air was clear with less of the humidity that summer had brought. The sun shined bright through the tree branches and onto the boys' faces. It was like someone was turning a light on and off as they walked down the tree-covered path. The road from the Calloway home was a mile of dirt and gravel, followed by another mile of paved road before it reached the school yard. Along the way, Tom came across a tin can and began kicking it as they walked. In between the clanging noise of the can skipping and tumbling across the gravel, Tom began to reflect on the events of the day before. Finally, with one swift, hard kick, Tom sent the can flying off of the road and into the ditch. Only then did either of the boys speak.

"Dee, why did you stop me and Jake from fightin'?"

"Well, cause I didn't want nothin' bad to happen to you."

"Aww, I'm a lot tougher than Jake Stephens."

"Maybe so, but what about Jake's friends? They wouldn't have let you get the best of Jake. They would've hurt you bad, Tom."

"Well . . . I didn't think about that," Tom slowly let out.

"I know. 'Sides that, that's what brothers do—they look out for each other, because sometimes one can see the bad stuff before the other one does. A good brother protects the other one from it."

Tom walked along in silence, staring down at the road below him—then, all at once, stopped. Dee, noticing it, stopped and looked back at Tom. With a look of complete enlightenment, Tom looked up at Dee and said, "So, that's why Uncle Frank fought in Pop's place over in that jungle? He saw the bad stuff before Pop did and wanted to protect him?"

The point had gone much deeper with Tom than Dee had intended, but his grinning reply showed his gladness that the point had been so well made, "Yeah, that's right, Tom. Now, come on, Munchkin, we've got to get to school."

They walked on in silence until they reached the school yard. Stopping again for only a moment, Tom looked at his elder and said, "Dee, I'm glad you're my brother."

Two

Caregivers and Caretakers

Dee and Tom ran across the field that was behind their house as fast as they could go, with a setting sun reminding them of the hour. While they hadn't received the summons yet, they knew that their mother called for supper only once—after that, you were out of luck. As Dee came in the back door, he made his way quickly to the bathroom. On his way back through the house, he noticed Doc Simmons sitting at the dinner table in a chair, across from Pop. Dee's appetite had put him in such a hurry that he had missed the scene on his way to go wash up. As he walked closer, he could see the doctor, calmly taking stitches out of Pop's arm. Dee's mother also sat at the kitchen table, watching the procedure—obviously, dinner would be served later than usual that night. Even in the mid-seventies, it was not that uncommon for a doctor to make house calls, especially in a small town like Pelo.

It had only been a few weeks since Pop had cut his arm while working on the barn roof. Dee recalled the day that it had happened and that he had never seen so much blood. He remembered the fear that he felt for his father and the worry that had shown on his mother's face. But today, all that remained was a thin, pink line, running down Pop's arm. Dee's twelve-year-old mind marveled at the good job that Doc Simmons had done. As the doctor prepared to leave, Dee asked him, "How did you learn to heal people?"

Doc Simmons, with a broad smile, replied, "Son, I truly appreciate the compliment, but God does the healin'—we're just here to help with the stitchin'."

That evening, as the Calloway family sat enjoying their supper, Dee's mind couldn't escape the impact of the doctor's visit. He sat in silent thought, his chin resting in the palm of one hand. As he twirled his fork between his fingers on his other hand, he pondered the conversation that he and Doc Simmons had earlier that day. The idea of helping God appealed to Dee. But he struggled to understand it. The silence of Dee's thoughts was broken by his father's booming voice, "Dee, you'd better stop that daydreamin' and eat. Your supper is gettin' cold.

"Yes, sir," Dee distantly replied, beginning to stab away at his green beans. Dan could tell that Dee was consumed by something.

"Dee," Dan's voice broke through again, "What's got ahold of your mind, Son?"

Dee, slightly shrugged his shoulders. "Nothin' . . . I guess." He had replied not really knowing how to answer the question.

"Well, it's bound to be somethin'. You've hardly touched your chicken, and I know that's your favorite."

Dee scooped up a mouthful of mashed potatoes and swallowed them down before answering his father.

"Well, Pop, you know when Doc Simmons was over here, workin' on your arm?"

"Yeah, what about it?"

"Well, me and Doc talked for a bit on the porch before he left," Dee's appetite found itself again, as he began to open up to his father—in between an increasingly steady procession of chicken, beans, and potatoes—about the profound conversation that he had with Doc Simmons.

"Well, he told me that, to him, bein' a doctor was callin'. I told him that I had only ever heard of a preacher bein' called—not a doctor, or anyone else, for that fact."

Dee stopped talking just long enough to take a big drink of tea to wash down his supper, then he continued, "He told me that what doctors do and preachers do was alike in some ways, because it was all about healin', and healin' comes from heaven. But I don't really understand what he meant by that. I mean, I've never seen our preacher give someone medicine or fix a broken bone or stitch up a big ol' cut or any cool stuff like that. So, how's it the same?"

Dee paused again to reach across the table for a piece of cornbread. Dan thought for a minute about what Dee had just told him. If his twelve-year-old son was going to be that inquisitive about such a serious subject, then Dan owed it to him to give some serious thought to it before he replied.

"Dee, let me ask you somethin'. Do you know what a *callin'* is?"

Dee thought for a second, then answered, "Well, when I was little and I heard a preacher say that God called him, I thought that he actually got a call from God. But I found out that wasn't true after I couldn't find God's number in the phone book."

Dan smiled at his son's honesty and began to do his best to explain what Doc Simmons had meant. "Dee, a callin' is when you feel somethin' pullin' you toward a task or a job. In Doc's case, that somethin' is actually God. He believes that God wanted him to be a doctor. Because he believes that, he wants to do the best he can for his patients. A preacher is the same way—he feels God's pullin' him toward the task of preachin'. He believes that God wants him to be a preacher. Does that make sense?"

"Yes, sir. But how is it all about healin'? I mean, how is it the same?"

"Dee, what Doc Simmons meant was that doctors like him help with the healin' on the outside and preachers help with the healin' of our spirits—what's inside," Dan said, first motioning toward the long, pink line running down his arm and then to the space on his chest where his heart was. "In both cases, God brings the healin'. That's why he said that it was all about the healin' and that healin' comes from heaven."

The Pelo Rangers and the Niobi Cougars had been big rivals for years, one that had been spurred on by the social and economic differences in the towns. While Niobi had seen much growth with large business and manufacturing, Pelo had remained predominantly a farming community with only small, local businesses. So, when these two met, it was like "the country came to town."

Dan enjoyed watching his nephew play ball, and the family rarely missed a game. Most every Friday night, you would find Dan, Dee, and Tom cheering on Frank Jr. Dee looked forward to the time that he would be able to play football in a few years, and he was always excited to watch his cousin play. The announcer would give the names of each player as they made their way onto the field, "Now playing linebacker for our Pelo Rangers, number forty-eight, Frankie Calloway!"

One night, Dan came to Frankie with a challenge, "Nephew, I'll tell you what—every time you sack the quarterback, I'll pay you two dollars."

"Two bucks! You mean every time I sack the quarterback, you're gonna give me two dollars?"

"Yep! But YOU have to do it, no assists."

With shoulders back and chest out, Frank Jr. replied, "No problem, Uncle Dan!" On the first defensive play, Frank Jr. shot through the line and introduced the visiting quarterback to the freshly cut sod. The home crowd roared. Frank Jr. looked up and searched the crowd until he found Dan, who was sitting next to his dad. He smiled and raised up two fingers. By the end of the game, Dan was out fourteen dollars.

Friday night came, and the air was electric. Frank Jr. and the rest of the Rangers, including Bobby Ford, lined up to take the field. They all stood there, trying to control the excitement in their gut, like gladiators waiting to enter the arena for battle.

Bobby Ford played running back for the Rangers, and he was one of Frank Jr.'s best friends. They had grown up together. Bobby's family had farmed for a few years before going bankrupt. Frank Jr.

remembered the day that all the Fords' farming equipment was auctioned off. He remembered how Bobby's mom had wept. Mr. Ford eventually found a job, which was driving a truck for a local stockyard. Bobby's family had been through a lot of ups and downs, but Bobby never seemed to be phased by the bad times. He was always caught up in his big dreams—dreams of being a professional football player. He would spend hours talking about the game and the players. He even had a list of the teams that he wanted to play for after he graduated from college. The idea of not being a football star had never entered his mind. It was his ticket to a better life for his family.

Bobby was definitely in his element this particular night. He could barely contain his excitement. Right before they ran onto the field, he turned to Frank Jr. and said, "Good luck, Frankie!"

"You, too, Bobby—now, let's show them what the Rangers can do! Oh yeah—don't forget, pizza at my house after the game tonight!"

Back and forth the game went—finally, late in the fourth quarter, the Rangers took the lead, 24 to 17. Frank Jr. and the rest of the defense held the Cougars to a three and out. The Ranger offense took the field, and Bobby moved into position, through the noise of the crowd Bobby heard the quarterback "Down, set, hut-hut-hut!" The line moved, and, like a thousand times before, Bobby felt the ball jam between his hands as he ran to the outside.

Frank Jr. screamed with all of his might, "GO, BOBBY, GO! RUN, MAN, RUN!" following him down the sideline. The announcer called out play by play, "He's at the forty! The thirty-five! The thirty! The twenty-five! And stopped at the twenty-yard line! What a great run by Bobby Ford!" The referee blew his whistle, ending the play, and the players began to make their way back to the line.

Bobby's mom was the first one to notice that her son was not moving. What had started out as cheers soon became her frantic screams that silenced the crowd. The staff, along with Mr. Ford, ran onto the field and over to Bobby. Time ceased as both teams knelt and prayed there in the grass. The sick feeling in Dee's stomach began to grow with the sound of the approaching ambulance. The shock of the scene muted everyone as the EMTs loaded Bobby up and drove away. Niobi won that night, but no one seemed to care.

Funerals are a strange thing to a teenager. They are so out of place in their lives, because, for young people, everything is new and great and hopeful. But at a funeral, that everything is gone. Mr. and Mrs. Ford had never known about Bobby's heart condition—a congenital condition that had remained hidden until . . . it didn't. It was hard for any to comprehend. All that Frank Jr. understood was that his friend was gone.

Frank Jr. walked up to the coffin, but he couldn't look at his friend. He turned to Mrs. Ford and managed to get out what he had rehearsed, "I am very sorry for your loss," before he broke into tears.

She held him as they wept together. Frank Jr. whispered through his tears, "He was my friend."

Mrs. Ford looked down at him, her face worn with pain and tears. She said, "I know, Honey. Just knowin' that he had good friends like you is helpin' me get through this." She paused, looking off somewhere in the distance, somewhere eternal, while she gathered her next words. "I know that God has a plan for all of us. Bein' Bobby's friend was your part in God's plan for him. His dad and I got to share our love with him for seventeen years. I try to focus on that—that was our part. You know, Bobby told me about you givin' him your cleats last year. His dad was out of work then, and we couldn't afford to buy him any. He also told me that they were the new ones that your parents had bought for you." Finally, she said, "Thank you, Frankie. Thank you for bein' a good friend to my son."

Dee watched it all from the light-blue sofa that was sitting in the waiting area just outside of the viewing room. It was the first funeral that he had ever attended. He and Tom sat and watched all the visitors file in, sign the visitor log, then line up to see Bobby laying there in that box.

Most of them, Dee knew; but some, he didn't. He struggled to understand it all. Bobby was young—why did he die? What would Mr. and Mrs. Ford do now? Their son was . . . *gone*. These and many more questions flooded Dee's mind. He imagined what it would be like if he were to lose Tom and how it would make him feel. Then, he thought about how painful it must be for Mr. and Mrs. Ford. His eyes began to well up with tears. For the first time, he understood what his dad meant when he talked about hurting on the inside. Eventually, everyone slowly made their way to the auditorium. There, Dee watched the pallbearers wheel Bobby into the room. There were songs sung and kind words spoken. It was those words that made Dee understand how a hurting heart could find healing.

As the lessons in life—both large and small—continued for Frank Jr., Dee, and Tom, Frank Jr. would be the first of the trio to graduate from Pelo High School. Much to his mother's dismay, he enlisted in the U.S. Army on his eighteenth birthday.

Three

Life Is the Land, and Land Is the Life

Dan Calloway was a true farmer. Farming was all that he had ever known. He and his older brother, Frank, were fourth-generation farmers. It was a way of life that had started with their great-great-grandfather, Lucian Calloway.

Lucian Calloway's parents had died when he was eight years old. He and his sister, Delores, who was three years his junior, would spend the rest of their young lives in an orphanage in Ireland. It was a difficult childhood, to say the least. They were thirteen and ten when the Irish Potato Famine hit—what some would refer to as the Great Hunger. It ravaged the land, and along with it came the typhus epidemic, which would take Delores from him in the fall of 1847. With no one and no reason to stay, Lucian decided to try and build a home in the New World. So, in 1850, at the age of eighteen, he—like so many others—boarded a ship bound for America.

He found work on the docks in North Carolina, then later worked in a foundry in Virginia. While in Virginia, Lucian frequented a pub owned by a German couple known by the name of Schteinhaus. It was there that he would meet the love of his life.

As was Lucian's custom on payday, he made his way to the Schteinhaus pub for a pint—and a glimpse of Hannah. Every Friday, he entered the pub and made his way across the smoke-filled room to his favorite spot. This darkened nook was positioned directly across from the kitchen, located behind the bar. Lucian knew that if there was any hope of Hannah noticing him, this was the place to be. Unfortunately, Lucian was not the only one vying for her attention. The thing about German pubs is that there are far more Germans than Irishmen. Consequently, thanks to alcohol and too much pride, Lucian found himself in what the Irish refer to as a brannigan. Even though Lucian held his own for a short time, he realized that it is never smart for an Irishman to start a fight in a German pub.

Mr. Schteinhaus, being the kind man that he was, had his daughter administer the much needed care to Lucian. The dish rag, dipped in cool water, stung as Hannah wiped away the blood, dirt, and sawdust from Lucian's swollen face. As his eyes opened slowly, her image came into focus. He recognized her blue eyes, blonde hair, and gentle smile. Lucian smiled and said only one word, "Angel."

On Christmas Eve, 1854, Lucian Calloway asked Hannah Schteinhaus for her hand in marriage. By the next year, he had saved enough money to move to a land that was said to be prime for farming—a place called Mississippi. There, Lucian purchased a hundred acres and began growing cotton. He favored the land in this area because it reminded him of his childhood home in Ireland before the orphanage.

By the start of the Civil War in 1861, Lucian was on his way to becoming a successful cotton farmer. But the years that followed would take their toll. When Lucian finally returned from the war, his house and most of his land had been lost to "the Northern Aggressors." Ironically, Lucian had never owned any slaves. He had witnessed—and experienced—much oppression throughout his youth, and causing others misery just was not his way.

He, like many a farm owner in the South, was not a wealthy plantation owner. A good number of them were simple farmers who fought for their homes. Upon his return from the war, he found that his house had been burned to the ground and that Hannah was gone. Without any traces of her whereabouts, Lucian feared the worst but hoped that she had traveled back to Virginia to stay with her parents, perhaps once the fighting had become severe. In hopes of being reunited, Lucian made the arduous journey north to Virginia. He had little money or possessions, and food was scarce after the war.

It took him ten days to make it to the home of Franklin and Greta Schteinhaus. There, he found that the Schteinhaus home had been commandeered by the Union army and then converted into a medical triage post. Mrs. Schteinhaus had died from fever soon after the war had begun, and Mr. Schteinhaus had nearly gone mad after losing Greta and witnessing so many of the horrors of war. To Lucian's dismay, he found that Hannah had not returned to Virginia. So, brokenhearted, he steered his horse southward and began the journey back to Mississippi, wondering how to pick up the pieces of what was left of their former life.

Each night, by his campfire, he would take out his only portrait of Hannah. When Lucian left to join the Confederate army, the only personal items that he had taken with him were the portrait of her, a Bible, and a hunting knife that Mr. Schteinhaus had given him. These items never left his side. Each evening, he would talk to the portrait. He would tell her how much he missed her and how he wished that he would have had more time with her. He would talk about the children that he wished that they could have had—the son who would have been named Frank, after his grandfather, and two girls named after both grandmothers. As he talked, tears rolled slowly down his cheeks, leaving lines through the dust on his face. In the night, he would dream of Hannah, seeing her standing there in her flower garden. She would look up from the lilies and smile at him—just before he would awaken to the realization that it was all gone.

The third day into his journey home, Lucian came upon a troop of Union soldiers. They were part of a cavalry that had been commissioned by General Grant to apprehend and bring to justice any remaining Confederate loyalists. They had been given freedom to arrest anyone who they deemed to be a threat to the Union. Seeing his knife and long rifle, they arrested Lucian. As they shackled him, he was informed that he was charged with being a member of Bloody Bill Quantrill's Confederate Militia, some of whom had reportedly fled to Mexico and not surrendered to the Union.

Lucian was repeatedly whipped and interrogated. For three days, he traveled with the soldiers, south into Georgia. One night, the troop decided to bivouac next to a small stream. The guard in charge of the prisoners seemed to take pleasure in pilfering through their personal belongings. He sadistically joked about how funny it would be if he were to kill Lucian with his own knife. Through it all, Lucian managed to keep Hannah's portrait hidden from the guard—until, one night, the guard overheard Lucian talking softly to it. Immediately, the guard seized the image and made note of Hannah's beauty, remarking next that she was better off dead than married to an ignorant "mick," especially one that was "Rebel trash." Though it took all of his remaining strength, Lucian stilled his anger until he was sure that all the troops had bedded down for the night.

Prisoners were not allowed to bathe and were often made to walk behind the pack horses. The dust and filth from the horses not only covered the prisoners with a hard stench but would also get into their cuts and abrasions, causing infection. Consequently, they were made to sleep away from the camp of soldiers, usually resulting in only one guard being assigned to watch them all—a guard who sometimes fell asleep. On the third night, Lucian eased through the darkness and up behind the guard, who was nodding to stave off his drowsiness.

Lucian knew the danger of waking the other soldiers, but, in his mind, if he got shot, then at least he would see Hannah again in the next life. Lucian's heart pounded as he raised his shackled hands up behind the guard. In one swift motion, his arms rose up and over the soldier's head, he sank the links between his locked cuffs into the soldier's neck and tightened them with all his strength. The soldier flayed his arms about, clawing and grasping at the chains. He opened his mouth to scream but Lucian tightened the chain, silencing his attempt to cry for help.

Seconds seemed like hours. Finally, all that was heard in the stillness was the soldier's heart beating, as well as his own. Both pounding and both seeking escape. Then, only Lucian's remained. Instantly, the sounds of night returned: crickets chirping, horses shuffling a little from the disturbance, and water flowing over the rocks in the creek nearby. As quietly as possible, Lucian frantically searched the guard until he found the key to his chains. He freed himself, gathering Hannah's portrait from the guard's shirt pocket and then any supplies that he could carry. It was too risky to try and retrieve his horse, which had been seized and placed in the Union herd. Slowly, he slipped into the stream and off into the darkness.

Traveling on foot, surviving on whatever he could scavenge or catch, and chewing on the bark of toothache trees to stave off his pain from his still-healing wounds and infections, Lucian made it three weeks later to the small road leading up to his farm. He walked slowly down the road, across the sandy ford, and through a row of trees into a clearing. There, in the distance, he could see the charred remains of what had been his and Hannah's home.

As he came closer, he saw it—Hannah's flower garden . . . in full bloom. He hesitated for a second, as if waiting for Hannah herself to appear. If only his dream of her could come true. Quickly dismissing those thoughts, he continued toward the home place. The smell of honeysuckle floated through the air. Lucian's mind recollected how much Hannah loved that smell.

Suddenly, he caught a glimpse of someone in the garden. As he drew nearer, he perceived that it *was* a woman, watering the flowers. Lucian stopped in his tracks and rubbed his hands over his eyes, as if wiping away the last bit of last night's dream. Hannah sat the water can down as her eyes met his.

"Lucian! Lucian!" she yelled as she began to run frantically down the path toward him. They both began to weep as they fell into each other's arms. Hannah kissed his face and caressed his arms and neck with her hands, reassuring herself that he was real. "Lucian, I prayed—I prayed for you. I prayed for God to bring you home again. I prayed for Him to bring you home when the flowers bloomed." Lucian was speechless. Overwhelming joy silenced him. He surveyed his wife's face, her hair, and her eyes. God had sent her back to him. Kneeling there in the path, he simply held her and wept.

After some time, Lucian told her all that had happened and how he had feared her to be dead. Hannah explained that she had gone to Natchez. Early in the war, the Union army had destroyed the farm, including the house. In the process, she had been taken as a prisoner, but was later released unscathed. The Union soldiers had fled into the night after being overtaken by a large troop of Confederate infantry, near the Mississippi River. She and the rest of the prisoners were put on a boat headed to Natchez, where they would be safe. Once the war was over, she had returned home.

In time, Lucian and Hannah rebuilt their home and life together. In the spring of 1866, she delivered a baby boy, named Franklin Schteinhaus Calloway, followed by a daughter, named Jewel Beth Calloway, in 1869; and another, named Greta Fleur Calloway, in 1870.

Dan told this story to Dee and Tom often. He wanted them to understand the connection that they had with the land and the part that the flower garden, which remained on the Calloway property, had played. Hannah's garden was still worked and planted every season, along with the fields that Lucian had tended, serving as a reminder of the miracles that God brings with the harvest.

Four

Jody's Story

Dee first met Jody Simms when he came into Mrs. Jones's fourth grade class as a new student. The first thing that Dee had noticed about Jody was his huge mass of dark, wavy hair atop his lanky, pale frame. His hair, parted directly over his right eye, looked as if someone had tried to half-heartedly tame the wild out of it. His unkempt locks were actually a good thing, because it distracted the attention away from his clothes. His shirt, stained and tattered, looked as though it had been found along the side of the road. It had been repaired so many times that no two buttons matched. His pants were even worse. Long since outgrown, the seams on the sides had been cut, and strips of old denim were sewn in, to make the legs bigger. More strips were sewn to the bottom of each leg, to give the needed length. The embarrassment of it all made Jody a timid child, with his appearance screaming poor, ignorant, weird, and backward. It seemed less painful to be quiet, so as to not draw more unwanted attention.

As the days passed, Dee noticed something else about Jody. Every day, when the lunch bell sounded, Jody would come alive with excitement. It was as though he had been waiting for that time all morning. As Mrs. Jones's class formed their military-style march to the cafeteria, Jody was always first in line. There was never a complaint about cold vegetables, runny potatoes, or what the students described as mystery meat. He was always excited to devour all that was on his tray. Each day, he would solicit any unwanted sides from his class-mates: whether it was mashed potatoes, green beans, or fruit salad, Jody turned nothing down.

One day, he approached Dee about his untouched peas. "Hey, man—you gonna eat them peas?"

Dee had been blessed with a few things in his life, one of which was a mother who knew how to cook and did so well. So, school lunches were something that Dee dealt with, not something that he enjoyed. "Naw, you can have them. They taste like chalk dust compared to Mama's," Dee replied with a broad smile.

"Thanks, man." Though Jody's voice was always quiet, his grateful response seemed to have an enthusiasm. "Hey, what'd you say your name was?"

"Dee, Dee Calloway—and you're Jody Simms, right?"

"Yep . . . that's me," Jody replied in between rapid spoonfuls of green peas.

"Man, you like eatin', don't you?" Dee said jokingly, but not as if to mean any harm.

In an instant, Jody stopped, his spoon perched in mid-air. He searched for a safe reply. He turned to Dee and, without making eye contact, said, "Momma says that it's a sin to waste food."

Suddenly, the bell sounded, signaling the end of lunch. Jody frantically tried to consume as much as he could before turning his tray over to the lunch lady. Children are never as naive as we believe; and Dee gleaned from Jody's response that something else was behind his insatiable appetite—something that Jody did not want to talk about.

As time went on, Dee would leave more and more items on his tray for Jody. Out of this act of kindness, the boys' friendship grew. Eventually, Jody began to confide in Dee about what he called his broken life.

In the fall of the following year, Dee and Tom prepared for their annual camping trip with their father, their uncle, and their cousin,

Frank Jr. As the time drew near, Dee approached his dad, "Pop, you think we could invite Jody to go with us?"

"Well, that's fine with me, Son—if that's okay with his parents. I wouldn't let you boys go off with just anyone, and I'm sure Jody's parents feel the same way," Dan replied.

"Great! I'll ask him."

The next day at school, Dee told Jody about the camping trip and asked if he wanted to go with him. Jody was overcome with excitement, "Man, yeah! I would love to go—I've never been campin'!"

"Great, but Pop said you have to get the okay from your mom and dad first."

Jody's expression changed. "Well, that's okay, I . . . uhhh . . . I don't even have a sleepin' bag. Mm-maybe . . . I . . . I better not go," Jody said nervously.

"Aw, man, don't worry about that, you can use mine. I can use my Papaw's old sleepin' bag. You oughta go, it'll be fun."

Jody's eyes moved about, as though searching for a way out of the moment.

"Jody, what's up? You goin'?" Dee asked, interrupting Jody's thoughts.

"Dee, I gotta tell you somethin'."

"Sure, what's up?"

"Well . . . I can't ask my dad."

"Well, why?" Dee asked, his eyebrows furrowing in curiosity.

"Cause I ain't got one." Jody drew a breath as he spoke, "He died a couple years ago."

Dee stood for a moment, temporarily silenced at the realization. Jody had hardly ever mentioned his father, and suddenly several things were starting to make sense to Dee. "Dang, Jody—I'm sorry. I didn't know."

"It's alright."

"Well, what happened to him?" Dee asked.

Jody shrugged as he continued, "He got sick one winter and just died."

"I'm really sorry, Jody. What about your mom? Can you ask her?"

"No, Momma never lets me go anywhere without her, and she works a lot 'cause we have a lot of bills," Jody replied.

Dee didn't reply, seeming to let the matter rest. Then, widening his eyes as if he were visualizing an idea, he said, "Hey, why don't I get Mom and Pop to ask your mom for you? We could come to your house, and they could meet your mom, and she could meet Mom and Pop, and—"

"No, no, I don't think Momma would like that," Jody interrupted, shaking his head, his ever-messy locks flailing about as he did so. "She doesn't like people to come to our house. It's real small and run down, and kinda smells bad and—"

"Jody, it'll be fine. Mom and Pop don't care about any of that stuff. Tomorrow is Wednesday, so we'll come by on our way to church, okay?" Dee asked.

"Okay . . ." Jody's tone was filled with reservation.

That night at supper, Dee explained the details of the conversation between Jody and himself earlier that day.

"So, Pop, do you think you and Mom could go by Jody's house and ask if he can go campin' with us? I have his address," Dee asked anxiously.

"Now, Dee, there may be a reason that Mrs. Simms doesn't like company. You never know about these things, and it's not polite to just go over there," Dan tried to reason.

"It's okay, Pop. Jody really wants to go. Mrs. Simms works a lot, and she probably just doesn't have time to clean—that's probably all there is to it!" Dee said, desperately pleading his case.

Dan looked at Elizabeth momentarily. After an exchange of glances, he then looked back at his son, "Okay, Dee, we'll go. But if she says no, then no it is."

"Alright, Pop, I can't wait to tell Jody!" Dee replied with excitement.

The next day, Dan, Elizabeth, Dee, and Tom all made their way across town to the Simms home. It took Dan and Elizabeth a few minutes to realize where they were going. It was a part of town that had seen its better days. The east side of Pelo was, at one time, the sharecroppers' "Capitol of the South" and originally only four square blocks. It had been built by the state during the Great Depression in the hope that it would help folks get back on their feet by supplying work and shelter. At first, it was a Godsend, and the neighborhood grew by another three blocks. Unfortunately, over time, the area had become a breeding ground for crime and despair. Oddly enough, the very place that had been built to save society from depression was exactly where it took up residence. The little shotgun houses had seen so many families come and go that it was now known as Gypsy Square.

As the Calloways turned left off of Main Street and onto the road leading down to Jody's house, Dan and Elizabeth took note of the irony of the street names: Faith Street, Peace Street, Joy Street, and the street where Jody and his mom lived—Hope Street. When they pulled into the driveway, Dan was struck by the small size and fragile appearance of the Simms home. To Dan, it looked more like an old corn crib, ready to be demolished and burned, rather than a place to raise a child. "You sure this is the right place, Dee?" Dan asked.

"Yeah, Pop. This is the address that Jody gave me. Let's get out!" Dee's excitement had not yet been dimmed, in light of the prospect of having his friend join in his upcoming adventure.

As the Calloways all exited the car, a grim picture began to unfold as they took in the surroundings. The smell of burning garbage was the first thing that they noticed, followed by the desolate look of everything. The tiny yards were mostly void of grass and shrubbery. Homeless people with homeless pets slept on the porches of condemned houses. Dirty children played in the streets with thrown-away toys. It resembled a third-world country, that of which you see on the news. All of the houses were whitewashed, and most were beyond repair. Dan led the Calloways up to the front door and knocked.

After several moments, a frail-sounding, female voice asked, "Who is it?"

"Mrs. Simms, it's Dan and Elizabeth Calloway. Your son, Jody, and our son Dee are classmates, er, friends," Dan answered.

"Okay. What can I help you with?" was the dry rejoinder.

Dan turned to look at Dee and his mother.

"Well, Mrs. Simms, we don't need anythin'. We've come to ask you somethin'."

"Well, what do you want to ask?"

Dan, becoming ever more frustrated while attempting to conduct a conversation through a closed door, said, "Mrs. Simms, I'd prefer to talk face to face, if you don't mind."

Silence followed, then it was broken by two voices arguing in hushed tones from behind the door. Then, there was silence again. The door slowly opened as it creaked and popped. Jody's mother appeared. She was as frail looking as her voice implied, and there was no doubt about from whom Jody got his looks. She had the same wavy hair and pale, skinny frame.

"Hello, I'm Helen, Jody's mom," was the greeting.

Helen Simms reluctantly invited everyone into her house. It was as strange to Helen as it was to Dan and Elizabeth. The inside was a reflection of the outside—empty and desolate. There were only two pieces of furniture in the living room, a folding lawn chair and an old love seat that looked as if it had been found along the roadside. The room was embellished with an old curtain. The walls were all bare except for three small, unframed pictures: one of Jody's grandmother in her wedding dress, a school picture of Jody in the third grade, and a picture of the Lord's Supper that Jody had cut out of a newspaper and given to his mother as a Christmas present.

The familiar silence returned momentarily and then was broken by Helen, "Y'all can sit, if you'd like." Elizabeth and Tom both took a seat as Dee and Dan stood next to them. Helen began the conversation, "Y'all had a question? Jody hasn't done anythin', has he?"

"No, it's nothin' like that," Dan replied. "My brother and I take the boys, well, our sons," gesturing toward Dee and Tom, "campin' every year. This year, Dee wanted to invite Jody along. I thought it'd be appropriate for us to meet you first. We'll be gone for three days and will be doin' some huntin' and trappin' and—"

Helen stopped Dan, "I don't know, it sounds a bit dangerous." Looking at Jody, she said, "Mr. Calloway, he's all I have." Jody just sat silently, looking as though he would explode if she said anything but yes.

"Well, Mrs. Simms, I can assure you that he'll receive the same protection that my sons will," Dan replied.

Helen just sat silent for a moment, then Elizabeth spoke, as though she had just come out of a trance—consumed by the thought of raising a child in such desperate surroundings. She appealed to Helen as only a mother could, "One thing that Dan failed to mention is that they always bring plenty of food with them. That's one of the things the boys always look forward to: eatin' three meals a day cooked over a campfire. Plus, Dan always surprises them with marshmallows or some other fun food the night before they head home."

A mother's intuition is a powerful thing. Three meals a day was something that Helen struggled to provide for Jody. She knew what Elizabeth was saying, and it was exactly what she needed to hear to tip her decision in Jody's favor. "Well, Jody's never been campin', so I think it would be a good thing for him," Helen replied, as she hesitantly smiled at Jody.

Jody erupted, "Alright! Thanks, Momma!"

Dan smiled, too, then said, "Good deal—we'll be there Friday after school to pick him up."

It was to be the first of many camping trips for Jody and the Calloway men. It would also be on one of these camping trips that Dee found out the true story about Jody's father.

Everyone had settled down for the night, except for Dee. It was his turn to stay up and keep the fire going. As Dee sat alone with his thoughts, the crackle and warmth of the fire seemed to feel like an old friend. It was as though it was staying up with him, keeping him company. As the night drew on, Jody emerged from his tent, wrapped in his sleeping bag. He shuffled over to the fire, yawning and scratching his head.

Dee looked up, "Can't sleep?"

"Nah, can't sleep," Jody replied.

From time to time, Jody struggled with sleeplessness. Dee and Jody were teenagers now. Most of the time when they talked, the conversation turned to girls, trucks, or hunting . . . but tonight was different.

Jody just started talking, and the conversation turned to his deceased father. "Hey, Dee, you remember when I started school at Pelo? Remember that first day?"

"Yeah, I remember," Dee replied.

"Man, I must have looked like some kind of weirdo." They both paused and quietly laughed for a moment, knowing that if they were too loud, they might wake up the others. Then, Jody turned somber. "Dee, you know how I told you that one time my dad got sick and died?" he asked, picking up a stick and beginning to push around some of the embers at the edge of the fire.

"Yeah, you said it was durin' the winter."

"Well, that's not really true . . . I mean, he did die durin' the winter, but he wasn't sick. Well, not sick like you think. He drank a lot and took a lot of pills. Sometimes, he would hit Momma and me. Once, when I was five, he came home drunk and accused her of flushin' his pot down the toilet. He slapped her a few times and then broke a window out. He took a piece of the glass, came to my room, jerked me out of my bed and carried me up the hallway to the livin' room, where she was sittin', holdin' her face. I remember she didn't look up at him right away. She just sat with her hand over her eye that had already begun to swell.

Dee's pure heart cringed at the mental image that was forming before him. The love that he had always known in his own childhood made it hard to wrap his mind around such a grim history in Jody's short life. Jody's next words continued to unfurl the depth of his experiences, "He screamed at her, 'Helen!' That's when he put the glass to my throat. He told Momma if she didn't get him some more stuff, he was gonna cut me open like a fish. She began screamin' and cryin', tellin' him to stop and put me down. After a while, he just laughed and tossed me onto the couch. He said to her that I was a mistake and that she was a whore and that neither one of us was worth goin' to jail over. Momma told me that he wasn't always like that . . . but that's all I remember."

Dee's eyes filled with tears as his mind continued to picture everything that Jody was describing. A long pause served as the introduction for Dee's few but heartfelt words, "Jody, I'm so sorry."

"I guess that's why Momma stayed with him—she remembered how he used to be. He died a couple of years after that. It was my birthday and one of the coldest winters—'least, that's what she said. He'd been gone all weekend, and we hadn't heard a word from him. Finally, the police showed up at the house and asked if her husband was Darrell Simms. Momma said yes and asked why. Turns out, he had been over in Alabama, drinkin' and druggin'. He took one of his buddy's cars and tried to drive himself home. The car was a convertible, and he was so wasted he let the top down. Halfway home, he passed out and froze to death. They found him and the car down in an embankment. I heard one of the cops say there was an empty whiskey bottle frozen to his hand. We found out later, from one of his drinkin' buddies, that he was tryin' to get home to give me my birthday present." Jody stopped for a moment and looked up at Dee. "You know, lookin' back," he began, a strangely stern expression coming over the boy's face as he uttered the next several words to his friend, "that was probably the best present he could've given me." Jody looked back down at the fire and pushed the last of his collection of embers back into the flames, followed by the stick in his slender hand.

Dee was silenced by the harshness of Jody's revelation. The two just sat by the warmth of the fire. It was the last time during their boyhood that Jody and Dee ever talked about his father. From that camping trip on, Jody became a familiar face around the Calloway home.

Five

Bobwhites and Braves

Summertime around the Calloway farm was never a vacation for Dee and Tom, because there was always some kind of work to do. They both had learned how to drive tractors not long after learning how to read and write. Throwing hay bales, driving seed trucks, and running errands were common summer activities for the brothers. On occasion, Jody would come and spend a couple of weeks with them, helping with whatever he could. To Jody, it was a vacation—a chance to step out of the incessant poverty and depression that composed his home life.

Oftentimes, it was during these summers that life lessons were learned. On one such occasion, it was late evening and approaching suppertime. The boys filed into the back of the Calloway home, one at a time. A barrage of boyish chatter filled the air. It could best be described as incoherent rambling about trucks, guns, girls, and football.

Elizabeth momentarily interrupted the racket with her list of recipe instructions as she moved about her kitchen, making the last-minute details to the meal. "You boys wash up good, no dirty fingernails or rusty hands at my table," she declared in a slightly elevated voice.

A collective *Yes, Ma'am* was their reply. Dee, Jody, and Tom all made their way into the dining room and took their seats. Dan had already taken his place at the head of the table next to Elizabeth. Upon taking a quick survey of them, he could see where the soap and water had stopped halfway up their forearms and the tell-tale dirt lines around their eyes and mouth. Smiling, he turned to his wife and said, "Elizabeth, you might want to add arms and face to your wash-up list before supper tomorrow evenin'."

"I agree, Dan," she replied, peering over her glasses at the boys.

Dee, Jody, and Tom paid no attention to Dan and Elizabeth's subtle sarcasm about their hygiene, or the lack thereof.

Suddenly, as if just remembering, Elizabeth announced. "Speakin' of tomorrow, in the mornin', I need you boys to take your bikes up to Uncle Junnip's house and pick up some muscadines. He sent word that he has some for me. I'm goin' to put up some preserves for us and for the church bake sale this year."

It was always an interesting trip when they went to see their Uncle June. Even though he was their mother's uncle, all the family called him Uncle June. He lived about two and a half miles away from the Calloway home, back into some foothills, just up from a low-lying bean field. He was practically a hermit and not much of a people person. He was the great-great nephew of Lieutenant General Nathan Bedford Forest—or so he claimed. He never really had any proof. What was true was that he was a descendant of a long line of moonshiners. His father and grandfather before him had been known to cook up corn liquor. In fact, that was how Uncle June got his name.

It was the middle of June, and George Doyle Perkins was courting Miss Tyla Sue Bingham. Tyla had always heard that the Perkins crew brewed moonshine. One night, she finally got up the nerve to ask George about it.

The two had just left the Stringfellow County summer dance, and George was on his way to take Tyla home. The truck, still a relatively new invention back in those days, rattled, shook, and popped as it made its way down the road to the Bingham house. During the ride, Tyla slid over a bit closer to George. She felt that maybe she could woo him into telling her what she wanted to know. After several failed attempts, she just came out with it. "George, Honey," she said, sliding her hand under and around George's arm, "George, Honey—I heard somethin', and I was wonderin' if it was true . . . and I thought maybe you could tell me if it was or not."

George paused for a moment as he soaked up the extra attention and said, "Sure, Babe, what you got on your pretty little mind?"

"Well, folks say that you and the rest of the Perkins brew 'shine, and, well, I—I just need to know," she said, sitting up slightly in her seat and placing one hand on her hip, as if to emphasize her point.

George just smiled and didn't say a word—at least, not right away. Soon, he pulled off onto an old logging road. It was barely wide enough for the truck. He drove through a thick stand of pines and across a small creek, then he stopped.

Tyla, by then both irritated and slightly frightened, assumed that George had ulterior motives and slid back to her side of the cab, issuing him a stern warning, "George Doyle Perkins, you take me home right now!"

"Now, Honey, I'm just here to answer your question, so calm down," George said as he stepped out of the truck and walked off into the darkness. After about five minutes, he returned, carrying a glass quart jar that looked to be full of water. George made his way around to her side of the truck and raised the jar up for her to see. He gave it a slight shake, hoping to entice her to lean out of her window to make a closer inspection. As she did, he continued, "Tyla, Honey, I cannot lie to you—my folks make the best 'shine in these parts." He opened the jar and stretched his hand out, offering up the contents.

Tyla looked warily for a second, then leaned in and took a small sniff of the clear liquid. Snapping her head back sharply and wrinkling her nose, she said, "My goodness, that smells strong!"

George gave a little smile, tilted the jar toward her, and offered her a taste.

"Absolutely not!" Tyla said, with all the wholesomeness that she could muster.

"Aww, come on, Tyla, just a taste, then we'll go, I promise," he prompted with all the sweetness of a copperhead.

"Well . . . I guess it'd be okay. What harm could a lil' nip do?" Tyla said, with a slight grin, her desire to be in the know overtaking what she already knew. Nine months later, nearly to the day, Tyla gave birth to a baby boy, whom they appropriately named Junnip Alabaster Perkins—June for short.

The next morning, the boys headed out early to Uncle June's house. They laughed and talked as they peddled down the old back road. Eventually, their conversation turned to Uncle June and his eccentric look. It was Jody's first trip to Uncle June's, and he was very excited. "Well, he's a little bit weird," Dee said as he stood up on the pedals of his bike, feeling the momentum.

"Huh—I think he's cool!" Tom replied, with wide eyes and a big grin, "You'll see, Jody. He carries a pistol and a knife and wears this really cool hat."

"Seriously, Jody, Uncle June is a good fella but not too keen on strangers. So, when we get there, just let me and Tom do the talkin' and don't be askin' any stupid questions, okay?"

"Sure, Dee, don't worry," Jody replied.

The boys pedaled on; and with every turn, gully, and hill, the road got rougher and rougher. Soon, they topped the hill where the old, dirt road was that led to Uncle June's house. The tiny pathway was barely noticeable from the main road. It was close to becoming grown over by the branches of two huge water oaks. The path itself looked very old and more accommodating for a wagon than an automobile. It reminded the boys of some of the sunken roads that they had read about in history class, and it was all the things that appealed to the adventurous side of a young boy. So, one by one, they started down the trail. The further that they went, the smaller the path grew, or so it felt. The forest seemed to close in around them. The smell of untainted wilderness permeated their senses. The pines, oaks, magnolias, and dogwoods filled the air with their own brand of fragrance. In places, the pathway was still muddy from recent rains. The trees and vegetation were so thick that they blocked out the sun. Wildlife came into full view of the boys more than once, stopping only long enough to notice the three strangers before disappearing back into the endless greenery. The trio peddled their bikes down the path, swerving to dodge mud holes and ducking to miss low-lying branches and vines.

As they rounded the bend and rode over a small creek, they spotted the small house. It looked like something from the 1800s. Its plank roof and pine log walls had seen many years of Mississippi weather and, as a result, had long since turned gray. There was an old barn that housed a rusty Ford T Model pickup that had once been black. It still ran, but now it had been relegated to making only occasional trips to town and back. The old home place had been there so long that the forest seemed to yield itself to it, allowing it to stay as part of the land-scape. The only sign of life was a small, thin line of smoke that was slowly rising from the chimney. The trio slowed about twenty yards from the house.

"Alright, y'all stay here," Dee said, passing them as he rode his bike up closer to the front of the cabin. He stopped and stood, straddling his bike. All at once, Dee cupped his hands on both sides of his mouth and made two medium chirps and one high-pitched chirp. He waited a second and then did it again.

Tom and Jody waited down from the house, on the side of the creek closest to the abode. Both boys stood, straddling their bikes. Hearing Dee's call, Jody looked over at Tom and asked, "Hey, ain't that a bobwhite?"

"Yeah, just wait," Tom said, crossing his arms as he spoke, staring up the hill at Dee as he did so.

Dee made the call twice more. Then, it came—a reply identical to Dee's. Within minutes, a thin, older man with a long gray beard and long gray hair emerged from behind the house. He wore a white, cot-ton shirt underneath a tattered pair of overalls that had been stitched and patched many times. Time had given him a slight hump to his upper back, and his skin was tan and rough as leather. There was a thick, wide belt around his waist with a buckle that had two letters: "C.S." The belt held a .45 revolver and a large bowie knife that rode high on his left side. On his head was a WWI Cavalry hat that had belonged to his father. His steps were slow and deliberate as he walked up to Dee. As soon as the man came into sight, Tom turned to Jody with a triumphant grin and a knowing look in his eye and said, "I told you he was cool."

"Hey there, Nephew, suppose you've come after them scuppernongs," June said, looking past Dee at Jody and Tom in the distance as he spoke, examining the visitors.

"Yes, sir. Mama sent us."

"Uh huh," June replied, still peering down the hill toward the boys who were waiting for the okay to come on up. June scratched his chin and ran his fingers through his long gray beard. He was always leery of new folks, no matter the age. It was only then that he turned to face Dee and asked, "Who's that feller down there with Tom?"

Dee turned around, still perched on his bike, and motioned for the boys to come on up, "That's Jody. He's a friend of ours."

Dee never knew exactly why he had to greet Uncle June this way. He just knew that he was told by his mother to call for the bobwhite and to come home if June didn't answer.

The truth was, Elizabeth knew that her uncle still brewed moonshine. It was always a dangerous thing to come up on Uncle June while he was cooking liquor. He had been known to shoot first and ask questions later. The bobwhite call was a safe call from Elizabeth's childhood.

When Elizabeth was a child, her father had fallen ill from pneumonia, and it had progressed to the point of needing hospitalization. Her mother, who had been deaf from birth, awakened Elizabeth from her sleep one night and gave her instructions to run to her Uncle June's for help. Elizabeth was the eldest of her siblings and had learned to communicate with her mother through sign language. She could see the urgency on her mother's face as her hands spoke frantically to her: "Please tell June to come quickly. Papa is very ill and must go to the hospital."

Elizabeth watched her mother speak, then she hurried out and into the darkness. It was a quarter mile to her uncle's home. But the dense woods and her intense fear made it seem much farther. Once she got there, she could smell the air—thick with the aroma of corn liquor. She remembered stories of people coming up on her uncle's still and getting shot. She struggled to think of some way to let him know it was her. She just stood there, in the dark, crying. Her legs, arms, and face were covered with scratches from running blindly through the dark woods. As she stood, she thought of how Uncle June called her Birdie, because she had been so tiny when born. She had also been told that she would peep like a baby bird. The only bird that Elizabeth could call like was a bobwhite. So, there in the dark, she began to call as the tears rolled down her cheeks. She called over and over, pausing only for a second in between her attempts.

Suddenly, through the moonlight, she could see the figure of a man carrying a lantern in one hand while the other rested cautiously on the handle of his pistol. She could see him moving slowly through the darkness to her. Then, his voice called out, "Birdie, Honey, is that you?" It was Uncle June.

Elizabeth rushed to him, sobbing and frantically trying to tell him what was going on with her father. June knelt down to meet her as she approached. He knew that there had to be something terribly wrong for her to be out alone at this hour.

"Papa is very sick. He has the fever and has to go to the hospital. Momma sent me for you to come help. Please, *please* come help!" Elizabeth choked out, trying to control her tears and whimpering.

"Okay, okay, Honey! Try and calm yourself," June said, lifting her up with one arm as he carried her to his truck. From there, the two hurried down the dirt road back to Elizabeth's home. As they pulled up to the house, Elizabeth leapt from her seat and ran to help her father to June's truck. Her mother ran out behind them and climbed into the truck next to her husband. She removed the knitted shawl that rested on her shoulders and wrapped it around him, pulling him close to her. She turned and motioned for Elizabeth, who stepped up onto the running board to help her better understand her mother. Elizabeth watched intently as her mother moved her hands quickly through the air, motioning with her fingers. "Please stay here and watch over your brother and sister. You are my brave little girl. We will be back soon. I love you." Elizabeth replied to her mother using her hands, reassuring her that she understood her instructions and that she loved her too. Her mother reached out and pulled Elizabeth to her and kissed her on the forehead. Then, she and June sped off into the night. It was because of Elizabeth's bravery that they were able to get her father the help that he needed. Soon, he was well and back home.

Sometime after, June told Elizabeth how smart and brave she was to come through the woods on her own. He told her that, from then on, the bobwhite was her "safe call." He had instructed her to use it each time that she came to his home and that he would call back and let her know it was safe.

Tom and Jody raced up to the house and dropped their bikes in front of Uncle June's house. Dee turned to Jody as he properly introduced him, "Uncle June, this is Jody Simms. He goes to school with us. Jody, this is Uncle June."

Jody, completely enamored by the look of this modern-day outlaw, paused for a second before stretching out his hand to the man. "H-h-h-hey, sir . . . nice to meet you."

"Likewise, son," June replied, shaking Jody's hand.

"Well, you boys must be thirsty. Y'all get a seat here on the porch, and I'll get y'all a cold drink."

The boys all sat in a row of uneven height on the edge of the porch. After a few minutes, June made his way back out of the house and onto the porch, carrying three glass bottles of Coca-Cola. The three drank as though they had just completed a trek through the desert. As boys will do, they all tried to finish their drinks in one gulp. Immediately, each let out a large belch, as if trying to outdo the other. Meanwhile, June had gone back inside the house, retrieving the muscadines for Elizabeth. After a few more minutes, he emerged, carrying three cloth tote sacks. Reaching down, he handed Tom and Jody each a sack containing the grapes for his niece, then he turned to Dee and handed him the third bag, the one that was absent of the tell-tale juice stains that were visible on the bottom of the first two bags. "Dee, this one's for John Tuleeves, take it straight to him and no one else, and be careful with it. He'll be expectin' it," June said as he looked down at Dee.

"Yes, sir—I will," Dee said, sensing the seriousness in Uncle June's voice.

The boys all thanked Uncle June for their drinks and headed home. They eventually reached the end of the pathway from Uncle June's place and turned back onto the main road. The three rode for a while before a clanging noise coming from Dee's tote sack came into question. Being the youngest, Tom's innocence led into his curiosity.

"Hey, Dee, reckon what's in that bag for John?"

Dee and Jody could guess what was clanging in that sack: two full, quart jars of moonshine. But telling Tom was not something that Dee was willing to do. It's not uncommon among siblings who love each other for the elder to try and protect the younger one from those things that are perceived as wrong or dangerous, and such was the case with Dee. Jody, on the other hand, was an only child. So, when Dee murmured that it was probably peas or okra in some jars, Jody just laughed and said, "Dee—man, you know those jars are full of corn liquor!"

Dee turned his head sharply toward Jody, and the trio came to a stop all at once.

"Jody, you're an idiot!" was the first thing out of Dee's mouth.

"What? What did I say? I just said it was moonshine. I mean, it's for John Tuleeves. You know it ain't peas or okra," Jody hastened to say, trying to defend his words. Dee just shook his head, wanting to clip further conversation for the moment.

John Tuleeves was a full-blooded Chickasaw Indian, and he was a very proud Native American. He was proud of his heritage and, in the early years of his life, had been influential in promoting Native American rights for the Chickasaw Nation in Mississippi and Oklahoma. In recent years, though, he had fallen on hard times. Almost no one really knew what had happened.

Dan Calloway and he had been schoolmates back in high school. When things went south for John, Dan gave him a job, which consisted of helping on the Calloway farm. John was an excellent hand and had good knowledge of farming. But it was also no secret that he drank. Oftentimes, he would drink until he passed out, but Dan chose to see past this symptom of the real issue. He knew what it was like to battle with the bottle. Dan had deep compassion for John and wanted to help him anyway that he could. In recent years, he had let John live in the loft of their barn, to keep him off of the streets. If there ever was a tortured soul, it was John Tuleeves.

After Dee had shaken his head and started to peddle again, the boys were silent for a ways. Jody was the first to speak, "Hey, Dee—you think we could stop for a bit? It's hot."

Dee seemingly ignored his request at first, then suddenly pulled his bike to the side of the road, "We'll stop here for a few minutes, but we can't stay too long. Mama will be expectin' us," Dee said as he reluctantly laid his bike down and took a seat underneath a nearby tree.

The boys each took their place in the shade. The air had grown thick with the sounds and smells of summer. The light aroma of pine and cedar surrounded them. The smell of freshly broken earth burst into the air. Occasional dragonflies and grasshoppers danced and jumped around in the heat. The boys relaxed with their bare legs in the grass, enjoying the soft coolness of it. They took note of a trail of fire ants moving to and fro in a thin line from a discarded coke bottle to a huge, brown mound just a few feet away.

"I bet there's a thousand of 'em," Tom said as he peered down at the tiny workers.

"Shoot, I bet there's at least ten thousand of them. What do you think, Dee?" Jody asked.

"I think it's way too many to count, and you two think way too much," Dee said as he drew on the ground with a stick that he had sharpened with his pocket knife.

Several more minutes crept by before Jody got his nerve up, "Hey, Dee, you e'er tried any moonshine?"

"What?! I think the heat has gotten to you," Dee shot back with a look of disgust.

"I ain't talkin' 'bout gettin' drunk, I'm talkin' about a taste," Jody returned.

"Pop says that if it takes a man ten sips to get drunk and he only takes one sip, then he's already one-tenth drunk," Tom interjected.

"You shut up and stay out of this, Tom—nobody's listenin' to you," Jody glared, pointing his finger at Tom.

"You're the one that can shut up, idiot! Or maybe I'll just bust you in the mouth and shut you up!" Tom yelled as he stood to his feet.

"Why don't you just try and shut me up, you sawed-off retard!" Jody shouted as he jumped to his feet.

Nothing ignited Tom's temper like a well-timed insult about his stature. Instantly, the boys flew into each other and onto the ground punching, kicking, and biting. Dee leapt to his feet and into the melee. Reaching down, he grabbed Jody around his waist and hoisted him up onto his feet and positioned himself in between the two boys. Dee turned from Jody just in time to stop Tom as he rushed toward Jody.

"STOP! STOP RIGHT NOW!" Dee shouted, grabbing the opponents by their shirt collars and wrestling until he could finally hold them apart. "You two stop it right now, or I'll give you both a good floggin', understand?"

After the two boys briefly exchanged scowls, they acquiesced to Dee's threat. Sounds of exhaustion could be heard from each, and more than a little sweat sheened on all their faces as Dee's mind worked to figure out what to say next. "Okay, let's just get on home—and Jody, not another word about moonshine," Dee said as he cut a harsh look toward the instigator.

The boy's swatted and pawed at their shoulders and the seat of their pants, knocking away the dirt and grass. They mounted up on their bikes again and made their way back to the Calloway home. The rest of their journey was quiet and uneventful. The only sounds were the crunching of the rocks underneath the wheels of their bikes and the clanging of John's jars, along with the occasional bird taking flight or the whizzing of a startled cicada.

Elizabeth met the boys as they peddled into the driveway and across the front yard. She stood, feet planted, with her hands perched firmly on her hips. "Where have y'all been? I was just about to send your daddy to look for you," Elizabeth questioned with all of the authority of a loving mother.

Dee responded quickly, before either of the "wrestlers" could form a sentence of deception. "Aw, we got hot and decided to rest a bit by the Sullivan's corn patch." Dee's reasonable reply and the fact that the trio made it back completely unharmed seemed to satisfy his mother.

"Well, okay then. You boys bring those grapes on into the kitchen."

Each one dropped their bikes into the grass where they stood. Single file, they marched up to the front door of the house. Dee walked behind the other two, as if to try and conceal his contraband for John Tuleeves. As the boys neared the house, Dee tried to be as inconspicuous as possible when he made the sharp turn toward the barn with his delivery. He knew how much his mother loved Uncle June, but the idea that he would willingly make a "bootlegger" out of her teenage son was not a transgression that she would take lightly. Dee had made the trek to Johns's about halfway when he heard her first call.

At first, he pretended not to hear her. The second call came slightly louder and was followed by a question, "Dee, where are you goin' with that bag?"

In the past, it had always proven unwise to ignore his mother. But, given his present circumstances, Dee felt it better to risk suspicion and keep on walking than to admit to his mother what he was carrying. Then, the third call came.

"Jefferson Daniel Calloway! What do you have in that bag, and where are you takin' it?"

No child who expects to have a future ignores the full-name call of his mother. Dee stopped dead in his tracks and slowly turned to answer her. Visions of the stories about how this moment would be remembered for years to come passed through his mind. He could hear the town folk telling of his descent into the outlaw lifestyle:

"Hey, Joe—you hear about Dan Calloway's boy Dee?"

"Yep, it's a darn shame, Bob. He was such a good boy. Too bad he turned to the ways of Satan."

"Did you know he started runnin' 'shine before he even got out of grade school?"

"Man, that's terrible. Poor Elizabeth, it just broke her heart. And the way she cried when he got sent to Parchman."

"Terrible, Just terrible."

All at once, Dee came to himself and prepared to face his demise, but before he could utter a word, a booming voice echoed from behind him. "It is for me, Mother Calloway. It is corn seed from June. I asked him to send it to me by young Dee." It was John Tuleeves. He had seen the whole thing unfold from the barn and emerged from behind the barn door to save Dee—and his cargo.

"Oh . . . well . . . okay," Elizabeth reluctantly replied, unsure if she truly believed it. "Dee, don't dally—you hurry and come wash up for supper."

Once the blood returned to Dee's brain and legs, he replied with a relieved *Yes, Mother*, then he turned to hand the bag to John.

John Tuleeves was a tall, slender man with tan, leathery skin. He smelt of hay and horses. His face was as stone as he peered down at

Dee, asking in his thick, baritone voice, "Young Dee, you didn't look into my bag, did you?"

Dee's heart pounded like a drum. "Uhhh, well . . ." he began, searching for the words.

But again, John spoke for him. "I didn't think so," he said, the words were followed by a small wink. Then, he turned and walked back to the barn, carrying his package.

That night, Dee stepped out onto the porch to call for his hound, Bonnie. It was part of Dee's routine after supper to take Bonnie a treat from his own plate. He had raised her from a pup, and there is a special bond between a boy and his dog. As he stepped onto the wooden planks of the porch, he began to call, "Bon-nie! Bon-nie! Bonnie Blue! C'mon, girl!" Within a few seconds, the bluetick came running out of the darkness and onto the porch beside him. Dee knelt and gave her the small bit of beef from supper and began to rub her on both sides of her head behind her floppy ears. It was quiet that night—all of the sounds of nature had seemingly bedded down.

The calmness of the evening helped Dee to notice the sounds that were coming from the barn in the distance. It sounded almost like singing but different. There were no words—at least, none that Dee recognized. Dee's curiosity got the best of him as he decided it was worth the effort to investigate. He slipped off the porch and moved closer to the barn. He noticed the light coming from an old camping lantern that was sitting in the middle of the floor. Dee could see the glow through a crack in the doorway. The singing was stronger now, and it sounded like nothing that he had ever heard before. What started as a deep, guttural moan led to a high-pitched wail, then to what could only be described as syllables being repeated and formed into a melody. Dee, trying to make sense of what he was hearing, eased closer to see who would be making such sounds. It was John Tuleeves. He was dressed head to toe in his native clothing. He wore moccasins on his feet and had on what looked to be leather leggings. Around his waist was a loin cloth, which hung down in the front and the back. He wore no shirt, but an elaborate necklace of beautiful colors hung around his neck. His face was painted red with a black band across his eyes, reaching from temple to temple. There were black marks that started in the corner of his mouth and the center of his bottom lip and stretched down to the bottom of his chin. In his hair were three eagle feathers, pointing in different directions.

The sight was shocking, almost surreal. Dee had only seen something like it in a movie or read of it in a book. He certainly had never seen this side of John Tuleeves, as it was a far cry from his normally stoic persona. Dee watched as John danced around the light, his voice and movements kept time with one another. It was then that Dee noticed what John carried in his hands as he danced about. In his right hand was a handmade bow—a relic, a weapon, an heirloom, handed down to John over many generations. Above and below the handle was an inscription of two words: *unconquered, unconquerable,* which had long been the motto of the Chickasaw people. In his left hand was a half-empty jar of Uncle June's corn mixture. Dee watched for what seemed like a long time as John danced and stomped, sending small clouds of barn dust up into the air. He slowed for only moments at a time to take a sip from the jar. Occasionally, he would hold the bow up into the air and release what sounded to Dee like several high-pitched yelps. The whole scene was one of power and ferocity. It was only after John neared the bottom of the jar that the dancing began to slow and change. Dancing changed to stumbling and staggering. The melodic syllables began to change to words. "Lily! Lily! Lily! Spring Lily!" John repeated over and over. Suddenly, John's legs gave way, and he fell into the hay. The jar escaped his hand, creating a loud thud on the hard ground and spilling the remainder of the liquor. John just lay there, clutching the bow as he began to cry. Dee was frozen by what was playing out in front of him. The power and ferocity from earlier had been replaced with pain and despair. John continued to lay there—weeping—repeating the same words, though less and less clearly, "Spring Lily! Spring Lily! Spring Lily!" Soon, John's body gave in to exhaustion. His words began to come more slowly, softly, and less frequent. "Spring Lily, Spring . . . Lily . . . Spring . . . Lil . . . Spring . . . Spring . . ." Then, the crying finally ceased. Dee just knelt there, staring at John's unconscious body. It was more than his young mind could process. He wanted to say something or do something . . .

It was Elizabeth's voice, from back at the house, that pulled Dee from his trance. "Dee, it's late—come on in and get ready for bed!"

Instantly, Dee returned to himself. He sprang to his feet and began to back away from the barn. He stopped only for a second to quietly step in and extinguish the lantern next to John. Then, he quickly ran to the house.

Several days passed, and Dee couldn't shake the memory of what he had witnessed that night in the barn. Each evening, as Dee went to give Bonnie her treat, he would look for a tell-tale light shining through the cracks in the barn door. But it was not to be seen again. It was on one of those nights that, while there would be no further demonstrations from his friend, Dee would receive food for thought from his father about what he had seen.

The screen door cracked and popped as Dan stepped out onto the porch to have the evening's last cup of coffee.

"Well, hey, Dee. How was your day, Son?" Dan asked as he eased himself into the old rocker that was sitting on the porch.

"Aw, pretty good, I guess," Dee replied as he stroked the hair on Bonnie's shoulders.

"Well, good. I'm glad you're enjoyin' the summer." The two just sat for a while, feeling the cool breeze and content in each other's company. It didn't take Dan long to notice the look of contemplation on Dee's face.

"Dee? Whatcha got on your mind, Son?" Dan asked.

"Aw, nothin'," Dee said, fiddling with his fingers.

"Are you sure?" Dan pressed.

"Why do you ask, Pop?"

"Well, a couple of reasons. The first is the look on your face. It's a look that only a mama or daddy would notice. The second is the fact that you have been rubbin' Bonnie's neck in the same place for the last five minutes," Dan said with a slight grin.

Dee smiled at himself as he realized that he had been found out. He stared down at Bonnie, still smiling a little, trying his best to conceal his embarrassment. After a few seconds, Dee opened up, "Well, there is somethin' that I had on my mind."

"Go ahead, Buddy. I'm listenin'," Dan urged, his voice reassuring.

"Well, Pop, how long have you known John Tuleeves?"

"John? Oh, I guess we've known each other since grade school. Why do you ask?"

"Well, is he a good man?"

"Yeah, I think John is a real good man—why? What's botherin' you, Dee?" Dan's parental instincts were fully engaged, with his voice now carrying a bit of concern.

Dee hesitated only for a second and then began to tell his father what he had observed several nights before. Dan sat and listened attentively to Dee's every word. It was only after Dee had finished telling of his account that Dan spoke. As he slowly drew the cup up to his lips to take a sip, Dan paused for a moment, as if to prepare his thoughts, then turned to look at his son. "Dee, I had hoped to wait until you were a little bit older before we would need to have this kind of conversation, but since you asked—and because I believe you deserve a truthful answer—I'm goin' to tell you. First off, I know that John drinks, and I know that I've always told you and your brother that it's wrong and you shouldn't have any part of it. That is true, but John hasn't always been the way you see him now. Actually, he never touched the stuff until recent years. You see, his dad and granddad were both alcoholics, and that's why John was raised by his uncle. He swore to never drink a drop, for fear of becomin' like his father and grandfather."

"So, why does he drink now? I mean, what happened?" Dee asked.

"Well, about five years ago, John and his wife, Lily, were on a campin' trip—that was their way of celebrating special events in their lives. The two of them would go up to Pine Creek and camp for a couple of days. It was somethin' they'd done many times before. This time, it was to celebrate Lily's pregnancy. She'd found out the baby was a boy and wanted to surprise John with the news on this trip."

"So, she was the Lily that John called out for?" Dee asked.

"Yes, she was. John loved her very much. He once told me that he called her Spring Lily because she was bright and beautiful like the lilies in the spring."

Dee nodded in his newfound understanding.

Then, Dan continued, "It was the evenin' of the second day, and Lily had been restin' at the campsite. She decided to walk down to the water's edge for a drink. John told me that he tried to persuade her to let him get the water for her, but she insisted on gettin' it herself. 'I need to walk, and our little brave needs a drink,' she told John. Once Lily reached the creek, she decided to step her feet into the edge. John said that she had always loved the coolness from the rollin' water, that it felt good. She carefully knelt down to splash a handful on her face and neck. It was then that she lost her footin' and fell. Pine Creek is narrow but very deep. She screamed for John, but the current quickly caught her as she struggled against water." Dan's voice sounded distant as he recalled the details as John had shared them with him so long ago. Dee listened intently, trying to wrap his young mind around the reality of such a good thing gone wrong.

Dan continued his storytelling, his tone growing more and more sober as he shared with his son, "John ran as fast as he could down to the water's edge. But he only got there in time to see Lily go under for the last time. He told me that he screamed her name and dove in after her. He even nearly drowned tryin' to save her, searchin' for her in the water. He was finally able to pull himself up back onto the bank. Once he did, he ran to his truck and drove as fast as he could here and got me and your Uncle Frank to come help search for her. We looked all night, just hopin' for some sign that she was okay." Dan, feeling the full force of the emotion from the memory, paused for a second and looked down at his cup, swallowed hard and shook his head, as if trying to rid himself of the sad tale. "We found her the next day. She had washed up on a shallow bend about two miles downriver. It was like nothin' we'd ever seen. She'd traveled underwater all that distance and there wasn't a mark or a scratch on her. She looked so peaceful, as though she was sleepin'. It was like she was just lyin' there, waitin' on John to find her. I think it was God's way of easin' John's pain some . . . I remember when he saw her, he walked over, knelt down beside her, held her hand, and just wept. I'll tell you, Son, it was the saddest thing I've ever seen. Ever since then, John has struggled with the bottle. There were a few times he managed to quit for a while, but the grief was just too much. It always seemed to overwhelm him. He once asked me how he could do any good for his own people if he couldn't even save his own family. You see, he always blamed himself for lettin' Lily go down to the creek alone. That, Dee, is the source of his pain. He hasn't been able to find peace with it, even with time. It was just a random accident, but it crushed that man's heart. So, when the guilt grows too painful, he tries to drink it away."

Dan slowly stood to his feet and moved to the edge of the porch. He tossed the remaining sips of coffee out into the yard, then turned to Dee to finish answering his question, "You see, Son, sometimes bad habits don't always make a bad man. Sometimes, you have to look at his heart and realize that bad habits are sometimes a sign of a good heart that is trapped, trapped in tryin' to cope with what is bad.

It doesn't make what John is doin' right—not at all. But I believe John has a good heart. I also believe that God is tryin' to speak to John and tell him that it wasn't his fault. In fact, Dee, I believe God can take John, his pain, his loss, and do somethin' great, if John could only hear Him. That's why I let him stay here, so he has a safe place to listen."

Six

Sweet Caroline

When you are fifteen years old, there is not much that catches a boy's attention like a girl. Caroline Clarke and her family had known the Calloways for many years, as both families had attended the same church. Caroline's father, Forrest Clarke, was a deacon there. He was an excellent tractor mechanic and had often done work for the Calloway family. Her mother, Cornelia, taught music at Pelo High School and played piano at the church. Caroline had two siblings, a set of twin brothers, Bill and James. She was their senior by three years, and they loved to tease her incessantly anytime a boy came calling.

Every Sunday you could catch Dee and Jody on the back pew of Cotton Valley Baptist Church. There, they could see all that went on during the services. Once, Mrs. Ford slipped her hymnal out of the holder and tapped Bobby on the back of the head, prompting him to stop talking during the sermon. There had also been the time when Mrs. Phillips stood up during the invitation and the bottom of her skirt was stuck in her underwear. Everyone sitting behind her tried to ignore it—until Mr. Phillips tried to help her pull it out. But no one could ever forget the time that Mr. Jenkins held up the usher during the offertory hymn while he made change for a five-dollar bill out of the offering plate. They noticed everything about everyone. The duo had seen Caroline come in and sit next to her mother a thousand times before. She had always looked the same with her homemade dresses; her shorter, nearly bobbed hair; her quiet voice; and some-what gangly frame. She had more or less been rather unnoticeable . . . until today.

The church building had a life of its own when Sunday rolled around. The pews had been reupholstered at least twenty times. The walls still had scars here and there from Civil War bullets. If tears, laughter, joy, and mercy had a scent, it could be smelled wafting throughout the old structure. The plank floors creaked and popped as believers and non-believers alike moved across them. The huge, oak doors, which led to the foyer, stayed open all day on Sunday, as if they were an extended invitation from old friends.

Although the boys were familiar with all the sounds and smells, they could still be a source of distraction. Their mothers would tell them that "the devil would use anythin' to take their minds off the sermon." But today, there was a new distraction. Dee's focus was on one person, the beautiful, young lady sitting in Caroline's place. "How could this be?" he thought, "That can't be Caroline. Where is the boy-ish haircut, the homemade dress, and the clumsy shoes . . . and what happened to those stringy arms and legs?"

It was a good thing that the pastor did not give a pop quiz on the sermon that day, because Dee Calloway would have failed miser-ably. He couldn't take his eyes off Caroline. To say that he was smit-ten might have been an understatement. Eventually, the invitation to the altar came, and souls needing repentance, rebuilding, or just relief made their way down to the front. Prayer was offered up, and those who had entered to worship began to exit the sanctuary to go serve. But Dee never moved. For the first time in Dee's life, time slowed down. He watched every face, some more familiar than others, pass by. He would give a smile and a slight nod of the head to all those who greeted him, but Dee remembered none of it. He was waiting on her—that beautiful person posing as Caroline. Finally, she began to make her way up the aisle.

For Dee, it was hard to explain what had happened—in his mind, it was as if Caroline had left one Sunday as this plain, shy girl and somehow came back as a stunning and refined young lady the next. Her blonde hair had somehow—at some point—turned more brunette and found its way to her shoulders. The blue in her eyes remained, but they were different now. Gone were those round, bouncy, childlike eyes of wonder. These were the eyes of a young woman, and the blue was so striking that it reached out for Dee's heart. It was all strange and wonderful to him. Even the old church building seemed to acknowledge what was happening, as not a sound came from those old floorboards. As she walked, all at once, her eyes met his, and, for the first time, she noticed Dee noticing her. Then, without warning, she walked over and hugged him. It was unlike anything that Dee had ever experienced. It was a sweet and simple act, but somehow the brief hug made it seem to Dee as if her soul had wrapped itself around him. He did not know what "it" was, but, in an instant, "it" had become as important as breathing. He was sure that his heart was still beating, but Caroline's was the only one he could feel. Soon, she released him from her embrace, much to Dee's dismay. She smiled at him and slowly walked out. Dee just stood and watched her until she was out of sight. It was then that it hit him like a bolt out of the blue why he could not feel his heart beating . . . she had taken it.

The next day was lost. All that Dee could focus on was Caroline and the way that she made him feel. He could not stop thinking about that little hug that had somehow been so powerful. Why would she hug him that way? What did it mean? Chores would have to wait today. Dee thought about calling Caroline, but then he would not be able to see her face and read her eyes. "Nope, this has to be done face to face," he thought to himself.

Love moves us, and that is exactly what it did to Dee. He walked across their front yard and onto the front porch. His voice boomed through the screen door, "Mama, I'm goin' to Caroline's. I'll be back later." Without waiting for a reply, he began walking toward the Clarke home. He had never felt this determined in his life. A young man's heart was on the line, and questions needed answers.

Caroline was startled by a quick set of raps coming from the front door. She opened the door to find Dee staring back at her. He felt a small jolt shoot through him when their eyes met. It made him think of the first time that he touched an electric fence.

"Hey, Dee, what are you doin' here?" Caroline asked, with a degree of excitement.

"I came to see you." Dee replied.

It was the answer that Caroline was hoping to hear. Then, it was her time to feel the jolt.

"Can we talk?" Dee asked.

"Sure, I'd love to. Let's sit on the porch—it's beautiful outside," she replied.

"It is now," Dee thought to himself.

The two walked across the porch and took their seats on the old, wooden swing.

"So, what do you want to talk about?" Caroline asked.

Dee's mind went completely blank. The textbook full of questions that had been swirling around in his brain all day had suddenly evaporated. He sat silent for a second or two, though it seemed more like half an hour as he searched for something to say. Then, in an instant, his subconscious decided that it had no time for small talk. So, out came the million dollar question, "Why did you hug me yesterday at church?"

Dee immediately thought to himself. "What! What did you just ask her? You idiot! You sound like a weirdo, and I hope you enjoyed it, because it's the last time that she'll ever hug you."

Caroline's gentle laugh and honest reply interrupted Dee's self-deprecating thoughts, "Well, Dee, I guess it was because I wanted to."

"Oh, okay." Dee responded automatically.

"Why? Did you not want me to hug you? Did you not like it?" Caroline asked.

"Huh? Yes . . . I sure did want you to hug me, and I did enjoy it. Boy, did I enjoy it." Dee cringed slightly at his rather excited reply when he noticed Caroline's raised eyebrows, "I mean, I enjoyed it in a good way. Not a bad way."

"A bad way—what does that mean?" Dee thought to himself, then he noticed the slightly confused look on Caroline's face. He could feel himself losing control as he looked up at her earnestly, his eyes asking for mercy in light of all the awkwardness, "I'm sorry, Caroline. I know I sound crazy."

"No, it's fine Dee. You don't sound crazy. Maybe you just have too many thoughts goin' on at one time," Caroline answered kindly, trying to reassure him.

"Beautiful and smart—she'll kick me to the curb quick," Dee thought to himself. Then, as if in an attempt to calm his nerves, Caroline reached over and took Dee's hand as it rested on his knee. Then, she smiled at him. This single act instantly drew Dee's thoughts back into focus. He smiled back at her and said, "I really like you, Caroline."

"I really like you, Dee," she replied.

All the thoughts and questions that had filled Dee's mind suddenly didn't matter. His heart had found the answer he needed. There would be many more porch swing conversations between the two over the next many seasons. Unfortunately, not all of them would be easy.

It had been nearly a year since Dee and Caroline had started their relationship, and "like" had turned to love. It was a Saturday night, and—like most—Dee could be found at the Clarke house. He and Caroline were sitting in their usual spot on the porch after enjoying supper with her family.

"Caroline, your mother is a great cook. Seems like everythin' she prepares is delicious," Dee said, commenting on the night's meal.

"Yeah, she's great. She gets it from her grandmother. We used to spend a couple of weeks every summer at her house in Natchez. All the grandkids called her Mamie. She was wonderful and an awesome cook. She passed three years ago . . . we all still miss her, especially Mama."

"Oh, I'm sorry about that Caroline. I mean, I'm sorry for your loss," Dee murmured compassionately.

"Oh, it's fine, Dee . . . thank you," she replied.

The two sat silent for a few moments, enjoying the night air and each other's company. Caroline had carried something in her heart for some time, waiting for the right opportunity to share it with Dee. Truth be known, the time may have come sooner if it had been something that she had actually wanted to share. As much as she wished that she did not have to share it, this thing had chosen to take up residence in the front of her mind and would not be moved. She took Dee's hand and began to speak.

"Dee, I need to tell you somethin'. It's somethin' that's been on my heart for awhile."

"Sure, whatcha got on your mind?" Dee replied.

"Well, do you remember a boy named Chris Baronger? He didn't go to our school—he's a year older than us—but he came to church a few times."

Dee slightly squinted as he searched his memory for any recollection. "Oh yeah, I remember him comin' to church a time or two. Why? I mean, if you're about to tell me that you once liked him, well, I kinda figured that already. Every time he was there, you two were sittin' together."

"Well, yes, we sorta dated for a while. Of course, I wasn't allowed to go somewhere unchaperoned. So, a lot of times, we would go to his house or come here. But there's more to it, and that's what I want to talk to you about."

Dee could not deny the concern beginning to run through him about what he might hear in the next few minutes. But he was determined to not let it show in front of Caroline. Whatever she had to say was obviously important to her and difficult for her to share. So, he was not about to make things worse.

"Well . . . like I said, we spent some time together here and there for awhile, and I did like him. His mother was a sweet lady. She and I hit it off right away. She was a divorcee—it had just been them two since he was five. So, she was pretty close to him . . . I didn't know it at the time, but, lookin' back, I can see that they were much too close and that she'd spoiled him terribly. I found out later on that the reason Mr. Baronger wasn't around was because he was so abusive to Mrs. Baronger . . . and she had the scars to prove it. It was only after he started to be abusive to Chris did she file for divorce. But things were fine with me and Chris—well, at first anyway. It was after about a month when Chris started to become more aggressive. He wasn't content with us just spendin' time together, if you know what I mean."

Caroline paused for a second at the reality of what she had just said. She loved Dee, and the awkwardness of what she was saying—and, more importantly, what she was about to say—made her flush with emotion. Dee squeezed her hand a bit and gave her a gentle smile of reassurance. "I tried to make him happy. But . . . he always kept pushin' for more. I mean, I was fourteen, and he was the first boy that I'd ever really liked. I didn't know how to handle it . . . we did some things that we shouldn't have. But it wasn't because I loved him, it was because he kept pressurin' me and pressurin' me. He said that the more I did meant the more I loved him." Caroline could not fight off the tears anymore and began to cry as she spoke. Dee slipped off the shirt that was over his t-shirt and handed it to her.

"Sorry, I don't have a handkerchief," he said, trying to smile.

Caroline wiped her face and continued to speak.

"After a while, when I wouldn't do certain things that he wanted, he would get so mad and say that I didn't love him. Then, he would threaten to commit suicide. It wasn't long after that the threats included harmin' my family or me."

Caroline began to tear up again as her lip trembled. She wiped her face once more and began to speak, "I know you're wonderin' why I never told my family or anyone else. It's because he would've told my parents what we'd been doin', and even the things we hadn't done. I would rather have the broken heart than for my parents to."

Dee could feel the anger welling up inside him. He could not understand someone like Chris. Maybe it was the semi-solitary life that Dee had led on the farm, but it was hard for him to imagine someone being able to be so cruel and manipulative.

"So, how did you get away from him? I mean, how did you get out of the relationship?" Dee asked.

"Well, it all came to a head one night at his mother's house. His mother was supposed to be there. But she had a second job waitressin' and had been called in at the last minute that night. Instead of takin' me back home when she left, like he was supposed to, he pressured me to have sex. But I'd never done that and did not want to with him." Caroline struggled to speak through her tears, "He kept tryin' to get me to go with him to his room. He said that he wanted to show me somethin' . . . but I knew what he was doin'. Everythin' he said seemed so dirty and wrong, and it all made my stomach turn. He was so repulsive. I insisted on stayin' in the livin' room. Truth was, I felt safer bein' closer to the door. I finally told him that I wasn't feelin' well and wanted him to take me home. He just looked at me with this stupid grin and said, 'That's okay, I've got somethin' to make you feel better.' That was when he finally got up from the seat beside me on the sofa and went to his room. He came back a few minutes later, carryin' what looked like a sandwich bag. It had what looked like tobacco with a few hand-rolled cigarettes. That's when it hit me that it wasn't tobacco at all—it was marijuana. He reached into the bag and pulled out what he called a joint and asked if I wanted to get high. I was terrified! I'd never even drank any alcohol, and I had no intention of tryin' pot—especially with Chris. I didn't know what to do. So, I just turned and ran out the door. He ran after me for a little ways but stopped at the end of his street. He probably got out of breath." It was at this point that Caroline stopped and gave a brief laugh that was half-nerves and half-relief, "Chris wasn't much of an athlete." As he listened, Dee felt a tenseness on his body that he had not felt since the camping trip on which Jody told him the story of his father's tragic death. Caroline continued, "I walked all the way home. I didn't care how long it was. I would've walked a hundred miles to get away from him. When I finally got home, I told Mama and Daddy that Chris's car had broken down a ways down the road and that I'd decided to just walk the rest of the way. Daddy did not like the idea that Chris had let me walk all that way in the dark. But I convinced him that it was my idea . . . I hated to lie to them, but I just wanted to get home and for it to be over. Chris called me the next day and apologized. I thought he was tryin' to be a good person for once, then he started askin' me to please not tell anyone about the pot. He was afraid for his mother to find out. He was more concerned about that than whether or not I even made it home okay. But it turned out to be a good thing, because I knew then that he'd never say anythin' to me or my family for fear of his mother findin' out about his secret."

The two teenagers sat together in silence as the heavy story continued to move through Dee's mind. It was unlike anything that he had ever expected to hear from his sweet Caroline. Caroline's continuation pulled Dee once more into listening mode, "No one knows how Chris treated me but me—and now you. Please . . . please don't think less of me. I felt so broken, like I was damaged goods. I couldn't help feelin' like a failure after it all, for lettin' him take advantage of me. You know, I promised myself—before you and I ever went out—that I would never let another boy cause me to lose my self-respect."

Dee's somber presence spoke to the depth of his understanding. His father had taught him and his brother, as well as been an example of it, to honor women in general, and especially any ladies whom they dated. With this wisdom that Dan had instilled, Dee's sense of how

Caroline should have been treated by another was completely violated and vexed. Still, for all the frustration that he felt at the account, he found his feelings for Caroline as strong and clear as ever. He looked over at her with compassion in his eyes, then said, "I love you. You are my favorite person."

In response, Caroline reached up and gently touched Dee on the cheek. "I want you to know that, in the time that we have been to-gether, your care and respect has repaired any damage that Chris may have caused to my heart and spirit." She hesitated for a moment, try-ing to measure her next words between honesty and discretion. "You know, sometimes . . . sometimes, I think of us goin' deeper or further in our affection. But I know it would be a promise broken—broken to me, and, more importantly, broken to God. So, please, please know that it's not you—it's never you. You are wonderful and handsome, and your heart is beautiful. But when I choose to give myself in that way, it will be to my husband. It has to be to him."

Dee thought carefully about what Caroline had just told him. He wanted to choose his words wisely. She had just shared her heart with him, and he wanted to handle it with care. Dee looked out across the Clarkes' front yard into the darkness and took a slow, deep breath be-fore he began to speak. He placed Caroline's right hand in between his hands and held it as he spoke, "Caroline, first let me say that you're not a failure . . . and you're not damaged—to me, or God, or anyone else. You're strong and brave. More than that, you're good. You were strong enough and brave enough to walk away. The fact that you lis-tened to what God was sayin' to your heart means that you're good. I admire you for your commitment. I love you, and you're my favorite person. So, I want to be completely honest with you." Dee's turn for a pause had come. Though he was young, his instincts told him that he had most likely found his one and only. Still, he knew that caution was still needed, in his words and in other ways—for both of their sake. "I feel the same as you. And you're the most beautiful woman, inside and out. I'm honestly just blown away that you're even interested in me. So, I won't deny my desire for you. I think about you often. But I would never ask you to do anythin' that you didn't want to do—or pressure you in any way that would make you compromise your self-worth. Because as much as my body may want you, my heart needs you more. You are wonderful and beautiful, and when I choose to give myself in that way . . . it will be to my wife."

Seven

Deeds

The final buzzer sounded on the scoreboard. It was the last game for Dee and the rest of the seniors. It was a bittersweet end to the so-called carefree years of his youth. The boys walked slowly across the field. They took note of all the sights and smells, as if trying to commit this night to their forever memory, savoring this moment of life. The football field had the same aroma as the bean fields right before planting. It was the smell of freshly turned soil. Only this time, it was turned by thousands of cleats struggling to gain one more inch. The aroma of burgers and hot dogs escaped from the concession stand and floated through the air. The glow of the scoreboard lit up the night, announcing to the world: "Home 23, Visitors 17."

Reaching up to remove a piece of sod from the corner of Jody's face guard, Dee asked, "What's your plan for the weekend, Jody?"

"Ah, I don't know, probably ride into town with Nick. I'm stayin' at his house tonight. How 'bout you?"

"Caroline and I are goin' to the movies tomorrow night. Why don't you come with us? It'll be fun," Dee encouraged.

"Nah, that's fine. You know—third wheel and all," Jody said with a half-smile, winking at his friend.

The truth was, Dee knew exactly what Jody was going to be doing that weekend. In the last couple of years, he had started hanging out with Nick Travis. Nick was somewhat of a loner. His story had a lot in common with Jody's: a no-good father who had left long ago, leaving behind a mother to raise her child alone. Unfortunately, his mother lacked the heart to take up the slack and be a positive role model for Nick. Consumed with loneliness and depression, she had often left Nick to fend for himself. Other times, his mother had brought men into their lives—men who had portrayed themselves as would-be fathers only to have left after they had gotten what they wanted. It was no secret that Nick drank and smoked pot, so when he and Jody began hanging out, it was not a connection that Dee encouraged. He knew that in destructive relationships, rarely does one pull the other up.

Graduation day came quickly. A sea of green caps and gowns made their way to the corner of the football field. All hearts were beating with excitement and anticipation. Smiles and hugs were in abundance. A few tears made their way into the crowd as well. The girls made their last-minute touch ups, while the guys clamored about, discussing what was to come later in the night. It was then that Dee noticed Jody staggering across the parking lot. His cap was shoved under one arm while he fidgeted with his gown, trying to prepare himself for the ceremony. Dee stepped away from the crowd and hurried toward the parking lot to help his friend, "Jody! Man, what are you doin'?"

"Huh? Man, these thangs are complicated!" Jody said, still trying to put his gown on correctly.

"No, you idiot! I'm talkin' about you. You're drunk! How are you goin' to walk across that field like this?" Dee said as he helped Jody with his cap and gown. The two struggled as Jody stammered about, nearly laughing one second and seemingly on the verge of tears the next.

"What are you talkin' 'bout, man? I just had a few to help me get ready for our graduation, man! Woohoo!" Jody half-screamed as he threw his hands into the air.

Dee grabbed Jody by the shoulders and gave him one, hard shake, as if trying to remove the drunkenness from his body. Forcefully, he stood him up straight. "Dude, don't be a jerk. You know this is a special day for a lot of people, includin' your mother, and you're goin' to ruin it!" Dee was red-faced as he spoke sternly.

Jody paused for a moment, staring back at Dee with a slight quiver in his lip. "It's my life," was all he said.

"Yeah, well, that's exactly what a drunk would say," Dee replied.

The boys' words were interrupted by the first notes of "Pomp and Circumstance" coming from the speakers on the field. "Come on, we have to go NOW!" Dee exclaimed, grabbing Jody by the sleeve of his gown. Dee nearly ran, almost dragging his friend across the parking lot and onto the field. The boys rushed to the back of the line to find their places. As they came to Jody's place in line, Dee shoved him into place and paused just long enough to help him straighten his cap. Then, he ran to find his own spot, trying to avoid being noticed by the crowd.

It only took Jody a couple of steps before the sensation hit him, the thought briefly passed through his mind, "Maybe I shouldn't have run that far drunk." The nausea swept over him like a wildfire. Beads of sweat popped up on his forehead and behind his knees. There, in front of students and faculty, Jody began to vomit. The scene was not a pretty one as his classmates filed around him, staring and shaking their heads in disgust. All that Jody could think about was what Dee had said moments earlier about his mother—her disappointment. He prayed that she did not see what had happened. In that moment, he began to cry. The drunkenness, so prevalent earlier, began to leave his body and was increasingly replaced by shame and sorrow. As the students walked onto the field and took their seats, Jody just stood there, leaning over with his hands posted on each knee. Softly weeping, his tears fell into the grass below him. It was his friend that came to his rescue once again.

Dee, who was several spaces back from Jody, had witnessed the whole ugly scene. As angry as he was at Jody for putting himself in this position, he couldn't help feeling a bit of sorrow for his friend. "Jody, you got to do this, man," Dee said, placing his hand on Jody's shoulder, "There are a lot of people in those seats that have prayed for you and want to see you walk out there and get your diploma."

Jody managed to gather himself. After taking the sleeve of his gown and wiping his nose and eyes, he straightened up and said, "You're right, Dee, will you help me?"

"Absolutely. I'll walk behind you. Just keep the distance between us to a minimum. Maybe three steps, so if you get out of line and start to fall, I can catch you. You ready?" Dee asked with a face of assurance.

"Yeah, let's go," Jody replied as he adjusted the tassel that was hanging down from the corner of his cap.

The two fell in at the end of the line. Slowly, they walked across the field to find their seats. It wasn't until Jody heard his mother's voice—which was shouting out, "Hey, Jody! I love you! I'm so proud of you!"—that he began to settle down and feel better.

"She didn't see it! Oh, thank God, she didn't see it!" Jody thought to himself.

The boys were seated and waited for the ceremony to start. The rest of the evening went as planned. All the speeches of hope and encouragement were delivered; all the awards were presented. At the close of the ceremony, an explosion of green caps rose into the night sky and then fell back down to earth, keeping time with the screams and applause.

Helen Simms made her way down from the bleachers and over to her son. She could not contain her joy as she hugged him tightly and pulled his head down toward her to kiss him on the cheek. The overflow of love and pride caused her to dismiss the smell of alcohol that emanated from her son. Her heart was not going to allow anything to steal this moment.

The Calloways exchanged hugs, handshakes, and kisses with Dee as he stood alongside Jody. Caroline, who had one more year before graduation, nearly knocked Dee over as she ran over to him to hug him. No one in the Calloway family had to wonder what the future might hold for the two—their love for each other almost palpable.

Soon, the joy and adulation of congratulations of Dee and Jody's benchmark passed, and the boys found themselves facing the next phase in their lives. It was late July, and Dee, Jody, and Tom were deep into the day's work on the Calloway farm.

The summer sun had risen to its highest point in the sky, giving the boys permission to pause for a bite of lunch. Since the day's duties called for the clearing of the creek bank toward the end of the Calloways' property, lunch would be served from a sack and not from Elizabeth's dinner table.

The three rested in the shade, eating ham sandwiches and drinking sweet tea. It was a scorcher that day. It had been a wet summer, and the humidity was high. Heat from the sun seemed to press in on them from all directions, even up from the ground. But this was life in Mississippi, and the boys were no strangers to it.

They sat, trading jokes and stories. Soon, the topic changed to the future, specifically Dee and Jody's. College had never been a serious consideration for Dee. His plans had always been to stay on the farm, because, in his mind at the time, "That's what Calloways do—they farm." But the thought of taking another path had crossed his mind. It was the memory—the memory of that thin, pink line—that would not let him go. It would fill his mind with a thousand what ifs every now and then, but it was always quickly dismissed. One thing he knew for sure, though, whatever the days ahead held, he wanted Caroline to be part of it.

Jody faced the future with a certain amount of fear, as his short life had been plagued with a lot of mistakes. He worried that if he went to college, he might not have it in him to finish. He feared being alone like his mother. He feared loving someone only to have that person leave. He feared, most of all, becoming like his father. Ironically, it was these fears that caused him to turn to alcohol and drugs. Talk of the future caused much anxiety for Jody, and so, to steer the subject away from himself, he asked, "So, Dee, you just goin' to stay here and drive that tractor?"

"Yeah, I guess. It's kinda what's expected. It's a good life. What about you? You still thinkin' about community college?"

"Oh yeah, I figure I'll learn how to work on cars, you know," Jody said, trying to convince himself of the plan. He then took a long sip from the mason jar of tea. It was cool and sweet to the taste—a good distraction from the subject at hand.

At this point, Tom found his way into the conversation. He had been resting in the shade, at the foot of an old water oak. With his eyes still closed, resting his head against the tree, he spoke his bit of wisdom about the future. "I know exactly what I want to do when I graduate: farm. Farmers and farmin' are the backbone of this country—not to mention what an impact farmin' has on foreign trade and the global economy. Countries around the world depend on us for grain, corn, and beans. Yep! Farmin' truly is a noble profession," Tom declared with confidence. Then, he took a sip of tea and laid his head back against the tree. Dee and Jody stared at Tom for a moment and then at each other, their mouths nearly agape in bewilderment, both wondering if such a profound dissertation actually came from Tom Calloway.

Evening came, and Dee found his way onto the front porch to call for Bonnie. Dee called several times then patiently waited. Bonnie was getting on up in years, and sometimes it took the old girl a while to get to the porch. After a few moments, Dee called again, "Bonnie, Bonnie Blue, come on, girl!" Dee's call was followed by a short whistle, but there was still no Bonnie. He scanned the dark, searching for a glimpse of his faithful companion moving through the shrubs that lined the driveway. It was the route that she had taken every night to retrieve her evening treat for so many years before. Concern finally got the best of Dee. He rushed to get a flashlight from the house and then slipped out into the yard. He hadn't gone very far when he heard a slight and very faint whimper. Dee stopped dead in his tracks. He called one more time, "Bonnie!"

Her whimper was so weak, but Bonnie was giving it every ounce of energy that she had left. Dee caught the direction of the sound immediately and shined his light toward an old cedar. There she was, lying at the foot of the tree. Dee raced across the yard toward her. The beam from his light swung violently up and down, catching glimpses of Bonnie as Dee moved closer. He reached her and knelt down at the bottom of the tree. Now the reason that she had missed their nightly appointment was visible. She was sliced from head to toe. Her neck and torso were riddled with bite marks; ears, matted with blood, dirt, and grass. Dee surveyed the damage. He was devastated when he noticed that her left eye was punctured and part of her tail was torn away. Dee was in shock as he stared down at his friend, "Oh, Bonnie . . . I told you to stay away from those coyotes," Dee uttered softly as he instinctively reached out to gently stroke her under her chin, trying to think of what he should do next. Bonnie raised her head slightly and began to lick Dee's hand. With tears rolling down his cheeks, Dee realized that Bonnie's injuries were even worse than he originally thought. She had lost a lot of blood, and he saw that she could not move her hind legs. He felt the gravity of the situation, as if a ton of bricks had been dropped on his chest.

By now, Dan and Elizabeth were making their way out into the front yard. Dan shined his light in Dee's direction. Dee motioned for them to come over. Once there, Dan and Elizabeth could see the terrible sight of Bonnie's bloody body, lying next to the old tree. After a brief period of silence, Dan looked over at Dee, "Coyotes?"

"Yeah, I've been hearin' them at night. I've been tryin' to keep her away from them, Pop." Dee replied as the tears kept coming.

"Bless her heart," Elizabeth said, kneeling down to slowly stroke Bonnie's face.

Dan took note of the situation, then he looked over at Dee and placed his hand on his shoulder, "Son, she's in pretty bad shape."

"Yeah, I know, Pop," Dee answered, fully understanding what was meant. After a few moments, Dee looked over at his mother and father, "I'm goin' to stay here with her until she goes."

"Okay, Son."

"I'll bring y'all a couple of blankets," Elizabeth murmured as she leaned down and kissed her son and then gently touched Bonnie's paw, as if to say her final goodbye.

"I'm sorry, Dee," Dan said. He gave his son a soft pat on his shoulder, then Dan added, "But you know, Dee, Bonnie had a good life, and she was happy. Sadly, a lot of humans never get to experience that."

Elizabeth returned with the blankets. Dee carefully covered Bonnie with one and himself with the other. He was prepared for the night. A few hours passed, with Dee occasionally reaching over to stroke her chin. Soon, Bonnie began to breathe faster and take shallow, quick breaths—she stretched out her leg, as if reaching for Dee, then slowly exhaled for the last time. Dee gently wrapped his old friend in her blanket and, at first light, buried her there by that old cedar.

Weeks passed, and work continued as usual on the farm. It was late morning on one overcast day, around 10:30. The recent rains had made it nearly impossible to get into the fields. Dee and Tom had spent most of the morning trying to extract their tractor from the mire and muck. Dan and Frank were busy digging channels in the south end of the field, in hopes of diverting a sea of rain water away from the beans. They prayed that doing so would help dry out their waterlogged field.

"Where is Jody?" Tom asked in a tone of disgust.

"I don't know—was supposed to be here at six this mornin'. I'm not sure what's keepin' him," Dee replied.

Tom stopped shoveling the mud away from the tires of the tractor. He stood and stared at Dee for a moment, as if waiting for him to read his face. Dee, taking note, stopped his motion and acknowledged

Tom's silent reply to his statement, "I know, I know. I know exactly where he's at, Tom."

Truth was, Jody had been late several times over the last couple of months. He would always manage to come up with a reason. But the smell of liquor and bloodshot eyes told the real story about where he had been and what had kept him. "I don't understand, Dee, havin' a daddy like his, why would you ever start drinkin'?" Tom asked as he shook the mud from his spade.

"Well, Tom, maybe that's part of the reason he started drinkin'."

"What do you mean? That's crazy talk."

"What I mean is that Jody's dad was an alcoholic, and so was his dad. So, when hard times came, that's how they dealt with it. Jody has that in his blood, and that's how he deals with things," Dee answered, pausing to wipe the sweat from his face, and check his watch.

"But that doesn't mean that Jody can't make his own decisions. He doesn't have to drink—nobody's twistin' his arm!" Tom replied in a stern voice.

"True. He can make his own decisions. He chose to drink in the beginnin', but now, it chooses him. Unfortunately, when he chooses to stop, the decision will be a lot harder.

The brothers paused to get a drink and shake the sticky mud from their boots. It was then that they noticed Jody slowly walking across the field toward them. As he approached, they noticed his wrinkled, stained clothes and his disheveled hair. Then, the smell made it to their noses. It was the nauseating smell of vomit and whiskey. He walked up to the boys and sat down in the shade, without saying a word. It was painfully obvious that he was hungover. Dee and Tom watched him for a moment before speaking. Both of them were wearing a face of irritation. Tom was the first to speak, "Jody, you okay?"

Jody opened his eyes slightly, as if in slow motion. He reached up and placed his hand across his brow, as if to block out the sun. "Do I look okay to you? You idiot," was his reply.

Tom chuckled a bit and said, "You come out here like this, and I'm the idiot? Right."

"Shut up, just shut up. You don't even know what you're talkin' about!"

Dee had heard enough. He stepped out from behind the tractor and walked over to Jody and said, "Naw, he's right, Jody, you are an idiot. You take advantage of everybody's generosity. You care nothin' about the people who love you. You choose to always do the wrong thing, even when you know it's the wrong thing, and you've broken your mother's heart more times than you can count. Worst of all, you just don't care."

The sting of truth kindled Jody's anger, and he leapt to his feet with his fist clenched. Swinging wildly at Dee, he managed to connect one punch to Dee's left cheek, sending him staggering backwards. Dee regained his footing and reached up to rub his jaw. "Yeah, perfect Dee. Everybody loves Dee. Dee does no wrong. I'm sick of all your preachin' and crap. You have your precious mommy and daddy and brother. Who do I have?" Jody screamed.

Dee could not contain his anger anymore, Jody had hurt him—more than physically, he had hurt his heart. He had crossed the line this time, and Dee did not know how to hold back. His shoulder tensed as he swung his hand backward, striking Jody across the cheek with such force that it lifted Jody and sent him flying backwards and then to the ground. At first, Jody just lay there, trying to regain his senses, but before he could clear his head, he felt Dee's hands lift him back to his feet. Dee held him by his shirt and punched him repeatedly. With each blow, Jody's head shot backwards. He began to bleed from his nose and mouth, Dee held him and struck him over and over again.

Tom ran over to his brother, and jumped on his back, yelling for him to stop. "Dee! Dee! Stop! Stop before it's too late!"

The trio fell to the ground, and Dee loosened his grip on Jody. Dee lay there with Tom wrapped around him, who was still talking while attempting to calm his brother, not sure if it was safe to let go. Jody lay a few feet away in a crumpled heap, coughing and crying, trying to regain himself and absorb the pain that had been inflicted by his friend.

"Let go of me, Tom, let go of me now," Dee said with a quiver in his voice.

"Not 'til you promise to stop."

"I'm good, let me go."

Tom unwrapped his arms and legs from his brother, and both boys rose to their feet. Dee walked over to Jody, who was still lying on the ground but by now had raised up and was resting on his elbow and forearm, he was wiping the blood away from his face with the sleeve of his shirt, leaving streaks of mud and blood across his cheek.

After a few seconds, Dee began to sob, "Jody, I can't help that you didn't have a dad, or a brother, or a sister—but you had us. Maybe God wanted you to have all of us instead. Did you ever once think of that?" Dee's strong emotions carried him into his next, life-changing words, "Just go home. We can make it without you." Dee wiped the forming tears from his eyes, then turned and walked away. It was the last time that Jody worked at the farm, and although he and Dee stayed in touch, things were never the same.

Several months passed—the harvest had come and gone, and Christmas was approaching, along with winter. Most of the down season was spent preparing for spring planting. Repairing tractors, fertilizing fields, and maintaining the equipment were all part of preparing for the upcoming season. Dee was stopping in at Kyle's store to pick up a hydraulic hose and a new belt for the tractor. As he entered, right away he noticed Mr. Kyle sitting behind the counter—his usually boisterous and jolly personality was muted today. As Dee approached, he noted his pale countenance and the sweat beads across his forehead, "Hey, Mr. Kyle, how are you doin'?"

"Not too good, son. I'm afraid I may be comin' down with some-thin'. I feel as weak as tissue paper. But that's the way it goes. What can I do for you?"

"I'm needin' a hose and belt for that 1650 we have," Dee replied.

"I may have that hose in stock, but I'll have to order the belt for you. Shouldn't take long to get here," Mr. Kyle said as he reached for a pad and pen to make note of the order.

Dee noticed the way Mr. Kyle's hand shook as he began to write down the parts number. "Mr. Kyle, are you sure you're okay?" Dee asked.

"Oh yeah . . . I'm fine. By the way, you're old enough to call me Bull now," he replied with a forced grin, obviously trying to mask his ill-ness. As Mr. Kyle stood to go retrieve the hose, he paused after only a couple of steps. His shoulders began to tense as he clutched his left arm and fell to the floor.

Immediately, Dee raced behind the counter—Mr. Kyle lay there, seemingly lifeless. Other patrons hurried from other parts of the store to see what could be done. Dee remembered the first aid and emer-gency training that he had learned as a scout and volunteer for the lo-cal fire department. Leaning over to check, he could tell that Mr. Kyle was not breathing and had no pulse. "Please, mister, call an ambulance right now!" he instructed a fellow patron. Dee turned his attention to Mr. Kyle and began CPR. He prayed that he wouldn't make a mistake. He placed his fingers at the base of Mr. Kyle's rib cage and measured the distance to his sternum, where he would begin his compressions. Dee called out the numbers with each pump of the chest, as he pressed down on Mr. Kyle's body: "One! Two! Three! Four . . ." Dee pinched Mr. Kyle's nose and gave two breaths into his lungs before returning to his compressions.

The man at the counter was speaking to the closest hospital, "Yes, Bull Kyle's store, out from town. Please send an ambulance, he's not breathin'! Hurry!"

Dee continued nonstop. "One! Two! Three! Four!" he called as he frantically tried to press life back into Mr. Kyle's body. It was going on twenty minutes before the sound of the siren could be heard as the ambulance approached. Paramedics rushed through the entrance of the old store. They were led to the space behind the counter, where Dee was still performing CPR. By now, his body was feeling the fatigue, so the EMTs were a welcomed sight.

"Okay, son, that's good, we'll take it from here," the EMT said, as he began to assess the situation. Dee just sat there on the floor, with his hands laying across his lap as he tried to catch his breath, watching them place a bag over Mr. Kyle's nose and mouth. They began to squeeze air into his lungs and check all of his vital signs, then came the words that Dee was longing to hear: "We have a pulse!"

It took several men to lift Bull onto the gurney and load him into the ambulance. Dee just sat there for the longest time, staring at the place where the man had laid. It was all so surreal. One minute, they had been talking about tractor parts, and the next, they were scratching and clawing to hold on to life. Then, the thought struck Dee—out of all of the valuable and priceless things in the world, life trumps them all.

Two weeks had passed since the incident at Mr. Kyle's store. It was noon, and the Calloways were finishing their lunch when a knock came from the front door. Elizabeth rose from her dining chair to see Mrs. Kyle standing at the door. She was a small woman with a slight build as well as a proper lady who dressed accordingly. She always wanted to look the best that she could for Bull and those around her. She believed that a pleasant look encouraged a pleasant spirit.

"Mrs. Kyle, come on in. How is Bull doin'?" Elizabeth said in her most hospitable voice.

"Oh, he's doin' a lot better. The doctors are sayin' he might get to come home in another week."

"Oh, that's wonderful! I'm so glad he's doin' good," Elizabeth replied. "Would you like to have some dinner with us?"

"Well, that sounds very nice, Elizabeth, but I will have to say no. What I really dropped by for is to see if I could speak with Dee for a moment."

"Absolutely. Just have a seat, and I'll get him," Elizabeth said as she returned to the kitchen to retrieve her son.

After a moment, Dee walked into the living room, where Mrs. Kyle was sitting, "Hey, Mrs. Kyle, how are you doin'?"

The lady rose to her feet and gave Dee a tight hug. "I'm doin' well, Dee." Mrs. Kyle and Dee then sat down at opposite ends of the sofa. She looked over at Elizabeth and Dan, saying, "What I have to say is for Dee, but I would like for y'all to sit with us as well, if that's okay."

"Certainly," Dan replied as he and Elizabeth took their seats.

Mrs. Kyle turned back to the young man, "Dee, I spoke with the doctors yesterday. We discussed just how lucky Bull is to be alive. I thanked them for all they did and were doin' for Bull. They told me that it truly was those first, critical moments with you that saved him. I want to share a story with you—one that I've never told anyone."

Mrs. Kyle stopped for a moment to collect her emotions before she began her story. "When I was seventeen, my mother and I were drivin' from Little Rock down to Red Banks, a little ways this side of Memphis. We were goin' to live with my uncle, who supposedly had a job for my mother—sewin' in a furniture factory. My father had left us a long time ago, when I was barely three years old. I should have known that Mother would leave me, too, at some point. Well, that point came at a truck stop, just across the state line. We had stopped in to get some coffee and a road map. Mother gave me five dollars and told me that she would wait in the car. When I came out, she was gone. I found out sometime later that she had met up with a truck driver friend of hers—a friend who wanted Mother but not me; so, Mother made her choice." Mrs. Kyle paused to take a tissue from her purse. She reached up and blotted tears from under her eyes before continuing, "I sat there on the curb and cried for hours, not knowin' at the time exactly what had happened, but I knew that I was alone.

Then, this huge mountain of a man came up to me and asked if I was okay. It was Bull. He had been to Memphis to pick up some tractor parts. He introduced himself and asked me what was wrong and what he could do to help. I don't know why, but I told him my story of goin' inside the stop earlier only to come out and have no trace of my mother. Maybe it was because he was the first person to ever offer to help me without askin' for anythin' in return. He offered to take me on to Red Banks, to my uncle's home. Turns out, my uncle didn't want me either—seems that he was aware of what a tramp my mother was and figured I was the same. So, there I was, with no one, no money, and no place to stay. I remember sittin' there, in Bull's truck, cryin' and wonderin' what was so wrong with me that no one wanted me—no one, that is, but Bull. Rather than take me to a home or back to where he found me, he offered me a job in his store. Over the next few months, we began to really learn about each other—our dreams, our hopes, and what we wanted in life. Eventually, we found ourselves fallin' hopelessly in love with one another. We married and began a family. I thought all of my heartache was behind me."

"I didn't know you and Bull had any children," Elizabeth said, interrupting Mrs. Kyle's story momentarily.

"We don't . . . we lost the baby three months into the pregnancy. One mornin', I began to bleed terribly. Bull raced me to the hospital, but, by the time we got there, I had miscarried. It was heartbreakin'. What was worse, though, was the doctor advised us against tryin' again, due to my inability to carry a fetus. So, we decided to let that dream go."

Elizabeth, with tears glistening on her cheeks, murmured, "I'm so sorry."

"No, that's okay, Honey. Bull and I have lived a wonderful life. I like to think that all the love that we could've given a child was able to be shared with those around us. Dee, Bull is all that I have. He is my husband and my best friend, and, because of what you did, we'll get to share our journey together a little longer." With that declaration,

Mrs. Kyle stood and thanked the Calloways for their time. After exchanging hugs and goodbyes, she stopped and turned to Dee, who was trying to hide his tears. She said, "I wanted you to know this because when you do somethin' good for your fellow man, the world sees the act of the deed, but God knows the depth of it."

Eight

The Best Things

Dan noticed the white, spiral phone cord stretching from the receiver on the wall in the kitchen, across the room, down the hall, and into the washroom on the right. As he approached the door, the muffled voice of Dee could be heard coming from the opposite side. The words were unintelligible, but the easy tone in Dee's voice told Dan who was on the other end of the line—Caroline. Dan slowly opened the door to the small room as he peered over his reading glasses into the narrow opening. He could see Dee sitting atop the washing machine. The phone was sealed to the side of his face as he spoke in a soft voice. Dee noticed his father's stare from the corner of his eye as a small, vapor-like steam rising from the coffee cup in Dan's hand caught Dee's attention. The son took note of the slight grin on his father's face.

"Were we too loud, or did you just not want us to hear all of the mushy, lovey-dovey talk?" Dan asked, raising his cup up to his lips to blow away a bit of heat. Dee smiled and waved his hand at Dan, as if trying to shoo away a fly.

"Dan Calloway! Leave that boy alone," Elizabeth called from the kitchen, "It's the only bit of privacy he can get around here."

"Aw, I'm just pickin' at him a little bit." Dan said, heading back into the kitchen. He watched Elizabeth moving about the space, cleaning and putting away dishes from supper. He watched her dry each plate and cup and place them in their designated spots. He noticed the grace and care in which she stored her seasoned cookware. Elizabeth took special care of the old, iron skillet that had belonged to her grandmother—she took great joy in using it to feed her family. She used it in the way that a painter might use his brush to create a masterpiece or the way that a sculptor might use his hammer and chisel to make a work of art. Where most people would see a piece of iron that was blackened and worn from the years, Elizabeth saw an heirloom capable of spreading love.

Dan reminisced on these thoughts, beaming at his wife while she moved about the house that she had so lovingly made into a home. "You know, it wasn't that long ago that you and I would talk in such a tone," Dan said, interrupting his own thoughts.

"Oh, I remember. I remember it very well, Mr. Calloway," Elizabeth said as she turned to look at her husband of many years. Smiling broadly, she pulled the brightly colored apron up to dry her hands and walked thoughtfully across the room to Dan. He placed the coffee cup on the counter top and then gently wrapped his hands around his best friend and pulled her to him. They stood for a moment in each other's arms, staring at one another. A pure, honest stare that only comes from sharing a journey of love. Then, Elizabeth slowly leaned into her husband, and the two exchanged a warm kiss.

Just then, Dee rounded the corner, making his way across the room to hang up the phone. He stopped, as if frozen in terror at such a public display of affection from his parents. "Uhh, maybe you two should take the washroom. I'll talk to Caroline out here," Dee said with a tone of sarcasm.

Dan, looking to antagonize his eldest, squeezed Elizabeth tighter and said, "Hey, that sounds like a good idea, Honey."

"Gross!" Dee yelped in jest as he exited the kitchen.

The next morning, Dee had plans to go Christmas shopping with Caroline. She had just finished the first semester of the second year of her degree. Her dream of being a pharmacist would be an arduous journey, but she was prepared for the long haul. The only thing that meant more to her than meeting her career goal was Dee Calloway.

Dee's truck rumbled up the driveway to Caroline's home. The whole front of the Clarke house was decorated for the Christmas season. Each column along the front porch was carefully wrapped with deep-green garland, complete with bright-red bows hanging from the top of each one. The rails carried swags made from holly leaves and adorned with large, brown pine cones. The whole scene gave Dee the warm feeling of Christmas cheer. Despite the lengthening time of their courtship, he would often get butterflies when he saw Caroline, so he gave himself a moment before going in. Dan had done well to teach his sons that women in general were a unique and irreplaceable creation of God and that, no matter who they were or what background they came from, they were deserving of respect and honor. With such a perspective undergirding his sense of relationship, Dee found it easy to see and appreciate all the value and goodness that Caroline offered, to both himself and to those around her. When he had calmed himself, he stepped out of his truck and made his way to the steps leading up to the porch. He never honked and just waited. Caroline was way too special to be treated as if she were waiting on a cab. Dee noticed the large, wood carving of the Nativity that helped welcome visitors into the entryway of the house. It was nearly as wide as the door. That scene put him in mind of what this time of year was all about, and it made Dee thankful. Soon, he reached up and pressed the small, white button located next to the door's large, brass handle.

Caroline opened the door and greeted Dee with a large smile and a warm hug. "Come on in, Babe. I just need to get my jacket," she said. She then gently led Dee into the living room, where her mother was sitting.

"Hey, Mrs. Clarke, how are you?"

"Oh, Dee, these holidays are 'bout to wear me out," Cornelia replied with a tired smile. "By the way, I think you know us well enough to use first names, and you know you don't have to ring the bell every time you drop by."

"Sorry, Mrs. Clarke . . . I mean, Cornelia. Force of habit," Dee warmly replied with a smile.

Caroline returned wearing a gray, tweed jacket and carrying a red, plastic container. Dee noticed how the jacket made her look so elegant and refined. The belt buckled snugly around her waist and was reminiscent of the way that the actresses in old, black-and-white films dressed. She possessed a beauty and maturity far beyond her years.

"Mother, we'll be back this afternoon—love you," Caroline said as she leaned over and gave Cornelia a hug.

"Love you too, Honey. Y'all be careful out there."

The two walked out of the front door and hurried across the lawn to Dee's truck, which he had kept running so as to keep the inside warm. He hoped that Caroline would notice his effort.

"My goodness, that wind cuts like a knife! I'm so glad you left it runnin'!" Caroline said as she climbed into her seat. Dee smiled slightly to himself as he closed her door and made his way around to the driver's side.

Soon, the truck backed out of the Clarkes' driveway and headed down the road. Caroline held the container in her lap as she rode. Curiosity eventually got the best of Dee, "What's in there, Honey?"

"Oh, it's a gift for a friend."

"A gift?"

"Yes."

"A gift that smells a lot like chicken and dumplin's," Dee surmised with a grin.

"Well, good, because that's exactly what it is."

"So, who's the lucky person gettin' chicken and dumplin's for Christmas?"

"Oh, you're goin' to get to meet him."

"Him?" Dee replied with his eyebrows raised. "Well, where are we goin'?"

"Mount Pisgah Nursing Home—it'll be on our way to go shoppin'," was Caroline's reply, much to Dee's surprise.

Dee pulled into the circular parking lot of the home and found a space close to the entrance. As he killed the engine and pulled the key from the ignition, Caroline noticed a look of concern on Dee's face. "Dee, we won't be long, and then we can go on into town," she offered in a reassuring voice.

"Oh, it's okay, Honey. Isn't this where your great-grandmother stayed?"

"Yes, she was here until she passed last year. And that is how I met my friend. Come on, and you can meet him."

The two walked up to the entrance and rang the buzzer. The voice over the speaker invited them in as the door opened. Immediately, Dee took in the distinct smell of cleaning agents and urine. Uncomfortable feelings washed over him as he struggled to keep from making eye contact with any of the residents. But they definitely noticed him. It was the first time that Miss Caroline had brought someone with her. The lime-green sofa and chairs that lined the walls in the meeting area came alive with expressions of welcome. Those who could walk, shuffled across the floor toward the couple. Those who could not do so just smiled and waved from their seats.

With age come many thorns in the flesh. Some are physical, some are emotional, and some are mental, but all are a struggle. It was an eye-opening experience for Dee. "Come on, Dee, we're goin' to room B11," Caroline said, leading the way down the long hall.

Dee caught glimpses of rooms on either side as he passed by. All were adorned with Christmas décor, and the hallway itself was lined with long bows of red and green ribbon. Every would-be blank space had some sort of happy, Christmas greeting. "Wow, they make it really festive, don't they?" Dee said, responding to the overwhelming show of holiday spirit.

"Yeah, they always try to make each holiday special. Once you move in here, you never know which one will be your last," Caroline replied soberly as she glanced back over her shoulder toward Dee. The door to B11 was open, but Caroline knocked anyway, "Mr. Baker, are you awake?" she softly called.

Soon, a deep, hoarse voice responded, "Ahhh, yes, I'm awake. Is that you, Caroline?"

"Yes, it's me. I have a Christmas surprise for you," she replied.

The two entered the room, and Dee could see the gentleman whom Caroline called her friend. As they came closer, he slowly eased himself up in his bed. The old man looked to be around eighty years of age. His hands and face showed a life of hard work—both were spotted from sun damage and had many wrinkles. Even with the man laying in the bed, Dee could tell that he was a tall one—around six-foot-three or -four he guessed. Dee noticed that once the gentleman realized that there was a lady in the room, he raised his hands to button the top two buttons on his pajama shirt. Then, he placed a shaky hand on each temple and smoothed back his remaining gray hair. These were signs of an older generation, one that was more mindful toward modesty and respect, and it impressed Dee.

"Mr. Baker, this is my boyfriend, Dee Calloway," Caroline announced as she reached over and placed her hand on Dee's forearm.

Mr. Baker stretched out his hand to shake Dee's, "Pleasure to meet you, young man."

Dee clasped the old man's hand in his. Though his grip was gone, Dee could tell there had been great strength there at one time. "The pleasure is mine, sir."

"So, guess what I have for you today?" Caroline quipped, cheerily holding the plastic bowl up to her friend.

"I don't know—but I know it smells good. Mm-mmm . . . is that what I think it is?"

"Yep, your favorite, chicken and dumplin's."

Caroline pulled a bright, white napkin from the top drawer of his bedside table and placed it across Mr. Baker's lap. She then opened the container, releasing the wonderful aroma. A small wisp of steam floated up into the air. She proceeded to dip a spoon into the bowl, lifting the resulting spoonful to her lips, to blow away a bit of the heat, then feed it to Mr. Baker. She repeated these steps over and over. Dee watched the whole scene from a small chair at the foot of the bed. He was amazed at the depth of care shown by Caroline. He had always known her to be kind, but Dee had never imagined a situation quite like this one. She smiled throughout the endeavor, seemingly sharing in the joy with Mr. Baker. At the end, she took care to clean away any remains of his supper from the edges of his mouth, the way someone would while feeding a child. The level of compassion was uncommon, and it touched Dee to see it.

They were halfway through the container when Mr. Baker raised the corner of his napkin and wiped his mouth. He softly cleared his throat and said to Dee, "I haven't always been this way. I had a few strokes . . . I think. That's what they tell me anyway. I get a might shaky now, so it's best to have someone else handle the silverware." He then smiled at them both and patted Caroline's hand softly.

As he finished his Christmas meal, Caroline wiped his face and hands and helped him to get comfortable in his bed. Mr. Baker wished them Merry Christmas and slowly closed his eyes, drifting into a nap. They were back in the truck before Dee said anything. He twisted himself slightly to reach his seat belt and clicked it in on his opposite side. The whole process seemed to go in slow motion as Dee continued to absorb what he had just seen. It put him in awe of the beautiful lady sitting next to him.

Finally, he spoke, "Caroline, how did you meet Mr. Baker exactly?"

"Well, I used to come and feed Mamaw the same way. Do you remember Teddy Baker that went to school with us? I think he was a year or two ahead of us."

"Yeah, I think so. Wasn't he killed in a motorcycle accident a year or so ago?"

"Yes, that's him. He died a week to the day after Mamaw passed. Well, Mr. Baker is his grandfather. Teddy would always come to see him on the weekends and bring him chicken and dumplin's. When Teddy died, Mr. Baker was devastated, to say the least. Turns out, Teddy was all the family he had left. Once he was gone, Mr. Baker had nobody. Can you imagine that, Dee, spending the last years of your life like that? The whole thing seemed so sad. So, I decided to help Mr. Baker the same way that I had helped Mamaw for so long. It seemed like such a small thing on my part, but the way it made Mr. Baker feel was so important. He usually smiles and tells me stories about his kids and Teddy growin' up. Sometimes, I think I am the one bein' blessed by the whole thing."

Though he said little more about it in that moment, Dee was moved, to say the least, by the selfless commitment that Caroline had been so faithful to—and the blessings that she and Mr. Baker had gained from it.

It was the following week and Christmas Eve. The Calloways and Clarkes had both planned for a big Christmas: it was the first year that the families would be celebrating together. And, though not everyone knew it just yet, a big announcement was intended to be made. It had all been put into motion—three months earlier—by Dee. He had waited until Caroline was away at school, then telephoned the Clarkes, asking if he could drop by to discuss something. Having received permission to do so, Dee headed over. He could feel the blood pumping through his veins as he stepped up to the front door of the Clarke home. He inhaled deeply and then exhaled slowly, trying to slow his thumping heart. The door soon opened, and he was invited in. Pleasantries were exchanged before he and Mr. and Mrs. Clarke stepped into the kitchen to sit down and share some coffee. Dee noticed that the two took their seats in a fashion that would allow Dee to sit at the head of the table—a position that would normally be welcomed by him, but not today. It only served to magnify Dee's range of emotions.

Mr. Clarke started the conversation, "Well, Dee, what do you have on your mind?"

"Well, first, I've already spoken to my parents about this, and they know that I've come to speak to you." Despite his type of nervousness, Dee felt a certain peace about his next words, "I would like your permission to ask for Caroline's hand in marriage."

Mr. Clarke paused for a second, first turning his face to Mrs. Clarke and then back to Dee, who by then was starting to feel the weight of the father's pause. After a moment, Mr. Clarke finally spoke. "Dee, me and Cornelia have always liked you. We've always talked about what a good boy you are. But, you see, Dee, when a young man starts to take interest in your daughter, you make it your duty as a father to take an interest—in him. I have my suspicions that I haven't always done the best job at that," the father murmured thoughtfully, referring to a time before Dee was the one in Caroline's life, "So, I take it very seriously now. I know your father and mother, and they are both fine people. But that doesn't always mean that their children will turn out the same way. Sometimes, they turn out to be pretty rotten. So, Cornelia and I have to be pretty particular about who we allow to call on our daughter. God has blessed us with a remarkable young lady in Caroline. So, we couldn't trust just anyone to treat her with the love and care that we do."

It was at this point in Mr. Clarke's reply that Dee felt his back begin to sink a little into the spindles on his chair, thinking to himself, "Maybe this is not going to turn out well."

"So, Dee," Mr. Clarke continued, "Do you think that you can love Caroline as much as me and her mother?" A gentle intensity rested on the man's face as he asked the question, looking intently at the suitor.

Dee paused for a second before answering. He wanted to choose his words wisely, so that the pair could truly see his heart. "Mr. Clarke, I can't speak to the love between a father and a daughter—I have no experience in that. But what I can tell you is this, I know what my mother and father have together, and I've watched you and Mrs. Clarke. The Bible says that a husband is to love his wife the way Christ loves the church and is willin' to give Himself for her. I can see that in y'all. The examples I've had have shown me what true love is and told me about what a good marriage really takes. So, I can tell you this—that's how much I love her."

Mr. Clarke was pleased by such a heartfelt declaration—years of prayer over Caroline's future as she transitioned from a girl to a young woman had yielded the fruit of a truly God-fearing man for her to share her life with. Once again, Mr. Clarke paused and turned to look at his wife, who by now had teared up at the words that she had heard. Mr. Clarke smiled at her and then reached for her hand, pulling it to him and gently kissing it. He turned back to Dee and placed his other hand on the young man's shoulder.

"Dee, not only do you have our permission, you have our blessin' as well."

The trio exchanged a mixture of handshakes and hugs, and then, along with the Calloways, began to prepare for the big surprise. The decision was soon made to combine their Christmas gatherings, keeping some details secret from Caroline.

Caroline had taken a part-time job at a local charitable organization and, though she had to work on Christmas Eve, was about to get off for the holidays. Dee had arranged to drive her home for the Clarkes' Christmas. His truck was waiting next to the curb as Caroline dashed out into the cold, December air while Dee held the passenger side door. The two exchanged a kiss and drove away.

"Babe, I have to make one stop on the way. Pastor O'Neil asked if I could stop by the church and check the pilot light on the old gas heater," Dee announced as calmly as he could, initiating the first part of his plan.

"Sure, that's fine, but we can't be long—Mother, Daddy, and the rest of the family are waitin'," Caroline replied. She thought it to be somewhat odd that the pastor would call Dee instead of one of the deacons, but the thought was quickly dismissed as her mind gravitated to the festivities ahead.

Dee pulled into the parking lot of the church and killed the engine, "Do you mind comin' in with me? I'll need someone to hold the flashlight if I need to relight the pilot light," Dee asked, trying to coax Caroline back into the cold momentarily.

"If I have to," she replied with a slight grin. It obviously wasn't her first preference, but Caroline was also a consistently good sport about things.

The couple entered the old church, and Dee made his way to the small closet that was just off of the foyer. There, he began to flip the breakers, one by one, lighting up the sanctuary. He closed the metal door on the breaker box, turned, and walked into the large, open room. The presence of peace and grace poured over him as he reached back to take Caroline by the hand. The feeling served as a confirmation for Dee that what he was about to do was the right thing.

"You know what, this is an awesome place. You see that seat right there?" Dee pointed to the pew second from the back on the left, "That's where I was sittin' when I noticed you for the first time." Dee smiled as he walked over and put his hands on the arm of the bench. He turned back to Caroline and pointed past her to a Sunday school room, "That room, that's where it all happened. That's where I met Jesus and accepted Him into my life. He saved me, right there in that room, and has been changin' me ever since," Dee declared, still beaming with joy.

Caroline, by now feeling the joy as well, turned to look toward the doorway, at the small room where Dee's life had been changed. While her head was turned, Dee produced a small, blue box from his pocket and knelt down on one knee. Caroline turned back to Dee and, upon seeing him, knew exactly what was going on.

"You see, Caroline, all of the best things that have ever happened to me have happened right here. Tonight, I want to add one more thing to that list." Dee gently opened the small box containing his token of love. "Caroline Clarke, will you feed me chicken and dumplin's when I'm old?" Dee asked, smiling with his whole body.

Caroline, who had placed her hands over her mouth, gave a small laugh through her forming tears and said, "I certainly will, Mr. Calloway, I most certainly will!"

Dee placed the ring on her finger, and the two melted into each other for a joyful embrace. The drive from the church to Caroline's home was a blur.

The light of love seemed to shine all around them as they walked up onto the wooden porch that night. When Caroline opened the door and stepped into the house, she was met with the roar of congratulations. Caroline was overcome with joy at the sight of both families there, celebrating with them, and Dee proudly stood at his beloved's side, taking it all in . . . It was a good Christmas.

Nine

Half-Life

It was mid-July, around 9:30 in the morning, and the humidity was already as thick as stew. Dan and Frank were on their way back from surveying a new cotton patch. It was to be the first cotton crop in several years for the Calloway family. Beans had been the replacement crop for the past decade. But, as their father had always said, corn and cotton are never gone for good.

"What do you think, Frank?" Dan asked.

"I think the crop looks good and was a smart choice," came the reply as he wiped the sweat from his brow and adjusted his cap before continuing, "Yep, cotton's on its way, Little Brother."

As the two drove down the old field road, their conversation turned to the subject of friends and family, as usual. "Have you heard from Frank Jr. lately?" Dan queried.

"Yeah, got a letter last week. They have him stationed in Germany right now—doesn't know when he'll get home," Frank replied.

"I guess my nephew is goin' to make a career out of it."

"It looks that way. You already know I didn't want him to enlist in the first place—and neither did his mama. But, like I've said before, he has to live his own life." A sigh from Frank at his own words hinted that, no matter how many times he said it, he was sometimes still trying to convince himself of the reality of it. "Frankie has always been a good boy. He never gave me or his mama a minute's trouble. So, when he decided to join the Army, I just couldn't see not supportin' him, especially with it bein' peace time. You know what, Dan? He's made a really good soldier. I'm awfully proud of him, but I worry about him every day—there's not a day that goes by that me and his mother don't get on our knees and pray for him."

"I know. Elizabeth and I pray for him too. No matter how old your children get, they never stop bein' your babies," Dan said with a smile.

It was nearing noon when Dan and Frank pulled into the driveway at Dan's home. "Is that Dee's truck?" Frank asked.

"Yeah, I thought he and Tom were workin' down on the south end today. I hope everythin' is okay," Dan replied while a look of concern furrowed his brow.

"Hey, what's for dinner, good lady?" was Dan's usual greeting as he entered the kitchen. The good lady would always follow with, "Somethin' good." Today was different, though, as Dan and Frank made their way through the washroom and into the kitchen. Dan's uneasiness caused him to forget his normal greeting.

Entering the kitchen, the two noticed Dee, Caroline, Elizabeth, Tom, and Sarah, all sitting around the table and grinning with delight. Out of instinct, Dan blurted out, "Okay, what's broke, and who broke it?"

Elizabeth, in her normal, calm demeanor said, "There's not a thing broken around here . . . Papaw."

"Well, good—so what's everybody grinnin' about? Somebody tell a stor—" Dan stopped mid-sentence, looked at Elizabeth, and asked, "What did you call me?"

Frank, who had already picked up on what was happening, looked over at Dan, back to Caroline, then said, "I believe she called you *Papaw*—it's an old Indian word for *granddad*." He was grinning from ear to ear, partly in amusement at his own joke but mostly at the happy prospect.

It didn't take long for Dan's eyes to fill with tears. He looked at Dee and then at Caroline, "You mean . . . ?"

"Yep, Pop. You're goin' to be a grandfather!"

"Well, praise the Lord!" Dan said, with his voice overflowing with joy.

Through a mix of tears and laughter, the Calloway clan exchanged hugs and kisses, congratulating Dee and Caroline.

Seven and one-half months later, on an early March morning, Caroline delivered a baby girl. Dee and Caroline joyfully dubbed their firstborn Mary Elizabeth Calloway. Another child would follow around two years later, a baby boy whom they would name Joel Gray Calloway.

The fall after the birth of Mary Elizabeth was one of the best harvests that the Calloways had enjoyed in some years. But after every mountain top comes a valley.

The sun was just beginning to set, lighting up the horizon in tones of peach and purple, as the phone rang within Frank's house.

"Hello?"

"Yes, is this Mr. Frank Calloway?"

"Yes, it is—who's callin'?"

"Mr. Calloway, this is Sergeant Sheffield with the Stringfellow County Sheriff's Department."

As if in sync with the sun, Frank felt his heart sink. It was a call that he had gotten before.

"Mr. Calloway, I have your wife, Sarah, here at the station with me. It seems as though she made a trip to the grocery store today and now cannot remember what road y'all live on. Is there any way that you can come down here and pick her up?"

"Uh, ye-yes, sir, Sergeant, I'll be there shortly."

It was the third time in six months that Sarah had taken a trip into town and lost her way. As Frank walked through the doors of the sheriff's department, he found Sarah sitting in a chair with her head down, as if she was ashamed, weeping silently.

"Babe?" Frank spoke softly to her. Immediately, she sprang from her seat and into Frank's arms.

Through her sobbing, she whispered, "Frank, what's wrong with me? Am I goin' crazy?"

"No, you just lose your way sometimes . . . that's all," Frank uttered gently, stroking her hair as he said it. Frank motioned toward the officer behind the desk, "Do I need to sign anythin'?"

"Oh, no, sir, you're good to go, Mr. Calloway."

"Thank you. I'll be back this evenin' to get her car."

"That's fine. No problem," the officer sympathetically responded.

Sarah spent most of the drive home with her hand tightly clasped in Frank's. She didn't say a word. She just stared out of the window, repeating to herself house numbers and the families who lived there. It was her way of calming herself. "225 Foster Street, the Edwards . . . 182 Tree Sap Road, the Blairs . . . 193 Tree Sap Road, the . . . the . . .the . . ." Sarah closed her eyes tightly, as if wincing in pain. Then, she slowly turned to Frank with a look of despair. After they pulled into their driveway, Frank killed the engine. Sarah broke the silence, "Frank, I need to go to the doctor. Somethin' is wrong—I know it."

It was not the first time that Sarah had mentioned the desire to see a doctor. But it was the first time that Frank shared her concern. "Okay, I'll call and make an appointment with Dr. Rogers over in Niobi."

Two weeks after Sarah had been checked from head to toe and nurses had taken multiple scans, run tests, and performed blood work, Frank and Sarah anxiously sat in Dr. Rogers's office, waiting on their turn with the physician and praying for good results. Dr. Rogers entered the room, followed by another man, who was also dressed in doctor's attire. He was slightly younger than Dr. Rogers—the stranger was a tall, thin person with dark, brown hair. His mood seemed slightly darkened as well. Both men exchanged greetings with the Calloways before sitting down.

"Hey, Frank, Sarah—it's good to see you both," Dr. Rogers said, reaching out to shake the couple's hands. "This is Dr. Salther, he's a neurologist from Jackson."

"Hello, Mr. Calloway, Mrs. Calloway." A stiff nod from the youngest of the four seemed to somehow fit the moment.

"Dr. Salther is here looking at the possibility of starting a satellite practice here in Niobi and one in Tupelo." Dr. Rogers continued, "I've consulted with him regarding your test results. Sarah, there are some abnormalities that are a bit concerning. Dr. Salther is a specialist when it comes to illnesses of this nature. So, I've asked him to speak with you about your results and possible treatment options." Upon seeing receptive looks on the couple's faces, Dr. Rogers motioned toward the neurologist, "Dr. Salther?"

"Mr. and Mrs. Calloway, as Dr. Rogers just explained, there are some abnormalities in the results. Specifically, with regard to the brain scan." Dr. Salther turned and pulled two films out of a large, brown envelope and attached them to the view box that was hanging on the wall. "Mr. and Mrs. Calloway, if you will, notice these discolored areas," he continued, pointing toward the slides. "These are sometimes referred to as plaques and tangles, which are essentially protein fragments or Beta-amyloid. They start to build up between nerve cells, which damage and kill the nerve cells. Over a period of time, as the cells die, the areas of the brain that control memory, thought processing, and sometimes motor skills are affected."

"So, what are you sayin', Dr. Salther?" Frank asked, looking puzzled.

"Well, Mr. Calloway, we believe that your wife has Alzheimer's."

"Alzheimer's?" Frank murmured as he reached for Sarah's hand. He wanted to say something more, but the words would not come.

After taking a moment to let the news soak in, Sarah reached over and put her other hand on top of Frank's. Then, she smiled and stared at him for a moment as if to say, "It's okay." Sarah looked up at the doctors and asked, "Okay, so what do I do now?"

Dr. Salther looked over at Dr. Rogers, who was the first to speak, "Sarah, Dr. Salther and I have discussed this. Unfortunately, there is no cure. But there are some medications that we can try. Some have proven to slow down the progression of dementia in some patients. Otherwise, we just want you to take care of yourself. You need to eat right, exercise, and get plenty of rest."

"Okay, whatever you say, Doc." A tension in the corners of Sarah's mouth, though she tried to be neutral, betrayed her true feelings at the news. It was like nothing that she had ever thought possible.

Frank just sat there in silence, clutching Sarah's hand, trying to make sense of it all. Dr. Rogers, who was sitting behind his desk, looked at Frank and Sarah for a moment and then leaned forward and removed his glasses. "Frank, Sarah . . . I am speaking as your friend now and not your doctor. Spend as much time together as you can. Frank, hold her hand every chance that you get—talk to each other every chance that you get." Pausing for a second, as if to regain himself, he continued, "Pray together as much as you can, and love as hard as you can."

Sarah and Frank took the doctor's instructions to heart, but even so, all of the changes and medications proved to be too little, too late.

As time passed, Sarah's condition worsened more and more rapidly, her mind diminishing to the point where she would often not recognize Frank. She struggled with processing her thoughts. They would get jumbled in her mind and cause her to become terribly frustrated. She began to lash out often, usually at Frank. She would say vile and hurtful things to him, only to forget moments later what she had said. She would leave the house at most any time and begin walking. She could be almost anywhere around town, but, on occasion, Frank would find her just down the road in Mrs. Jenkins's flower garden. When he asked her where she was going, her answer was always the same. She would smile, oblivious to the mayhem or panic that she had caused him, and simply say, "Home." But there were also moments of clarity, moments when Sarah knew everything and everyone around her. It was those moments that Frank lived for. Those moments were refreshment for his parched soul. Eventually, he tried to describe to Dan, his main confidant, what those moments were like,

"In early spring, you can look out over a pasture. The grass is greener than it'll ever be again. As you look out across it, you see nothin' but green, with the mornin' breeze gently blowin' across the strands. Then, your eyes are drawn to this one little, perfect flower that the hay and grass just couldn't choke out. You see that flower, Dan? That's Sarah. I get up every day lookin' for one more flower."

Sarah stood in the middle of Mrs. Jenkins's flower garden, picking roses and lilies. She had slipped out during the early morning hours again, her mind now being left only with shreds of happy times and fond memories that came into focus. She had loved growing flowers back when she was whole and able to work the soil. The memories of those days led her more and more often to the flower garden down the road.

The ringing phone awakened Frank, and, out of instinct, he reached across the bed, searching for Sarah. Frank's heart began to pound when he realized that she was not there. He grabbed the phone and answered in a frantic tone, "Hello?"

Before another word could form from his lips, Mrs. Jenkins's inhospitable voice came booming from the other end, "MR. CALLOWAY, PLEASE COME GET YOUR WIFE."

"Mrs. Jenkins?"

"Mr. Calloway, this is the third time this month that your wife has destroyed part of my garden."

"Mrs. Jenkins, I'm so sorry—I'll be right there. Is she alright?"

"Mr. Calloway, she's well enough to destroy my property!" shouted Mrs. Jenkins. "Just come get her!"

Frank hung the phone up, then hurried to get out of the door and down the road. He found Sarah sitting on Mrs. Jenkins's front porch, surrounded by buds and blossoms. She was still in her nightgown. She smiled at Frank as he walked up to her, "Hey, Darlin', I picked us some flowers. Aren't they beautiful?"

"Yes, Honey, they're lovely. You did a great job," Frank said in a gentle voice. "Now, let's go home and have some breakfast. Does that sound good?" Frank helped her to stand up and start making her way to the truck. As he buckled her into the seat, Sarah clutched the bouquet as she would an infant cradled in her arms.

Frank walked back to the house to apologize one more time to Mrs. Jenkins. He stepped up to the screen door, but before he could knock, she appeared on the other side, "Mrs. Jenkins, I'm really sorry for—"

Mrs. Jenkins interrupted, "Mr. Calloway, save it. If you really are sorry, you should put her somewhere before she hurts herself or somebody. You know, there are places for people like her," she said, smirking through the screen.

Frank clenched his jaw and swallowed back down the words that he really wanted to say to his neighbor. Words that she would have deserved. Words that would have cut her as deeply as her words had cut him. There had been a time in Frank's life when he would have pulled that screen door out by the hinges and tossed it into the yard—but not today. Today, he would not waste a moment of the precious time that he had left with Sarah. He wouldn't let his anger steal a second of it. So, he simply turned and walked back to his truck.

Once they arrived home, Frank walked Sarah into the house and began to draw her a bath. As he did so, he gently pulled all the leaves and twigs out of her hair. Then, he thoughtfully gave her instructions for bathing, ending with, "Honey, you just sit there for a bit and soak. I'll go make us some breakfast." Frank had learned to discern between the moments that she could be left alone and when she could not be, and he sensed that she was more of her able self in that moment. A little while later, Sarah emerged from the bathroom, wearing the clothes that Frank had laid out for her. As she approached the table, she made note of the fresh bouquet that was sitting on it. "Oh, Frank, how beautiful! Where did you get those flowers?"

Frank smiled compassionately and said, "Someone special to both of us picked those."

"Well, how sweet," Sarah replied.

As the two were eating breakfast, Frank noticed that she became very quiet and began pushing her eggs around her plate.

"Honey, are they not good?" he asked.

Sarah paused for a second and looked up at him, with tears in her eyes, "Frank, I picked them—didn't I?"

Frank's expression changed to one of empathy, "Yes, Babe, you did."

Sarah reached over and touched one of the roses. A silence marked the moment as she regained her composure and said, "Frank . . . you know you're goin' to have to put me somewhere."

"Honey, you are somewhere—you're with me."

"But you can only do so much, and I want you to know—before I don't know anyone or anythin'—that it's okay to put me in a home."

Frank stopped her, saying, "Sarah, you are home." Then, he reached over and took Sarah's trembling hands into his own. "Honey, you remember what you told me when we got married?"

Sarah gave a slight smile through her tears and slowly shook her head, feeling angry with herself for not remembering.

"That's okay, Hon—I remember. You quoted Ruth to me."

Sarah's confused expression prompted Frank to quote the ancient vow:

Entreat me not to leave you,

Or to turn back from following after you;

For wherever you go, I will go;

And wherever you lodge, I will lodge;

Your people *shall be* my people,

And your God, my God.

Where you die, I will die,

And there will I be buried.

The LORD do so to me, and more also,

If *anything but* death parts you and me.

(Ruth 1:16–17)

A single tear rolled down Frank's cheek as he whispered, "Those are my words to you, too, Love. Only death parts us."

Winter came and went and, with it, took Sarah. She had developed pneumonia right after Christmas and fought it for days after. In the end though, the doctors said that her weakened immune system just could not handle the fight any longer. Despite his deep sorrow, Frank felt peace in knowing that the only other home that she would know was heaven.

Frank pulled the navy-blue dress out of his bag and handed it to Mr. Turner, the funeral home director. "This was one of her favorites. She really loved the white, lace collar. She thought it made the dress," Frank said as he slid his hand slowly across the stitching, many memories coming to mind as he did so.

"Frank, she'll be given the utmost care."

Frank reached his hand out toward Mr. Turner. "I know she will . . . thank you," he responded, with his voice quivering slightly.

The funeral was simple and sweet, just as Sarah would have wanted, and Frank was appreciative of all the family members rallying around him, not only in the first few days of his loss but also throughout the service and in the weeks after. But still, a certain loneliness, a certain something, haunted him. There was a depth to the pain that no one else in the family had quite known—that no one else in the family quite understood—and, as the days after Sarah's death clicked off one by one, Frank began to wrestle with the unanswered questions that he had been left with in her place.

Too often, when our heart has been fractured, old demons—long since thought dead—will rise up to torture us again. Four months after the funeral, Dan and Elizabeth found an empty whiskey bottle lying next to Sarah's headstone. That evening, Dan approached his brother about it.

Dan pulled up to Frank's house to find him sitting on the front porch in the dark. The faint glow of a half-smoked cigarette, wedged between his fingers, gave the only light. As he approached, he noticed the despondent look on Frank's face, and it pained Dan to see it.

"Frank, we need to talk," Dan announced as kindly as he could.

"What you have on your mind, Brother?" Frank replied, staring off into the distance.

"Well, I'll come straight to the point—I know you're drinkin' again. Elizabeth went to put some flowers on Sarah's grave and found your whiskey bottle. I'm sure it's not the first . . ." Dan uttered, searching his brother's face, trying to read his heart and mind as he spoke to him. "Frank, I know you're hurtin', but that stuff is like poison to our family. It destroys everythin'."

The rejoinder was a gruff one and far from what Dan had hoped to hear, "Let me just tell you somethin'. When I was in Vietnam, I saw friends—good men—lose their arms and legs. I've even seen them get their eyes burned out of their heads—some scarred beyond recognition. I always wondered how they could come home and live a half-life. Well, Brother, here I am, livin' it. Because that's exactly what it feels like without Sarah!" Frank's voice was punctuated with emotion, "Dan, I'm done talkin'—I'm goin' to bed."

The veteran stood and slowly let the cigarette that, by now, had burned down and began to singe the hair and flesh on his fingers fall to the ground. He turned away and, without another word, walked into the house, leaving Dan standing in the dark.

The next day, Dan drove over to Pastor O'Neil's house, "Brother Calloway, how are you?" the gentle man of God asked.

"I'm fine, Pastor, but I need your help."

"What do you need, Dan?"

"Well, I wondered if we could go over to the church and pray for Frank," Dan requested.

"Absolutely," the pastor answered, sensing Dan's urgency.

The two men entered the sanctuary and walked to the altar. The 150-year-old building had a calming effect. The smell from the old rafters and the paper from the hymnals was a distinct aroma. The altar was stained and worn from the weight of a century-plus of tears and burdens that had been laid down.

Once the two men knelt, Dan began to pray, "Father, it's Dan. I need your help. Frank is sufferin', and only You can stop it. I know You have Your reasons, even for his sufferin'. Please give him somethin', Father—somethin' that's greater or better—so that he knows You're there . . ." Dan's words left him at this point.

Pastor O'Neil reached over and placed a hand on Dan's shoulder and began to speak. "Lord, we're here for Frank. We're here, lifting him up to You, Lord. Pour out Your grace and mercy on him today, and open our eyes to our part in his healing. I ask it all in Your Son's mighty name."

It was a shorter session of prayer than either man had thought it would be, but somehow it seemed like enough, and Dan's heart felt more at ease.

Around 9 a.m. on the following Tuesday, a patrol car from the county sheriff's department pulled into Dan's driveway. Sheriff Mike Bode was a family friend. He had gone to school with Dan and Frank. As the sheriff stepped onto the porch, he was met at the front door. "Hey, Mike, what's goin' on?" Dan asked, a bit curious.

"Well, I got a situation with your brother that I could use your help with."

"Mike, what's happened? Is Frank okay?" Dan replied, his curiosity temporarily replaced with fear.

"He's okay, Dan. In fact, I'd say he's fine. It's just that we got a call from Mrs. Jenkins this mornin', and it seems that Frank stole her flowerbed," the sheriff explained, trying to control his slight grin. "So, we went to her house, and—sure enough—it's gone. I mean, every last bud."

Dan rolled his eyes.

"Any idea where Frank would've taken a whole bed of roses?" the sheriff asked.

"Yeah, I know exactly where he took 'em—Sarah's grave."

"Well, we're headed to Frank's house. I've known y'all my whole life, and I know Frank's not . . . not been the same since she passed," the sheriff said, pausing slightly as he picked his words regarding Frank's grief, "but I got a job to do. So, I wanted to give you an opportunity to go with us and talk to him first, so it doesn't get out of hand."

"Sure, Mike, I'll ride with you," Dan answered, grateful for the opportunity. "Who do you have with you?"

"That's my nephew Jerome. It's his first day on the job," Mike said, nodding toward a stocky, ruddy-faced boy with a flattop haircut who was sitting behind the steering wheel.

As the men stepped off the porch, Elizabeth emerged from the house, declaring as she untied her apron, "I'll be goin' with you." Dan knew better than to argue.

The group noticed tell-tale clumps of fresh soil in the bed of Frank's pickup once the cruiser had pulled into the driveway and they exited the vehicle. Dan led the way up to Frank's front door. He opened it and called out, but there was no reply. The house was dark and smelt of whiskey and cigarettes. Dan called again. This time, a gravelly voice responded with a solemn reply of "Backyard."

The four made their way through the house and into the kitchen. Frank's muddy frame could be seen through the screen door, which led from the kitchen to the back patio. He was sitting in a swing, still clutching a small garden spade in one hand and a freshly lit cigarette in the other. A half-empty bottle of whiskey sat on the ground next to him. As the scene came into view, the eager officer exclaimed, "I'll get him, Uncle Mike," exiting the house and nearing Frank before anyone could rebut his actions.

A feeling of concern poured over Dan as he watched from inside—concern not just for Frank but also for the officer. Dan knew that his brother, once he had spent some time in the bottle, was far from the gentle, good-natured man that everyone knew. It was because of that very reason that he and Frank had sworn off liquor years ago . . . . at least, until now.

The young man walked up to Frank, stopping at the appropriate distance according to his reserve training. With both hands perched on each side of his belt and the sternest face that he could muster, he began questioning Frank. "Sir, my name is Officer Jerome Bode with the Stringfellow County Sheriff's Department. Are you Frank Calloway?"

Acknowledging the officer's presence with a slice of sarcasm, Frank replied, "That's what my daddy called me."

"Well, Mr. Calloway, I need to ask you a few questions. Do you know a Mrs. Lola Jenkins that lives down the road?" The officer motioned in the direction of her home as he made the inquiry.

"Oh yeah, I know her, but I can't say that I'm any better off because of it," Frank said as he reached down to grab the whiskey bottle, turning it up for another drink. He sat the bottle back down and then quickly took a drag off of his cigarette. Just as the officer started to ask another question, Frank interrupted, "Hey—ain't you Mike Bode's nephew?"

"Yes, sir, I am. But this isn't about me, Mr. Calloway. Mrs. Jenkins has had some property stolen, and she identified you as the perpetrator. So, I need for you to—"

Frank interrupted again, "Mike Bode, I haven't seen ol' Mike in some years. How is he doin'?"

Officer Bode, having become irritated at Frank's insolence and lack of concern, slid his right hand slightly closer to his sidearm and shifted his body weight so as to take a more aggressive posture, hoping to show Frank who was in charge. "Mr. Calloway, I think it would be in your best interest if you'd stop talkin' and come with us down to the station."

Frank took another puff and said through a dismissive chuckle, "Son, I'm not goin' anywhere with you."

Officer Bode became more impatient and moved closer to Frank, "Mr. Calloway. I need you to stand and put your hands behind your back—please don't make me force you."

It was then that Frank's mood darkened. Frank took one last draw from the cigarette and thumped it into the yard. He slowly exhaled, letting the smoke out through his nostrils. The muscles in his forearm rippled as he tightened his grip on the small spade, which had remained in his muddy hand. Looking up at the officer, he said, "Son, you lay one finger on me, and I'll separate you from your manhood before you can palm that pistol."

Frank's coldness and lack of fear caught the officer off guard. He stepped back and searched for some words that might salvage his authority in the situation. "Mr. Calloway . . . Y-y-you just stay right here," was all that he could come up with as he stepped back into the house.

There, he found the sheriff and Dan discussing what had happened and what could happen to Frank. Elizabeth was moving about the kitchen, cleaning and straightening up as she went. She loved her brother-in-law, and it pained her to see him like this. Cleaning was her way of helping the situation.

Jerome stood quietly next to the sheriff, waiting for an opportunity to insert himself into the conversation. His timid, childlike demeanor caught the sheriff's attention. "Jerome? I thought you were goin' to apprehend Mr. Calloway," the sheriff said, taking note of his nephew's pale countenance.

"Well, Uncle Mike, he, uh . . . he . . ."

"Son, spit it out," the sheriff said, now speaking in a more serious tone.

Jerome turned his eyes first to Elizabeth and then back to Sheriff Bode, as if about to blurt out some kind of expletive. "Uncle Mike, I tried to apprehend the suspect, but he, uh . . . he," then, leaning into Sheriff Bode's shoulder, he said in a hushed tone, "he . . . threatened me," refraining from further detail out of respect for Elizabeth's presence.

Sheriff Bode's eyes looked up at Jerome's face and then over to Dan Calloway, who was caught between feeling the humor of the irony and his understanding of the increasing seriousness of Frank's situation. Sheriff Bode's expression changed to one of irritation as he turned back to his nephew, "Jerome, you mean to tell me, that you, an armed officer, could not apprehend a suspect because he threatened you while holdin' a garden spade?"

"Well . . . yes, sir, but—"

"Jerome, go wait on the front porch," Sheriff Bode replied, interrupting the young man's attempt to create a plausible reason for his breach of duty. As the sound of Jerome closing the front door behind him could be heard, the sheriff turned to face Dan and then moved closer to him, wanting to be clear about what he was about to say. His words came out in a low but serious tone, "Dan, I am tryin' to be patient here, but Frank is workin' against me. He just threatened an officer of the law—that's a little more serious than diggin' up some old lady's flower bed. As a friend, I'm givin' you one opportunity to go out there and talk your brother into comin' with us, or I am goin' to treat him like anyone else. You understand what I'm sayin'?"

"Yeah, I know, Mike. Just give me a few minutes."

Dan pushed the screen door open and walked up to Frank, then he sat down next to him on the swing. Frank cupped his hand around the flame of the lighter as he lit a fresh cigarette that was perched between his lips. He was the first one to speak. After taking a deep drag off of the cigarette and slowly blowing the smoke into the air, he said, "Little Brother?"

Dan didn't reply at first. His eyes turned back to the house and through the screen door where the sheriff was standing, intently watching the pair. Dan looked at the sheriff for a moment before turning his attention back to Frank. "Frank, why are you makin' this harder than it has to be?"

As Dan spoke, Frank gave a slight shake of his head, staring at the ground.

"Frank, if you don't walk with me to the sheriff's car right now, Mike's goin' to come out here with even more deputies and take you by force . . . all because of some flowers."

Frank, still defiant, said, "Let 'em come," reaching down for the whiskey bottle that was now sitting on the porch planks between the two brothers. As Frank's hand neared the bottle, Dan slid it further under the swing with the heel of his boot. The two brothers glared at each other, each waiting for the other to give an inch.

Dan broke the silence with the very words that Frank needed to hear, but the last words that he wanted to be said. "What would Sarah say about what you're doin'?"

A flash of coldness flew over Frank's face. He would have broken any other man in half for saying such a thing, but this was brother, and his brother knew his and Sarah's story. Frank dropped his cigarette and slid back into the seat. His face and body succumbed to his misery and loss. "Dan, I'm just so tired—tired of hurtin' and tired of missin' her," Frank said, through a quivering voice.

"Frank, it's okay to miss her. You don't ever stop missin' her. But she never would've wanted you to become this. She would want you to live your life and be as happy as you can be."

Frank nodded, tears beginning to gather at his lashes. A solemn, indecisive shrug gave way to the words of truth, "You're right . . ."

"Ready to go tell Mike what he needs to know and get this behind you?" Dan asked gently.

A silent but meaningful nod from the grieving signaled the needed surrender. Both men stood up together and walked to the back door where Sheriff Bode was waiting.

The screen door screeched and popped as Dan opened it for his brother. Frank stepped into the house and up to the sheriff with two outstretched, muddy arms, touching them wrist to wrist. "Frank, that's not necessary. Jerome will walk you out to the car."

Elizabeth, who had seen the whole thing unfold from the kitchen window, stepped forward to hug Frank tightly before he was taken away. "Frank Calloway, only God loves you more than we do," she said as her tears were pooling.

Jerome walked Frank out to the squad car. He was careful to let Frank walk in front, so that he could keep an eye on him. As the officer opened the door to the back seat and helped Frank into the car, Frank sensed the officer's uneasiness. Jerome opened the driver's side door and slid in behind the wheel. After he repositioned his gun and his flashlight, he fastened the seat belt. Both men sat in silence while Dan and Sheriff Bode talked on Frank's front porch. It was then that the gravity of the situation sank in. Frank thought about what Dan had asked him on the swing. He felt ashamed thinking about Sarah and what she would have said. Frank glanced up at the officer and caught him watching him through the rearview mirror. Once their eyes met, the officer looked away. They sat there for a few seconds, then Frank said, "Look here, son . . . I'm sorry about what I said to you earlier. That was the liquor talkin'."

The officer, stunned by Frank's apology, could only say, "Uhhhh . . . yes, sir . . . I mean . . . it's okay. I accept your apology."

"Thank you, son," Frank humbly replied.

As reconciliation occurred in the police car, Dan and Sheriff Bode were still on the porch, wrapping up details of the plan for Frank. "Well, Dan, we'll take him down to the county jail. He is bein' charged with destruction of private property, theft, and trespassin'. Plus," the gray-haired sheriff continued, rolling his eyes slightly, "Mrs. Jenkins said that, even though Frank never actually threatened her, she felt frightened by his 'crazed look.' I doubt anythin' will come of that. You can pick him up in a couple of hours."

The next morning, the brothers greeted the sun as they had so many mornings throughout their life. Both sat on the back porch of Dan's house, sipping coffee.

The morning solitude brought a certain clarity to Frank's mind. The fresh morning breeze swept across the field, into the yard, and gently across his cheeks. He closed his eyes and thought about Sarah for a moment. His eyes opened, and he noticed how the colors seemed to be brighter. The blue sky, the different shades of green grass, the pines and the oaks, even the pale blue of the wooden planks on Dan's porch. Those old, white rockers even seemed less old somehow. In that moment, he felt Sarah all around him. Frank could almost smell the scent of her hair. He closed his eyes once more as he held back his tears. Then, he imagined what she would say to him if she could. The words came to him, as if she spoke them herself, "New day, Honey."

Frank inhaled quickly, catching Dan's attention. "You okay?" the younger brother asked with a tone of concern.

Frank looked up from the coffee cup clutched between his hands and said, through the mistiness in his eyes, "I'm fine, Brother, just fine." The two smiled momentarily at each other, acknowledging Frank's newfound peace.

The following month, Frank's court date approached, and he prepared to stand before the judge to pay his fine. Pastor O'Neil stopped by Frank's house on the appointed morning. He tapped a few times on the aged, wooden screen door that was on the front of the home. Frank opened the door.

"Hey, Pastor, what brings you out this way?" he asked, first shaking the reverend's hand, then promptly inviting the visitor into his living room.

"Well, I know this is a big day for you, so I wanted to stop by and maybe say a quick prayer with you before you go."

"I would appreciate that."

Pastor O'Neil placed his hand on Frank's shoulder, and both men bowed their heads. The pastor petitioned the Father, asking Him to give Frank all the guidance, mercy, and peace that he needed for the day. He thanked Him for all that He had done in Frank's life and for all that He was about to do. The two men embraced, and Frank thanked him for coming.

"Frank, I have one more thing here for you," the pastor said, reaching into his coat pocket and pulling out a check, "The church wanted me to give this to you." He continued, "There should be enough there to take care of the fine and provide Mrs. Lola with a half dozen or so new rose bushes."

Frank reached up to wipe his eyes, which were forming tears of of joy, "Pastor, I just can't believe how God is blessin' me, especially given the way I've been actin' lately."

"Frank, that's all He wants to do—is bless his children." The pastor paused for a second and then said with a smile, "But I do believe this is the first time in the 150-year history of Cotton Valley Baptist Church that a love offering was taken to pay a court fine." After a brief chuckle, the pastor continued in a more sober tone, "Then again, it's not the first debt that we have owed that God paid for us."

Suddenly, the screen door screeched open, and in walked all the Calloway clan. Frank looked up, with tears in his eyes while still clutching the check. "Y'all knew about this, didn't you?"

"Knew about what, Uncle Frank?" Dee replied with a slight grin.

Frank just smiled and shook his head as he pulled the white hand-kerchief from his back pocket to wipe the tears away. After a few moments of shared emotions among the Calloway family, Frank walked over to Caroline, who was cradling her and Dee's new son. Frank had been so consumed by grief in the past few months that he had barely acknowledged the birth of his great-nephew.

"He just turned four months," Caroline said as she beamed down at her baby boy.

"Can I hold him?" Frank asked.

"Why, sure, I'd love for you to."

Frank gently picked up the child, being ever so careful to support the baby's head. "Oh my goodness," Frank whispered, "he is a fine boy." Frank pulled Joel close to his chest, to see his face. He noted the sweet baby smell and the spray of blonde hair atop his head. "It's true," Frank said.

"What's that, Uncle Frank?" Caroline asked.

"What Sarah used to say, 'Holdin' a baby is like medicine for the heart,' " he replied.

Frank held Joel for a few moments, gently swaying him from side to side. Under his breath, he whispered softly words from Job 1:21 as he smiled down at Joel, "The LORD gave, and the LORD has taken away; Blessed be the name of the LORD."

Ten

Brother John

Three years had passed since the birth of Joel, and life on the farm had carried on. Frank, although he still missed Sarah, was in a better place now. Frank Jr. continued his career in the military but stayed in touch with his dad more often. Dan and Elizabeth were enjoying the blessings of being grandparents. Tom was not married yet, but he was doing a lot of looking for the right lady. Jody Simms had been seen on occasion by the family. He had been arrested a time or two for drunken, disorderly conduct. Surprisingly, it was John Tuleeves who had bailed him out. It had been three years of sobriety for John. He would joke from time to time, saying that his life started at the same time that Joel's did. John's compassion for Jody was based on the fact that he knew all too well what it was like to deal with those kinds of demons.

It was the day of Joel's birth. All of the Calloway clan were at the hospital, soaking up the joys of a newborn baby. John was still at home at 8 a.m., sleeping off his habits from the night before. He was awakened by the screams of Mrs. Patterson, a neighbor, as she banged on the door of the Calloway home.

Lois Patterson was a widow who lived alone with her ten-year-old grandchild, Alice. Lois's husband, John, had passed away several years before. He had been a U.S. Navy lieutenant who retired after the birth of Alice, as their daughter had died immediately after giving birth to her. At that point, it had become their plan to raise Alice as their own.

John sat up in his bed and rubbed his face, trying to decide if the screams were real or in his head. He managed to pull on his pants and boots with his signature speed, then he began to climb down from the loft. He was halfway down the ladder when he heard the knocking again. It was real, very real. John peered through the space between the barn doors. There, he could see a frantic lady as she banged on the doors and then the windows of the Calloway home. John buttoned the last few buttons on his shirt and pushed his hand over his head, pulling his hair back and out of his face. He emerged from the barn and began to walk swiftly toward Mrs. Patterson, saying, "Mrs. Patterson, they are gone. There is no one home. Young Daniel and Mrs. Caroline have had a son. Dan and Elizabeth have gone to see the child. Can I help you?"

John's explanation of the whereabouts of the Calloways was all but interrupted by Mrs. Patterson's response—"HELP ME, PLEASE HELP ME! MY GRANDDAUGHTER! PLEASE HELP MY GRAND-DAUGHTER!"

John gently but firmly grabbed Mrs. Patterson by the shoulders, trying to calm her so that he could understand what she needed. "Mrs. Patterson, what is wrong with Alice?"

Mrs. Patterson, who was by now completely hysterical, shook free from John, and turned back to run toward her house, screaming, "SHE'S IN THE HOUSE! SHE'S IN THE HOUSE! IT'S BURNING!"

John followed after her. Once he got to the road, he could see the black smoke, rising from the old, two-story home. John ran as fast as he could down the road, passing Mrs. Patterson. He was horrified to see the house almost completely engulfed in flames. Mrs. Patterson ran up behind John and collapsed in the yard. In between the gasps of air, she screamed, "SHE'S ON . . . SHE'S ON THE SECOND FLOOR!"

John ran up to the house, "ALICE! ALICE! WHERE ARE YOU?" he bellowed, hoping for a response. "ANSWER ME!"

"HELP ME! HELP ME," a young voice cried out, as the girl peeked out of her partially opened bedroom window, smoke enveloping her.

As John heard the direction the voice was coming from, his heart sank as he realized the inferno that was burning between him and her rescue. "STAY THERE! I AM COMING TO GET YOU!" he called as he surveyed his surroundings. John could not help but think of the child whom he had lost so many years ago. He determined in his heart that he would not lose this one.

Looking about, he noticed a blanket lying on the front porch swing. He then spotted a barrel of rain water sitting nearby. John raced up onto the porch, took the blanket, dropped it into the barrel, then pulled the wet cloth out and over his head and shoulders. He flung himself through the doorway of the house. The heat filled his lungs and tried to force him back into the yard. He ignored the flames that were licking up the wooden staircase as he ran up them and called out to the girl, "ALICE! ALICE! I AM COMING!" John reached the top of the staircase only to realize the entire top floor was filled with smoke. "ALICE! ALICE! CALL OUT SO I CAN FIND YOU!" John yelled.

"I'M HERE, AT THE END OF THE HALL!" Alice shouted back as her voice gave way to sobs.

John ran in the direction of her voice as the flames followed him. He found Alice crouched down, next to the bedroom window. "WE MUST GO NOW!" he said as he wrapped the blanket, which was quickly becoming less wet, around her. John grabbed her in his arms and turned to try and find the staircase, but he found that it was completely engulfed. He could feel the floor creaking and popping below him. He turned back to the room at the end of the hallway. "ALICE, KEEP YOUR FACE COVERED!" John shouted as he ran the short distance down the hall and across the bedroom. He crashed through the window, with Alice clutched tightly to his chest. John immediately felt the cool rush of air, followed by the stinging pain from the small shards of glass which had cut into his face. He held her even tighter as they both fell from the burning inferno. With a sudden jolt,

John felt the hard ground slam against his back, slapping all the air from his lungs.

Mrs. Patterson, who had seen the whole thing unfold from the front yard, rushed over to them. She picked her granddaughter up and removed the partially charred blanket from around her face, which was still hot from the encounter. "Alice! Alice!" she cried out.

The girl began to cough. "Grandma! Grandma! I was so scared," were the words that followed.

John lay there wheezing, trying to recapture the air that had been forced from his body. The tiny cuts from the window glass had left thin, red lines across his face and neck. His long, black hair was now singed and starting to be matted in the trickles of blood. Smoke rose from his body. He held his forearms upright, bent at the elbows, to prevent his burnt flesh from touching anything that would make the pain worse. He remained motionless, with his eyes closed, as he focused on his breathing to divert his attention from the seething pain.

Shortly, there were two sets of hands reaching underneath his torso and around his upper arms. It was Alice and her grandmother, attempting to pull John away from the still-burning house. The two struggled at first, but soon began to slide his body across the grassy lawn to a safe distance. The pain shot through John's body with every movement. It felt as though his flesh was being torn away by their efforts. He thought of his wife and child. He thought that if death did come to him, how happy he would be to reunite with his family. That blessed thought passed quickly as a sad one replaced it: one which made him feel so ashamed that he began to weep. It was the thought of leaving this world and passing to the next while smelling of whiskey. It was not how he wished to meet his son for the first time.

The sadness was broken by the sound of sirens from the approaching fire trucks. John spent the next six weeks in the hospital. The doctor said that he had suffered three broken ribs, a ruptured spleen, a collapsed lung, multiple facial lacerations, and third- and fourth-degree burns to his arms. They were bewildered by the fact that a man of John's age could sustain such trauma and live. Rehabilitation was long and painful for John, but, as the days, weeks, and months went by, he began to return to his old self . . . with a few changes.

The fall revival at Cotton Valley Baptist Church had begun. The Wednesday night service drew a particularly large crowd. To the surprise of most, one of those faces belonged to John Tuleeves. Many years had passed since he had been in church. As a matter of fact, he had been a young boy during his last visit. This time was different, though, as the invitation had come from a certain young girl named Alice. During John's recovery, she had asked if he would attend just one service of the revival. John had promised her that he would, so, on this particular night, he was keeping his word.

Soul after soul filed into the old sanctuary. Smiles, handshakes, and hugs saturated the congregation. John received the biggest hug from Alice, "You kept your promise, John! You kept your promise!" Alice said, squeezing him tightly.

John found a seat next to Dee and the rest of the Calloway clan. The service began as usual, with prayers and songs of praise. Then, the visiting evangelist, Reverend Churchill Biggers, from Wiggins, Mississippi, stepped up to the pulpit. His large, booming voice echoed through the rafters of the old building.

"Brothers and sisters, please turn with me to the book of Daniel, chapter three. There, we will read the story of the three Jews who refused to bow down and worship the golden image of King Nebuchadnezzar. We will read how they placed their faith in the true, living God, because he is the only God. We will read how they defied the king, even when he threatened to throw them into the fiery furnace." A shuffling of pages could be heard throughout the room as the fingers of the faithful searched for the passage. As the sound of the search quieted, the preacher continued to read Daniel chapter three, verses seventeen and eighteen:

If that *is the case,* our God whom we serve is able to deliver us from the burning fiery furnace, and He will deliver *us* from your hand, O king. But if not, let it be known to you, O king, that we do not serve your gods, nor will we worship the gold image which you have set up.

Reverend Biggers went on to tell how this boldness enraged the king, so much so that he had the furnace heated seven times hotter than it had ever been before, then he had the three men bound and thrown into the fire. John began to create this image in his mind as he listened. He began to imagine the fear of such a punishment—and what faith the men must have had.

The reverend continued with the story. At times, he would step out from behind the pulpit and walk across the stage, holding his Bible high in the air. It was as if he was pointing a bright light to the heavens. He went on to tell how God delivered the men from the fire, and he proceeded to read from verses twenty-four through twenty-six of the same chapter:

Then King Nebuchadnezzar was astonished; and he rose in haste *and* spoke, saying to his counselors, "Did we not cast three men bound into the midst of the fire?" They answered and said to the king, "True, O king." "Look!" he answered, "I see four men loose, walking in the midst of the fire; and they are not hurt, and the form of the fourth is like the Son of God." Then Nebuchadnezzar came near to the mouth of the burning fiery furnace, *and* spake, and said, Shadrach, Meshach, and Abednego, ye servants of the most high God, come forth, and come *hither.* Then Shadrach, Meshach, and Abednego, came forth of the midst of the fire.

Reverend Biggers laid the open Bible gently on the pulpit, the edges of it were worn from many faithful years of use. Then, he reached into his back pocket and pulled out a white handkerchief. He wiped the sweat from his forehead and said, "Brothers, Sisters—what has God delivered you from? What golden image, what idol, are you willing to deny, so that God can use you?"

The preacher asked the piano player and music director to come down. The congregation stood to sing. John stood silent, studying the words that he had just heard. He knew all too well what he had been delivered from, and it was not just a burning house. As John stood there, deep in thought, he realized what God had performed in his life through a small girl in a burning house: John had not shown up to save Alice and her grandmother. God had sent them to save him.

The tears began to run down John's cheeks. He was completely overcome by God's love. He could clearly see the golden image in his own life, and it was shaped like a whiskey bottle. As the voices around him rose with song, he stepped out into the aisle and slowly walked down to the altar. John knelt down and placed his hands over his face as he began to pray. It seemed as if only a few seconds had passed when he felt a small hand on his shoulder. He knew it must have been Alice. "What a godly, compassionate, and loving little girl," he thought to himself. "How wonderful it would be if more people were like her." John's heart cracked and broke open. All the burdens spilled out as he knelt there, petitioning to God. He laid his last bit of pain and loss at the foot of the cross, and he asked Jesus to be his Savior. The songs came and went throughout the sanctuary. By the time that the last one softly ended, John felt light as a feather. He was so thankful for God's miraculous grace and mercy.

John stood, wiping the tears from his face. When he turned to walk back up the aisle, he was frozen with awe. Not only had Alice knelt there with him, but also a multitude of strangers. John began to weep again as he looked at each face. One by one, they hugged and congratulated him. An ocean of *God bless yous* washed over him. It was the first time that John had felt such love.

Eleven

A Dream to a Calling

The winter following his conversion, John Tuleeves returned to the Chickasaw Nation with his sobriety in tow. He traveled throughout the reservations, counseling other Native Americans who were struggling with alcohol abuse. He would return each year, though, to the Calloway farm to help with the planting and harvesting seasons.

After one such visit, Dee was inspired by the change in John. It consumed his thoughts for the next several weeks. He thought about the difference that John was making in the world around him. It made Dee think of his own life and what, if any, difference that he might be making. His mind wandered back to the dreams of his childhood. The dreams that were so much larger than himself; dreams that drive our youth, but somehow get consumed by the reality of life, instead of becoming a part of it. There was one dream that remained. The biggest dream, the one which always seemed to be waiting patiently for Dee: the dream of being a doctor. He thought about the time that his father was injured and had to have stitches . . . and the time that Bobby had passed away . . . and the time that Mr. Kyle had been saved. Dee even thought about when his old dog, Bonnie, had died. All of these events drew his mind and heart back to the dream that he had always felt was an impossibility.

"A doctor—oh, Lord, help me," Dee thought to himself one quiet afternoon, when Caroline and the kids were away. The idea seemed too overwhelming. The fact that he was even thinking about such a feat filled him with emotion. "What a difference I could make, what a holy profession," Dee marveled. His joy and hopefulness were soon replaced though by fear and doubt. "What am I thinkin'? Startin' medical school at my age? Besides, I'm not smart enough. And how would I tell Pop, or Mom, or Uncle Frank, or Caroline? Oh gosh, Caroline—how on earth would I tell her? She just finished school herself. We have all this school debt—they'd all think that I'd lost my mind!" The fear and doubt did what it often does when we begin to imagine greater than ourselves—it painted Dee's dream as silly and unrealistic. He felt foolish for even thinking of it.

It was spring, and the Calloways were preparing for the Sunday morning church service. But it was not just any service. It was Easter. Joel pulled and tugged at his tie, which was striped in blue and yellow. "Joel, stop pullin' on your tie. It looks nice, and you'll have it twisted and crooked." Caroline declared as she tried desperately to comb her son's hair.

Dee and Mary Elizabeth sat in the swing on the front porch. They were waiting patiently on mother and son to appear, so that they all could make their way down to the church. Mary Elizabeth took note of her father's light-gray suit and blue tie. "You look nice, Daddy," she said, peering up at his face.

"Why, thank you, Honey, you look nice too. I love that new, yellow dress."

"Thanks, Mom bought it for me for Easter."

"Well, you make it look lovely," Dee replied.

Eventually, the remaining family members made it out onto the front porch. "My goodness, you're lookin' sharp there, Mr. Joel. And you, Mrs. Caroline, are a vision of beauty. What do you think, Mary Elizabeth?" Dee asked as the two made their appearance.

"He's right, Mom. Y'all both look real good."

"Why, thank you, Mr. Calloway and Miss Calloway," Caroline said as she gave a slight curtsy in response to the overflow of accolades. "Now, let's go before we're late," she continued.

The four filed into the church entrance. Mary and Joel hurried to their seats and waited for the music. Mary looked around to see if there was anyone new present today, while Joel pushed his little car toy—the one piece of contraband that he had been able to sneak past his mother's seemingly all-seeing eyes—around in the seat next to hers. Soon, Dee and Caroline took their seats after gathering a program and exchanging a few handshakes, hugs, and welcomes with some well-known faces.

The congregation sang to the top of their lungs. Special after special followed. Mrs. Harper's daughter played "How Great Thou Art" on the piano, and Mrs. Jones's twins sang "I'll Rise Again."

After the special music, Pastor O'Neil walked up to the podium. He laid his Bible down on it and flipped through the pages until he came to the scripture that he had marked earlier. He paused only for a second, looked out across the audience, and smiled. "Happy Easter, and welcome. Today, I want to speak about three people: David, Daniel, and Mary. In particular, I want to speak about something that they all had in common . . . trust. Their steadfast trust in God is the reason you know who they are today. The book of First Samuel, chapter seventeen, verses thirty-seven through forty-six, tell us about David's trust." Pastor O'Neil went on to read the words from the chapter aloud:

Moreover David said, "The LORD, who delivered me from the paw of the lion and from the paw of the bear, He will deliver me from the hand of this Philistine." . . . And the Philistine said to David, "Come to me, and I will give your flesh to the birds of the air and the beasts of the field!" Then David said to the Philistine . . . "I come to you in the name of the LORD of hosts, the God of the armies of Israel, whom you have defied. This day the LORD will deliver you into my hand, and I will strike you and take your head from you." . . .

The pastor continued on, "David's trust in God slew the giant in his life. It was Daniel's trust that shut the mouths of the lions. The book of Daniel, in chapter six, verses sixteen through twenty-two, tells us this:

So the king gave the command, and they brought Daniel and cast *him* into the den of lions. *But* the king spoke, saying to Daniel, "Your God, whom you serve continually, He will deliver you." Then a stone was brought and laid on the mouth of the den, and the king sealed it with his own signet ring and with the signets of his lords, that the purpose concerning Daniel might not be changed. Now the king went to his palace and spent the night fasting; and no musicians were brought before him. Also his sleep went from him. Then the king arose very early in the morning and went in haste to the den of lions. And when he came to the den, he cried out with a lamenting voice to Daniel. The king spoke, saying to Daniel, "Daniel, servant of the living God, has your God, whom you serve continually, been able to deliver you from the lions?" Then Daniel said to the king, "O king, live forever! My God sent His angel and shut the lions' mouths, so that they have not hurt me, because I was found innocent before Him; and also, O king, I have done no wrong before you."

You'll notice that when King Darius called to Daniel and asked if he was okay, Daniel's reply was one of surety. He was still in the den when he spoke to the king. There was no fear. He was not screaming, 'I'm okay, just hurry up and get me out of here!'"

A wave of laughter rolled across the crowd. But Dee's laughter was tempered with a grain of self-reflection. "Could I trust God that much?" he wondered to himself.

"No! Daniel didn't do that," the pastor continued. "You see, Daniel had slept in confidence among the lions. He had laid side by side among the beasts all night. He trusted God, because he had seen Him in action. Then there's Mary—oh, Mary. Scripture tells us that she was highly favored among women. How awesome is that? You know, Mary had to have more trust than anyone. Here was a young woman who was not married, she's promised to Joseph, and then finds herself miraculously pregnant. Now, you know where your minds go when you hear of unwed mothers. Don't think that Mary wasn't aware of what people would think of her. But Mary—bless her heart—she trusted. The book of Luke, in chapter one, verses twenty-six through thirty-five, tells us of Mary's encounter with the angel Gabriel:

Now in the sixth month the angel Gabriel was sent by God to a city of Galilee named Nazareth, to a virgin betrothed to a man whose name was Joseph, of the house of David. The virgin's name *was* Mary. And having come in, the angel said to her, "Rejoice, highly favored *one,* the Lord *is* with you; blessed *are* you among women!" But when she saw *him,* she was troubled at his saying, and considered what manner of greeting this was. Then the angel said to her, "Do not be afraid, Mary, for you have found favor with God. And behold, you will conceive in your womb, and bring forth a Son, and shall call His name JESUS. He will be great, and will be called the Son of the Highest; and the Lord God will give Him the throne of His father David. And He will reign over the house of Jacob forever, and of His kingdom there will be no end." Then Mary said to the angel, "How can this be, since I do not know a man?" And the angel answered and said to her, "*The* Holy Spirit will come upon you, and the power of the Highest will overshadow you; therefore, also, that Holy One who is to be born will be called the Son of God.

I love the way that Gabriel just lays it all out for Mary: 'God has chosen you. This is what's going to happen. And trust me, Mary, it's going to be the greatest thing ever!' " Pastor O'Neil said with passion in his voice, raising his hands in the air.

Amens filled the room, acknowledging the joy in the truth that had just been spoken.

"I tell you, friends, God is still calling people to trust Him today. He has something great in mind for those who step out on faith and trust Him." The sweat rolled down each side of Pastor O'Neil's face and gathered on the bright-white collar of his shirt, leaving would-be stains all around his neck. Dee pondered the words that he had just heard. As the pastor continued with his sermon, Dee hung on every word. It was as if he was the only one in that sanctuary.

Pastor O'Neil reached down under the pulpit and pulled out a small cup of water, took a sip, then placed it back into its spot. After wiping away the sweat from his brow, he added, "In closing, let me say this; when you come to the point where you decide to trust God, I want you to understand some things. He may take you to some scary places, but He'll be there to protect you. He'll shut the mouths of the beasts. He may give you some big obstacles to overcome, but He'll equip you with all that you need, so that you can slay your giant. He may even entrust you with a great, great task—one which you feel is too great to carry out. But He'll be with you every step of the journey, so that, in the end, those around you might see Him in you."

With those words, the sermon ended. A song was sung, and the altar was opened. Soon, Dee, Caroline, and the kids were on their way home.

Mary and Joel chattered back and forth from the back seat about things of relevance in a child's mind. Questions such as "How is bubblegum made?" and "How old is God?" and "Why does the Easter bunny bring you colored eggs?" could be heard coming from the backseat.

Caroline talked about what she was cooking for lunch. "Dee, do you want peas or green beans with the roast? I prefer peas, but it's up to you. And what about bread—what kind of bread? Rolls or cornbread? I prefer cornbread, but it's up to you," she said, barely pausing for a reply from Dee.

Dee failed to register any of it. He just drove on silently as he thought about the message. He thought about how he felt like God had been speaking directly to him. "Is God askin' me to become a doctor?" he wondered to himself. A series of questions came to his mind following the first one: "Why would He do that? What purpose would it serve? How can I know? Am I not too old? What about the farm? I mean, really, I thought God only calls us to places of ministry." It was then that it struck him—"That's what He's doin'!" Dee's thoughts went back to the words that Doc Simmons had spoken to him so many years ago: "It's all about the healin', and healin' comes from God."

"Dee! Are you listenin' to me?" Caroline's raised voice cut in, jerking Dee out of his state of deep thought.

"Huh? Yeah! I heard everythin' you said—peas, rolls, cornbread. Yeah, I heard everythin', Honey."

Caroline sighed deeply and rolled her eyes.

Dee continued to wrestle with all of his thoughts. The emotions, questions, concerns, fears, and doubts moved inside him until they all came together and rested in his heart. By the time that he pulled the car into the driveway, he had settled within his soul what must be done. For the next several weeks, he prayed about how he would tell Caroline and the rest of the family. Soon, the time came, and Dee felt in his heart that it was the right moment to share.

It was late on a warm, spring evening. The honeysuckle laid on the air like a soft blanket. Dee had always liked the smell of honeysuckle. It smelt of home. It gave him a certain peace about the decision he had made—and sharing it with his wife. Dee and Caroline sat in the swing on the front porch, slowly swaying back and forth as they watched the kids play in the yard. "Caroline, I have somethin' I need to tell you," Dee said.

"What is it, Babe?" she asked.

"Well, this has been on my mind for quite some time. I've prayed about it, and I'm confident that this is what God wants."

"Honey, what do you want to tell me?" Caroline asked, with a noticeable look of concern.

"I've decided that I want to go to medical school. I want to be a physician. I know that I'm a little old to be doin' this, and I know that we still have a lot left to pay on your student loan. I know that it will be hard on us, but, Caroline, God has spoken to my heart . . . I know that He wants me to do this. I don't really know why right now instead of ten or twelve years ago, but I know He has a purpose in it." Dee's emotion finally overtook him. The tears began to well up in his eyes. "Honey, it's like God spoke to my soul and said, 'I want to show you what I can do with your dream. Just trust Me.'"

Caroline paused for a moment, to prepare her words before she spoke. She took Dee's hand, and, as her blue eyes—as beautiful to him as ever—met his, she spoke, "Dee, I've known you my whole life. I've loved you nearly my whole life. When we got married, we promised that we would try to be to each other all that God expected us to be. Since then, I've watched you pray for God's direction for us—every day. I've watched you love me the way God loves the church, and I've seen you be a godly father to our children." She took in a breath, as if to prepare herself for her own words. "This will not be easy, Dee. It will most likely be the hardest thing that you—that we—will ever do. But if it's what God wants . . ." Caroline leaned in, her face coming slightly closer to Dee's—her voice lowering with subtlety, punctuating her honesty, ". . . then how could I do anythin' other than support you? I'll be right here, every step of the way."

Thankfulness flooded Dee's heart as he wrapped his arms around his wife and held her tight. Never had he been more sure that Caroline was a gift straight from God.

The next morning, Dee drove to his parents' home. He was unsure about how his father would take the news about his decision to quit the farm and go to medical school. Dee opened the old screen door that led into the kitchen, Elizabeth was busy putting the final touches on breakfast. "Hey, Mama," Dee said as he gave his mother a kiss on the cheek.

"Hey, Sweetie. What are you doin' out so early?"

"Ah, I need to talk to you and Pop about somethin'."

"Honey, is everythin' alright? One of the kids sick? Is it Caroline? She just works too hard, that girl." Elizabeth expressed in an urgent, motherly tone.

"Mama! Mama! Everythin' is fine. I just need to tell you somethin'," Dee said as he reached out and placed his hands on his mother's shoulders, to calm her.

Dan made his way into the kitchen and took his normal seat. "Hey, Buddy, what are you doin' out so early?"

"Hey, Pop. I have somethin' I need to tell you and Mom."

Dee took a deep breath, pulled the wooden chair away from the kitchen table, and sat down. Even though Dan and Elizabeth had looks of concern on their faces, they patiently waited for Dee to speak. "Pop, Mom, I've decided to go back to medical school and get my degree. I want to be a doctor." Dee's announcement was short and to the point.

Dan and Elizabeth paused for a moment before responding. Elizabeth looked at Dan, then back at Dee, then spoke, "Dee, Honey, are you sure? I mean, have you prayed about it?"

"Mama, I haven't been this sure about somethin' since I asked Caroline to marry me. And yes, I've prayed about it. As a matter of fact, not only did I talk to God about it, but He also talked to me," Dee answered, with an ever-so-slight chuckle.

Dan didn't say a word at first, he just raised his coffee cup to his mouth and took a sip. It was always that way with Dan in a serious moment; he was never one to speak without assessing the situation first. Finally, he looked at Dee and asked, "How long will it take you?"

"Well, Pop, it'll take four years here in college, and then six in medical school, and about three years of residency."

Dee read the look on Dan's face as he added up the years in his mind. "So, by the time you finish completely, and are practicin' on your own, you'll be forty-eight?" The length of the process was something that Dee had always known, but there was something quite sobering about someone saying it out loud. "What does Caroline say about this?" Dan continued.

"She's fine with it. I mean, we both know it's not goin' to be easy, but nothin' important ever is."

Dan paused for another moment. "So, what about the farm? Where does that fit in with all of your plans?" he asked.

"Well, Pop, nothin' will change right away. I'll start school in the fall, and I'll have my summers to work."

Dan sat back in his chair, a grave expression washing over his face as he did so. Finally, he said, "Dee, I just don't know what to say. I mean, this farm has been such a big part of our lives for so long. It's who we are, and, honestly, Son, at your age, I don't really understand the reasonin' behind turnin' your back on it. I know it's somethin' you talked about when you were a boy, but that's all I thought it was—talk."

"Pop, it's not about not wantin' to be a farmer anymore. I'll always be a farmer. But this is different. It's about wantin' what God wants. And no, I don't understand His timin', and, honestly, I've stopped tryin' to understand it. I'm just tryin' to trust."

Although the look of disappointment did not leave Dan's face, he knew that the talking was done. He gave Dee a hug and said, "I understand." It was his way of trying to make Dee feel better about things and give himself time to process it.

The next morning, Dan awakened early. He was seeking some time to talk to God about everything. He found himself walking among the rows of the old flower garden that had been such a part of the family story. It had become the family's "thin place"—a place where heaven and earth seemed closer. A place where God's voice was more clear. Dan walked slowly, taking time to notice all the beautiful colors. He paused at the end of each row and closed his eyes as he took a breath, savoring all the smells. He walked the rows for quite some time, occasionally reaching down to feel the texture of a bloom, until God and he had reasoned together.

That evening, Dan drove down to Dee and Caroline's house. "Papaw!" was the response from Mary and Joel as he pulled into the driveway. The two ran to meet him before he could make it to the front door. It was their usual greeting. He gave them both hugs, lifting them off their feet. "Did you come to see us?" the duo inquired.

"I always want to see you two, but I need to talk to your daddy first. Then, we may go pick up Mamaw for some ice cream. How about that?"

"Yaaaayyyy!" shouted the two.

Dee had already made his way onto the porch as Dan was making the bargain with Mary and Joel. "Hey, Pop. What's up?"

"Dee, I want to pick up where we left off at breakfast yesterday."

"Sure, Pop," Dee replied, then he turned to his youngsters, "Would y'all let me and Papaw have a talk? We'll come get you when we're done."

Father and son took their seats on the porch as Mary and Joel headed back into the house. Dan was sure in his thoughts, so he wasted no time getting started.

"Dee, I thought about what you said yesterday. I won't lie, Son. It hurt me to think that somehow farmin' was not for you anymore. I felt that your decision to be a doctor meant that the way you grew up wasn't good enough. I know now that's not true. It was all in my way of thinkin'. At first, I thought of how selfish of you it was and how you were too old to start somethin' like this. To me, it all seemed kind of wasteful and unnecessary and, if I'm bein' honest, even a little silly. I was afraid that you might be havin' a midlife crisis. I thought, 'Lord, help us—why doesn't he just go buy a motorcycle or somethin' like that.'" Both men gave a chuckle at Dan's bit of humor. "But then I thought about what you said, about how God was puttin' this on your heart. I know you well enough to know this is not somethin' you would decide without certainty. It made me think of how God moves people to do for Him—different things at different times. When we decide to live our lives by His will and not our own, we accept those things. The flip side is that when we are all in for God, He is all in for us. He does nothing halfway, and His timin' is always perfect. You know, Dee, it puts me in mind of Abraham. God asked him to leave his home and move to a faraway land and said that He would bless him. He was seventy-five years old when God asked him to do that. Then, He told him and his wife, who was barren, that he would be the father of a nation. He was one hundred years old when Isaac was born." Dan paused for a second as father and son looked at one another. "Yeah, when we listen and let Him lead, He always leads to greatness. I am so, so proud of you for havin' the courage to follow Him."

The two stood and embraced. Dan hugged his son tightly for a moment, as if sensing the rough road that would lie ahead for him, then he kissed him on the forehead, "The family supports you in this, Dee. We love you very much," Dan said somberly. Then, he turned his attention back to Mary and Joel, "Well, let me make good on my promise to them." Dee nodded his agreement as Dan made his way to the front door, gently opened it, and called out, "Hey, Booger Bears, let's go get some ice cream." The cheerful response was a fitting description of how all four of their hearts felt in that moment.

The next four years proved to be difficult, at best. It was quite a learning curve for Dee. Returning to school after so long brought its own, unique problems, one of which was money. Schooling costs are expensive, especially when you are starting from scratch. But Dee made the grades, Caroline made the bills, and God blessed.

Finally, graduation was in sight. Dee worked to complete his last year. If all went well, he would be accepted into medical school in the fall. It meant the completion of the first leg on his journey with God. But it also meant that Dee needed to make a final push to score as high as he could on his MCAT, which meant sacrifice on the part of Caroline and the rest of the family.

Tom was pulling double duty on the farm while Dee was spending most of his time studying. Tom never backed down from a hard day's work, but sometimes his better judgment was replaced with impatience.

He knew that the willow bridge was too small and too old for the tractor, but with all of the rain that they had gotten lately, the creek was up too high to cross over in the shallows. The only other way to cross over to another field would be on the main road, which would have taken an extra hour.

The old bridge had been thrown together years ago by Dan and Frank. And it had long since lost its usefulness. Tom slowly inched onto the bridge, first with the front tires and then the back. The bridge creaked and popped with every movement, as if complaining about its unexpected load. Tom knew that he had gone too far when he felt the bridge shift and drop a few inches. He decided to shut the engine off and then try to climb down from the tractor and off the bridge. Just as Tom stepped off the tractor and onto the bridge, he felt it give way underneath him. The next thing that Tom felt was the muddy creek water all around him. He gathered his senses enough to decide to try to get to the bank, but before he could move, a timber from the bridge crashed down on his legs, pinning everything from his waist down underneath the water. Tom, writhing in pain, at first thought that the tractor had fallen on him, then he almost instantly realized that it hadn't fallen at all—but it had started to roll off the edge of the broken bridge. One broken timber, sticking out from the base of the bridge, was all that was keeping that massive green machine from crushing Tom. He sat there, trapped in the water, contemplating how to escape, thinking, "If I lay here too long, the timber could snap." He also thought about how foolish it was to have tried that old bridge anyway . . . and how if Dee had been there, he would have been telling him just how foolish it was. "If he'd been here in the first place, it wouldn't have happened anyhow," he said to himself. Just as that thought passed, Tom heard a loud pop.

It had been two hours before Uncle Frank found Tom. It took a couple of backhoes and another tractor to pull the John Deere off of him. He was barely recognizable and barely breathing. The helicopter flight to the hospital seemed to take forever. When Dan and Elizabeth made it to the hospital, the doctors were still assessing the damage.

Dee was still at the library, up to his elbows in books, when Caroline called. All she could get out was, "Tom's hurt! Come to the hospital!" Dee's heart sank. All he could think was the worst.

After all the family had arrived, Frank tried to explain what had happened, trying to hold back his tears as he did so. The crew jumped to their feet when they spotted the doctor coming toward them. They immediately felt the gravity of the situation simply by the look that the physician carried on his face. No words were to be minced, "Tom has some serious injuries: two fractures on his jaw, compound fractures to both legs, several broken ribs, multiple lacerations to his torso, but what I'm most concerned about is his head injury. He has suffered a lot of trauma to his cranium; subsequently, there is a lot of swelling. But we do have him stable . . . for now. We will keep you informed. We've done all that we can. He's in God's hands."

"Thank you, Doctor," Dan said. Elizabeth could not stop her tears. Tom was a grown man to everyone else; but, to her, he was still her baby.

Dee would be one of the first of the family to see Tom. Before entering the room, the attending physician, who was a friend of the Calloways, caught Dee by the arm. "He looks bad, Dee. He doesn't look like Tom."

"I understand," was the older brother's only response. He barely took time to process the warning, but nothing could have prepared him for what he was about to witness.

As Dee entered the room, the first thing that he noticed was the sound of the respirator, pushing and pulling the air from Tom's body. Tom's body shook violently with every breath. The doctor was right—Tom did not look like himself. His face was swollen beyond recognition. What little was showing through the bandages was black from bruises. His hair was matted with dried blood. Both legs were set with splints. Dee could still see leftover mud on Tom's hands, which were one of the few areas that had escaped significant harm. The smell of creek water emanated from Tom's skin and permeated the air. Dee could feel it all over his body. The shock caused him to momentarily stop at the foot of the bed. He then stepped closer and slowly rested his hand on Tom's. He fought as hard as he could against the tears. He knew that Tom could not hear him, but he still searched for something to say. "I . . . I want . . ." Dee paused to catch his breath. Each word was difficult. He felt as though someone was choking him while squeezing the air out of his lungs. Dee's emotions finally defeated him. He began to tremble silently as tears trickled down his cheeks. His heart ached at seeing Tom this way. He stood by the bed for several minutes without saying a word. The only sounds were from the machines of life that were beeping, hissing, and breathing for Tom, accompanied by what had turned into nearly childlike weeping. Dee cried until he felt himself emptied, then gathered himself, raised his head and attempted to speak once again. Through the wetness of his eyes, all he could manage to push out was, "Love you, Brother." He then turned and left the room.

Caroline was waiting on Dee as he came back into the hallway. "You okay, Babe?" She already knew the answer.

"No."

"Let's go get some coffee. I need to talk to you," she replied, gently taking him by the arm and leading him down the hall. The two settled into a small booth in the hospital cafeteria. The coffee was good—black and strong, just like Dee liked it. The sense of something comforting and familiar helped him regain himself. "You know, this is not your fault," Caroline said, in her ever-calming voice. "Tom is a grown man. It was a choice he made that put him at the bottom of that creek, not yours." A half-shrug, half-nod spoke of the inward wrestle that Dee felt . . . he wanted to believe Caroline—and, deep down, he did—but it was little comfort to him at that moment.

Several weeks passed by and there was no change in Tom's condition. Dan and Elizabeth were at the hospital each day, watching and praying, hoping for any sign of improvement.

Dee stopped by one evening to see his parents and to check on Tom. There had still been no response from the younger brother. As Dee entered the hospital, he saw Dan sitting by himself. "Hey, Pop. Where's Mom?" Dee said as he took a seat next to his father.

"She's up in the room, with your brother," Dan answered, a weary tone in his voice.

"Has there been any change today?" Dee asked.

Dan could not speak for several moments. He just sat, staring out of the window. Then, with all the strength that he could muster, he turned to Dee and said, "No."

Dee had never seen his father this distressed. The look on Dan's face was that of a man whose very life was slowly being pulled out of him. The past several weeks had taken their toll. "Pop, how are you and Mom holdin' up?" Dee asked.

After a deep, long breath, the answer came. "We're here, Dee—that's about it," Dan said, tears welling. "Your mother does what any good mother would do. She rarely leaves Tom's side. She helps bathe him. She talks to him. She reads to him. She prays for him. And, at night, she cries for him. Me . . . I just sit here—stuck between fear and hope. I hope that this will all be over soon and he can come home with me. I hope that God will see and understand just how much I love him, that He will heal him and make his father happy and joyful to have his child come home again. But my fear . . . my fear, Dee . . ." murmured Dan as he looked up, his cheeks now damp and his lip quivering, "is that God feels the same way."

Twelve

Blood Brothers

It was a bright, clear morning, and Elizabeth Calloway was up early. Today, she was bringing her son home from the hospital. It had been three, long months since Tom's accident, and he was going to make it home for Christmas. She had worked tirelessly to prepare the spare bedroom, the one that had actually been Tom's back when he lived at home as a child, in order to accommodate his wheelchair and crutches. She thought briefly about how bad things had been only a month earlier. She had never prayed so hard in her life or cried so many tears. The weeks following the accident had taken a toll on the whole family. For so long, there was no response from Tom, and it had looked as though they would lose him. But God had other plans, and He used a child to do it.

When the doctors approached Dan and Elizabeth about Tom's condition, several weeks had passed since he was taken to the hospital. Even though Tom's body was healing, he was still in a coma. The doctors encouraged Dan and Elizabeth to try what they could to draw Tom out. They tried over the next few weeks to revive him. Family members talked to him whenever they visited. Dan and Dee would read Old Western novels to him. They even bought a CD player to play some of his favorite songs, but nothing seemed to work.

It was evening time one day when Caroline and Mary stopped by the hospital. They entered Tom's room and witnessed Elizabeth softly singing to him. As they entered, Elizabeth stopped mid-verse to greet them. "Hey, Hon. How are you, Sweet Pea?" she asked, addressing the mother and daughter. They could see the worn look on Elizabeth's face. It was obvious that she had been crying. She took a tissue from the box and wiped her eyes and nose. Caroline pulled up a chair from the corner of the room, so that she could sit close to Elizabeth while Mary sat on her mother's knee.

"How is he? Has there been any change?" Caroline asked.

Elizabeth didn't speak. She just shook her head, reached up, and cradled her hand inside Tom's. They sat in silence for a few moments, just two mothers, holding their children.

Finally, Mary spoke up, "Mamaw Bett, can I sing to Uncle Tom?"

Elizabeth cleared her throat and said, "Honey, I think that would be wonderful."

"Okay, I'm gonna sing a song that I heard Momma sing in the choir last Sunday."

"Okay, Babe," Elizabeth replied lovingly.

Caroline smiled at Mary as she stood up and walked around to the other side of Tom's bed. There, she reached out, took her uncle's hand, and began to sing:

Somebody's praying, I can feel it,

somebody's praying for me.

Mighty hands are guiding me,

to protect me from what I can't see.

Elizabeth began to cry as she listened to her granddaughter sing. She could not carry the weight of her pain anymore. The agony of her heart—which over the last few weeks had felt just as broken as her son's body—came to fruition in this one moment. Mary noticed her grandmother and paused for a second. Then, Caroline, by now fighting her own tears, nodded to her, giving her permission to continue:

Lord, I believe, Lord, I believe

that somebody is praying for me.

Angels are watching, I can feel it.

Angels are watching over me.

There are many miles ahead

before I get home,

still I'm . . .

Suddenly, the sweet notes morphed into a different sound as Mary exclaimed with excitement, "Momma! Momma! Uncle Tom is squeezing my hand!"

"What did you say, Mary?"

"Uncle Tom! He's waking up!" she replied with even greater excitement.

Elizabeth stood to her feet and took Tom's hand again as she leaned over his bed. "Tom! Tom! It's me—it's Mama. Can you hear me, Baby?" Elizabeth said frantically as she searched for a response from her son.

There was a deafening moment of silence while Elizabeth waited, staring down at his face. Then, Tom slowly squeezed his mother's hand and began to try to speak, "Mmmm . . . Mmm . . . Mmmaa . . . Mama?"

Elizabeth erupted into tears of joy, "OH, THANK YOU! THANK YOU, LORD! THANK YOU! THANK YOU! THANK YOU!"

Caroline and Mary joined in with their own tears, praise, and thanks. All of them cried and hugged one another. It marked the second time in Tom's life that his first word was *Mama*.

Once home, Tom began the lengthy process of rehab. There were many days of physical therapy. The pain overwhelmed him at times as he slowly regained the strength and range of motion of his legs, but Tom was determined to get back to his former self. The daily improvements, no matter how small, helped him push through the painful exercises. The process was a long one, but Tom's body was healing, and the physical pain seemed to lessen every day. But not everything in Tom's life was healing like it should. His relationship with Dee had remained strained, and it all came to a head one evening at Dan and Elizabeth's.

Dan and Elizabeth had made plans to take a trip to Natchez for their anniversary. The therapist had given Tom exercises to do at home to increase his leg strength. Tom had been advised to not try them without assistance at this point in his rehabilitation. It was Dee who volunteered to help his brother. Dee knew that Tom still had hard feelings toward him, but he loved his brother, despite Tom's animosity. More than once, Dee had attempted to talk to Tom, in an effort to get down to the root cause of his irritation. Each time, though, Tom refused to open up about what was bothering him.

The reception was less than warm when Dee arrived at his parents' home. Tom was sitting in the living room. Although the television was on, he paid it little attention. "Well, glad to see that my babysitter made it," Tom uttered in the most sarcastic tone.

"Take it easy, Brother. I brought plenty of Pampers and Similac," Dee replied, trying to liven the mood.

Tom said nothing, but his stare said it all.

"Seriously, Tom, I'm just tryin' to help."

"Okay, let's get this over with, so you can feel like you've done your part," Tom replied, pulling himself up from the chair as he placed a crutch under each arm for balance. He slowly walked to the staircase that led up to his parents' room. The plan was to make three trips up and down while Dee spotted him. A truly tender-hearted man, Dee struggled to keep his composure as he watched him begin. He simply could not get used to seeing his brother in such a weakened state. He followed Tom up the stairs. The look on Tom's face gave evidence of the pain. He took one step after another until he made it to the top and then back down again. At one point, he stumbled, and Dee caught him. Tom pulled his arm away in anger and said, "I'm good!"

Dee kept silent as he shook his head, turned, and walked toward the front door.

"I don't understand!" Tom said aloud, hoping to make Dee respond.

Dee stopped but did not turn to face his brother. He stood there, with his hands perched on each side of his waist. "What do you not understand, Tom?"

"Why would anyone decide to abandon their family and start school to be a doctor at thirty-four?"

Dee turned and faced his brother, with a trace of tiredness in his voice, "Tom, we've already talked about this. And I didn't abandon anyone."

"No! No, Dee! You talked to Pop, Mom, and Uncle Frank—but you never once talked to me about it. I'm your brother—your only brother. Dee, we're blood—blood!" Tom said, tapping his chest. "We've lived our lives together, but somehow I wasn't important enough to come talk to about this—it affected my life too! It was me, Dee, I was the one that was abandoned." Tom struggled to conceal the quiver in his lip and the thin stream of tears that had begun to run down his cheeks.

Dee stood for a moment. He had been prepared for his brother's bitterness but not his outburst. It was possible that two or three minutes passed before Dee finally found the words that he needed to say. "You're absolutely right, Tom—I should've come to you and talked to you, brother to brother. We built our lives here on this farm. I just didn't think about how all this would affect you. I was wrong, but please understand . . . I'm just tryin' to follow God's plan—His will for me." Dee slowly walked up the handful of steps, embraced his brother, and then left for the night. He hoped that Tom would not only come to forgive him in time but also understand why he was pursuing this dream.

They say that time heals all wounds. But among brothers, fishing is a good supplement. It had been nearly a month since the brothers had spoken when Tom's phone rang at 5:45 a.m.

"Hello!" a slightly irritated Tom answered.

"Mornin', Brother, get dressed—the fish are bitin'," Dee replied.

"What? Wait. What? The fish are bitin'? Dee, you know that I can barely get around. How am I goin' fishin'?"

"Don't worry about it, Little Brother, I'll carry you—I'm used to it." Dee continued with a bit of brotherly sarcasm.

"Carry me? Whatever!" Tom responded.

"No, but seriously, Tom, we are goin' fishin' today. I'll be there in about a half an hour. Be ready."

Dee hung up before Tom could give a rebuttal.

Tom waited in reluctance on the front porch for Dee to arrive. Dee could see his brother's face as he pulled into the drive. The look of irritation coupled with the fact that he was actually ready to go, with a pole in hand, made Dee laugh to himself.

"Well, let's go—hop-a-long." Dee said as stepped out of his truck and up onto the porch.

"Not funny," Tom replied as he reached for his crutches.

The two made their way back down the porch steps and across the lawn to Dee's pick up. Tom noticed the old, familiar craft that was sitting in the bed of the truck.

"Is this Papaw's ol' crawdad boat?" Tom asked.

"Yep, it's a classic," Dee answered.

"*Antique* doesn't always mean *classic*," Tom said as he surveyed the artifact. "Are you sure it'll float?" he continued.

"Absolutely," Dee said, then he muttered the words *for a while* under his breath.

"Wait, what did you say?" Tom asked.

"Nothin'. It's gettin' late—we gotta go," Dee hurriedly replied.

Tom stared at his brother for a moment with a look of uncertainty before pulling himself up into the passenger seat of the truck. The two made their way across town to Ritter's Lake. It was a familiar fishing spot for the brothers, as they had fished there for many years. The lake was quiet that morning. One or two small bass boats skimmed across the glassy water.

While Dee and Tom puttered their two-seater slowly across the calm lake, the sun had long since found its way above the tree tops and began to warm the cool lake water. Dee pulled the small boat up into a familiar cove and pitched out the rusty, makeshift anchor. The brothers prepared their lines and began to cast out into the water.

There was silence for a while as they took in the peace of the morning and their surroundings. Only the songs of nature could be heard. Fish popped the surface of the water and snatched up insects that rested ever so lightly on the barely perceptible waves. Mother birds cawed and flew from the thick canopy of the trees. Squirrels, searching for food, rustled through the leaves along the hillside that led up from the bank. A crane slowly navigated the soft mud of the nearby shoreline as it stealthily hunted for breakfast. A slight breeze danced across the tender branches of the tallest pines. All the sounds worked together to produce a living melody.

Tom watched his line rise and fall back into the water with the motion of the boat. He paid little attention, though, as his mind was elsewhere. He was the first to speak. "Dee, I know why we're here, and it ain't about catchin' fish."

"Mama always said that *ain't* ain't a word," Dee countered nonchalantly, flinging his line out into the water through a skilled flick of the wrist. He knew full well where Tom was going with his thoughts, and, as much as Dee wanted resolve between them, he also didn't want the needed conversation to happen until it was truly the right time . . . until Tom was truly ready to have it.

"Dee, please—let me say what I need to say," Tom said.

Dee settled his posture, nodded his head, and quietly replied, "Okay."

Tom continued with his back to his brother, staring out at his line, "I know why we're here. There are some things that need to be said between us—some things that need to be settled. I've been thinkin' a lot about our conversation that we had at Mom and Pop's a few weeks ago. Actually, it's pretty much all I've been thinkin' about since then."

Dee could hear Tom clearing his throat before he spoke further. "I was wrong, Dee. I was wrong to feel the way I did. I was so angry at you for leavin'. Plus, when I found out that you had talked to everyone but me . . . it made me feel like the little brother—like I was insignificant or not worth the trouble. All our years growin' up, you'd never treated me that way. In my mind, we'd always been more than brothers . . . we were *friends.* But it was like you were somehow concerned with everyone else's opinion but mine. I let it make me bitter . . . and that led to frustration . . . which led to impatience, which," Tom let out a sigh, "led to me at the bottom of that creek . . . I wanted to blame you so badly for all of it. I couldn't understand why you were choosin' to leave now—it didn't make sense. It wasn't like you. You were always the steady one—predictable, solid, and dependable. It seemed so far out of your character that, on some level, it troubled me. I guess, I guess the best way I know how to say it is that it was like you had betrayed my image of you somehow."

Tom could feel Dee looking at him.

"I know, I know—it sounds stupid," he said, turning his head slightly to look over his shoulder in Dee's direction. "But I want you to know how I felt . . . I didn't say that it would make sense."

Dee took a moment to collect his thoughts before responding. "It doesn't sound stupid. You're right—I should've talked to you like the others . . . because you do matter, and it affected you, probably more than anyone. For that, I'm sorry, Brother."

"I know you are. It's alright. I'm the one who needs to apologize. You know, Dee, you said somethin' to me that has stuck in my mind, and I just couldn't get it out of my head. You said that you were just tryin' to follow God's will for your life." The morning sun, now glimmering through nearby treetops across their faces as the boat gently bobbed on the water, made Tom's hazel eyes look even greener as he spoke, "I've heard preachers, deacons, and even Sunday school teachers say that a hundred times in my life. It sounded almost cliché. I mean, we expect that from them. But, until we talked, I'd forgotten that it's what we all should be doin' . . . but you were puttin' it in action. Even though it was probably goin' to turn your life upside down, you did it anyway. If that's the case, Dee, you didn't have to say anythin'—to any of us. And then, once I thought about it, I felt so ashamed for actin' like you were supposed to answer to me, as if, somehow, you needed my permission or somethin'." Tom's voice cracked as he finished his sentence. He ran his shirt sleeve along the tip of his nose and paused only for a second before he continued to speak. "I've been doin' some readin' since the last time we talked. You know that verse that says, 'No one, havin' put his hand to the plow, and lookin' back, is fit for the kingdom of God'?" Tom paused for a moment, to make sure that his brother was understanding him.

Dee nodded his head, murmuring, "Yeah . . . that's from somewhere in Luke . . . Luke chapter nine . . . verse sixty-two, I think."

"Well," Tom continued, "that's a verse I can relate to . . . I can remember Papaw plowin' with an ol' mule. I asked him one time how he kept the rows so straight. He said that he would pick somethin'—like a big tree or a small mound at the end of the field—then he would guide the mule to that point. He had somethin' to focus on or aim for, I guess. The point is, if he wasn't diligent, that mule would wander off to the first apple tree. He couldn't do what he needed to by lookin' over his shoulder. I know now what you were focused on and why it was so important." As he spoke these words, Tom's voice quivered once more.

Dee sat still, simply taking in his brother's description of the recent years . . . there was an unusual clarity in it, hearing it from Tom's perspective, which was coming from a place of deep bond, deep pain, and now, finally, a deep understanding.

"You weren't showin' a lack of love for the family, the farm, or me. You were showin' the depth of your commitment to God." Tom paused for a moment, pulled a faded bandanna from his back pocket, and wiped the tears from his cheeks. He then turned to Dee, saying, "I'm sorry I missed that, Brother. I see it now."

Dee reached over, placing his hand on the back of Tom's neck, then pulled Tom to him.

"You are a good man and good brother, Tom Calloway. Always remember that I love you, and I'm proud of you, and I love the family and the farm. There's no way I could ever separate myself from it. If I grow into anythin' fruitful for God, it's because He planted me here."

A deep sigh from each man indicated that what had needed to be said for so long had finally made its way into the daylight of things. The two wiped their faces free of the salty tears as they returned to their forgotten lines. There was only a couple seconds of silence before Dee spoke, "Man, all I wanted to do was a little fishin'." Both brothers burst into laughter—the healing had begun.

It was a beautiful spring day in Stringfellow County. The lilies were in full bloom with vibrant shades of yellow, pink, and crimson. The hanging petunias swayed softly in the breeze. The scent of freshly cut grass wafted through the air. It was graduation day for Dee, and that reality made it even more beautiful. It was the culmination of years of studying, of sleepless nights, of endless prayers, and of countless odd jobs. God is always good, but days like this day serve to remind us of how much He loves us. The family, who felt as eager for this day as Dee did, filed into the auditorium and took their seats. Soon, the procession of graduates made their way in to take their places at the foot of the stage.

"Jefferson Daniel Calloway," were the next words that Dee remembered hearing. Every step up to the podium seemed to be in slow motion. His joy seemed to carry him across the stage. Dee collected his diploma and began to walk back down the aisle. He could see his mother sitting in the crowd. Next to her was Pop, Uncle Frank, and Caroline, and they were all beaming with pride. Dee looked down for a second and said a quick prayer of thanks, then looked back up. He searched the crowd, looking for his brother. As he walked past Caroline, he mouthed the question, "Where is Tom?" Caroline shrugged her shoulders, mouthing back at him, "Running late." Dee smiled to himself and rolled his eyes. At that moment, his eyes caught the image of a thin man with a cane, standing at the back of the room, just next to the entrance. Dee instantly recognized the familiar frame as his brother's. As he took his seat again with all his fellow graduates, he motioned to Tom, tapped his time piece, and then held his hands up and out slightly, as if to say, "Where have you been?" Tom just smiled and shook his head.

After the ceremony, Dee found his way through the crowd and over to his family and brother. Hugs and handshakes were exchanged. Caroline's smile somehow seemed as if it might have been even bigger than it was on their wedding day. Then, Tom pulled a small box from the bag that he was holding.

"Here you go, Doc." Tom said, offering the item to Dee. "This was why I was late. I had to pick somethin' up on the way."

Dee took the box from Tom's hand and began to open it. To his surprise, inside was a new wristwatch. "Tom! This is too nice. You shouldn't have spent this kind of money on me," Dee said as he beamed at the exquisite timepiece.

"Yeah, I know. But, hey, how many doctors do we have in the family . . . and we can't have you representin' the family with that ten-dollar, Wal-Mart digital," Tom replied with a smile and a chuckle. "But it does come with a request—turn it over."

Dee glanced up at Tom, then back down at the watch as he turned it over—he could tell from Tom's tone that there was meaning in the request. There was an inscription with the words *Keep your hands on the plow.* Dee's eyes filled with tears as he looked up at Tom and said, "Absolutely, Brother, absolutely."

Thirteen

Fathers, Friends, and Funerals

The years that followed had their share of mountaintops and valleys. There were great harvests, and there were lean times.
Those who were young grew up. Those who were old grew older.
There were those who were added and those who were taken home.
Dee was in his third year of residency. He had chosen surgery as his
specialty and was earning his way in the trauma room at Niobi Baptist. Caroline still worked as a pharmacist there in Pelo.

The two worked many hours, but they always made time for one
another. Every day, they spent breakfast, lunch, or supper together.
Mary Elizabeth had graduated from high school and was in her first
year of college. Joel was in high school and played quarterback for the
Pelo football team. Tom had completed a very successful rehabilitation. He had married his physical therapist. He and Hayley Jones had
wed the previous spring—Dee was the best man.

Also, in true fashion, God sometimes likes to bring additional
blessings to a table that is already overflowing. In the case of Dee and
Caroline, that blessing was in the form of a brand-new Calloway. A
baby girl was on her way. Dee had already started calling her the child
of his old age. Family and friends alike would often ask the same question, "Another child? Did you guys mean to?"

Dee would always smile and say, "Well, God meant to, so that kinda settles it for us."

So, here they were, a little over seven months into their third pregnancy, patiently waiting on her arrival.

Caroline stopped her car in the driveway and got out to retrieve the day's mail. She opened the box and pulled out all the different-sized envelopes, got back in her car, and drove the rest of the way up the gravel drive to the house. Inside, she found Mary and Joel working on homework. "Hey guys, good day?"

"Yeah, pretty good," they replied almost in unison, never looking up.

Caroline sifted through the mail and weeded through the normal "resident" junk to the more important items. One particular envelope, postmarked El Reno, Oklahoma, caught her attention. It was addressed to Dee, Caroline, and family. She opened the envelope, pulled the letter out, and began to read:

Mr. Calloway,

My name is George Nashoba. I am a good friend of John Tuleeves. We worked together here on the reservation. He asked me to be sure and contact you if ever something happened to him. I am most saddened to inform you that John passed away and was laid to rest two days ago. He died peacefully in his sleep. My apologies for not contacting you sooner. John was always very private, so I did not have a number to call. I am sure that John had intended to provide me with a number sometime. However, I found this address on some mail in his room. He also wanted you to know that he had remained sober. Also, when you receive this letter, please call the number below, as I have a package of some of John's effects and wish to confirm the address of delivery. Again, I offer my condolences. John spoke often and highly of you and your family.

Sincerely,

George Nashoba

Caroline slowly placed the letter back down on the table among the other envelopes and then took a tissue from the box that was sitting on the counter. She wiped the tears from her eyes. She was saddened at the loss of such a great family friend but also comforted to know that he had died among friends, feeling loved. Dee and the rest of the Calloway family were equally saddened about this great loss and the fact that they were unable to be present for his funeral.

Three weeks passed before the package reached the Calloway home. Dee opened it carefully, not wanting to damage any of the contents. After he carefully bent back the flaps on the top of the brown box, he found John's denim shirt and pants, folded up neatly and placed inside tissue paper, along with John's belt and a buckle that had the Chickasaw Nation seal etched into it. Also included were his pocket knife, wedding ring, and three eagle feathers. Dee smiled to himself as good memories flooded his mind.

It was then that Dee noticed an envelope that had been folded and stuffed into the front pocket of John's shirt. He carefully pulled the envelope from the pocket—he could tell that it was several years old. The tattered and stained envelope was addressed to him. He gently unfolded the letter inside. According to the date on the paper, John had written it the day that Dee had started medical school:

Young Daniel,

I know that you are not a child anymore, but, as I have been able to watch you grow from a child to a man, I can and will only think of you as young Daniel. In some way, I can see my son in you, and it makes me very proud. It takes much courage for us to change when we are older, when we have seen many sunsets and we have become content with our accomplishments and our flaws. It is then that we are reluctant to move. But you have conquered this. You have chosen to listen to God, the Great Spirit, the great I Am. That is why you have great courage. I draw strength and courage myself from your journey with God. So, continue, my friend, because when we change for God, the world is blessed by it.

Your friend,

John Tuleeves

Dee felt tears coming as he folded the letter back up and slid it into his own shirt pocket. For the rest of his journey, Dee often kept the letter with him. Whenever he felt discouraged, he would pull the letter out and read it. It renewed his strength and reminded him to be courageous.

Dan started every morning early, and this one was no exception. He made the slow walk out to the barn with his coffee cup in hand. He thought of the work ahead and laughed to himself as the thought crossed his mind, "I don't know who needs maintenance more—me or the tractor." The air was cool and extra crisp for an October in Mississippi, which made it seem odd when Jody Simms showed up at the Calloway home in nothing but a tattered t-shirt and jeans.

Dan peered through the open barn door and watched an old, beat-up car pull into his driveway. It was tan, or at least it used to be. The doors were dented and rusted out. The back glass was gone, along with all the hubcaps. It rattled, clanged, and smoked as it came to a stop. A thin, pale man stepped out. He stood for a moment, just staring at the house. Dan emerged from the barn, wiping the grease from his hands, then he called out, "Hello! Can I help you?"

The man gave a slight jerk, as if he had just been startled. "Hey, Mr. C.—it's me, Jody, Jody Simms!" Jody walked across the small field to the barn where Dan had been working. As he approached Dan, Jody pulled one of his hands from his pockets, stretching it out toward Dan, "Hey, Mr. C., it's been a while."

"Hey, Son. How have you been?" Dan replied as he shook Jody's hand. He was in shock at Jody's appearance. Gone were his boyish good looks. His face was pale and gaunt, and his eyes were sunken and flanked with dark rings. The shirt that he was wearing was torn and dingy, as if maybe he had found it in a dumpster, and it looked like it was covering a skeleton. The needle tracks in his arms told a story of how alcohol had led to other things. It all made Dan feel sad and sorry for Jody.

"I'm doin' o-o-o-okay, Mr. C," he said with a slight quiver.

"Where is your jacket, Son? Ain't you cold?" Dan asked as he began to return to his work.

"Nah, I'm good. Mr. C.—but I wanted to see if I could borrow a few dollars from you."

"Well, sure, Jody, but can I ask what it's for?"

"Ah, just a few things, you know."

Dan had seen this before. He knew all too well what Jody was going to spend the money on. "I tell you what, Jody—why don't you ride with me to town, and I'll buy you some food and a new change of clothes?"

"Nah, I appreciate that, Mr. C., but that's too much trouble. You can just give me the money."

"Jody, you know I can't do that. You need to just let me help you," Dan replied in a stern tone, his pity for Jody beginning to turn into frustration as Jody's attempt to pull one over him showed through more and more.

Jody did not say a word. He just rubbed his face and fidgeted for a moment. Then, he asked again, "Please, Mr. C., I-I-I really need it . . . the m-money, I-I mean, the money—I need the money."

Dan completely stopped what he was doing and wiped his hands on a shop towel before lying it across the seat of the tractor. He stepped over to Jody and placed a hand on his shoulder. "Son, why don't you just let me help you? I know and you know that you're goin' to use that money for drugs. It's time to stop, Jody. Think of your mama."

Jody looked down at the ground and began to cry. Inside, a war raged between the friend and the addict. He started to tremble and cry for a moment as Dan embraced him like a son. Then, Jody quieted himself. His regret, though, suddenly turned into rage. "Okay, okay . . . you can help me." In an instant, he grabbed Dan by the throat and screamed, "GIMME THE MONEY!"

Dan instinctively grabbed Jody's right hand with his left, snatching it away from his throat. He simultaneously struck Jody under the chin with his right hand. The blow sent Jody flying to the ground. Dan was an older man, well into his sixties, but he was still very capable of defending himself. Jody laid on the ground for a moment, completely still and bleeding a little from the mouth.

"Jody, you need to leave now," Dan uttered as calmly as he could as he turned and walked back to the tractor.

Jody pulled himself up onto his hands and knees. As he spotted a shovel leaning against the tractor, the addict defeated him once more. He leapt to his feet and grabbed the shovel. He swung it at Dan, striking him in the back of the head. Dan fell to the ground, unconscious. Jody frantically searched Dan's pockets until he found the cash that he had come for. Then, he ran to the old car and sped away.

The noise of screeching tires and flying gravel caught Elizabeth's attention as she stepped out onto the front porch. She could see Jody driving away. Fearing that something terrible had happened, she turned and walked out into the side yard, just within sight of the barn. There, she could see Dan lying in the dirt next to the old tractor. She screamed in horror and ran as fast as she could to him. As she drew closer, she stumbled and fell to her knees next to him, then she gently rolled Dan over onto his back. He groaned and moved his arms in a lethargic but defensive manner. "Honey, Honey! It's me, Elizabeth!" she said loudly as she pulled her apron from her waist. She placed it on the back of Dan's head, where he was bleeding. Once Elizabeth managed to calm him, she ran back to the house and called Frank.

Minutes later, Frank came to a screeching halt in the drive and came running across the field to the barn. "Dear Lord—no! Elizabeth, who did this!?" he asked.

"It looked like Jody, Jody Simms. But I just can't believe he would do such a thing. It's awful, just awful!"

Frank made the decision to drive Dan to the hospital rather than wait for an ambulance. Soon, the trio made it to the entrance of the emergency room at Niobi Baptist. A stretcher was raced out to Dan, then he was quickly rolled away.

The beeper on Dee's waist sounded, summoning him to the emergency room. Once there, his heart sank as he found his mother covered in his father's blood. "Mama, what is goin' on?"

Elizabeth explained, and Dee's heartbreak turned to fury. "If I could get my hands on that piece of trash right now—" he thought to himself.

After some time, the other resident on duty approached Frank, Elizabeth, and Dee, "Mr. Calloway, Mrs. Calloway, Dr. Calloway—Mr. Calloway has suffered a concussion. He also has a three-inch laceration on the back of his head. We've stitched him up and taken X-rays. There doesn't seem to be anything broken, but he'll need to stay here a couple days for observation." The attending doctor, who was a friend of Dee's, looked at Dee and then said in a slight tone of amusement, trying to lighten the mood, "I'll tell you, your dad is a tough old bird . . . I think he'll be fine."

"Thank you, Doctor, when can we see him?" Elizabeth asked.

"As soon as they get him to his room, you can go on up. He'll be in room . . . 428," the doctor replied as he searched for, then found, the room number listed on his chart.

Dee's attention was broken by the buzzing of his cell phone in his coat pocket. He noticed that it was Caroline's number. "Someone must have contacted her about Pop," Dee thought to himself as he answered the call. "Hey, Babe, how'd you hear about Pop so soon? We just got the results from his x-rays."

"Pop? Wait—hold on. What's wrong with your father?" Caroline asked with alarm, interrupting Dee.

"What? Wait, I thought that's why you called me?"

"No, it's not. I was callin' because I've been in an accident."

"What? An accident? What kind of accident? Are you okay? Is the baby okay?" Dee flooded the conversation with questions, barely giving Caroline a chance to reply.

"Dee! Dee! I'm okay, and the baby is okay," Caroline said, reassuring him that everyone was fine. "But I can't say the same for the car—the tow truck just pulled it out of the ditch. It looked pretty beat up on one side."

"Oh, Lord have mercy, Caroline, I nearly fell out on the floor," Dee said as he regained his emotions. "So, what happened? How did you end up in the ditch?"

"Well, I was on my way to the ob-gyn. So, I'm comin' around that long curve on Fergeson, and there's this car on the wrong side of the road. And it was either hit the car or hit the ditch . . . I chose the ditch."

"Oh, gosh, Honey—I'm just glad that you and the baby are okay."

"I didn't see who it was, but I gave a description to the police."

"Well, maybe they'll find the person before they hurt anyone else," Dee replied. "So, you're goin' on to the doctor right?" Dee continued.

"I feel fine. But yes, just to be on the safe side. So, what's goin' on with Dan? Is he okay?" Caroline asked.

"Well, he's been in an accident, but he's goin' to be fine. I'll give you the details tonight," Dee answered, trying to conceal the anger in his voice.

Dee joined his mother in his father's room and tactfully brought them up to speed on what had happened to Caroline. Once Dee was sure that the two were settled and comfortable, he stepped out. He then noticed that Caroline had left him a voicemail.

"Hey, Babe, just left the doc—everythin' is a-okay. Alice's grandmother has been my chauffeur this evenin', She's droppin' me off at the house. I'm sure it'll be a late night for you . . . may be asleep when you get in. Talk in the mornin'. Love you."

Later that night, as the three sat in Dan's room, Dee's beeper sounded again, calling him to the trauma room once more. "Mama, I've got to go. I'll be back later to check on Pop. I love you."

"I love you too, Hon," Elizabeth replied.

Dee stepped off of the elevator and rounded the corner. The nurse uncharacteristically caught him by the arm, signaling the urgency of her message. "Dr. Calloway, I'm the one who paged you. We have a patient who came in awhile ago. He was in a car accident and has several deep lacerations across his face and shoulders. Dr. Hault wants you to take a look at him. He is going to need extensive surgery."

"Absolutely. Where is he located?" Dee replied.

"I'll take you to him, Doctor."

The two walked down the hall to the first operating room on the right. When they entered the room, Dee was taken aback by the amount of damage that the man had received from the wreck. He lay unconscious, and much of his face was concealed by bandages. He was virtually unrecognizable.

Dr. Hault entered the room behind Dee. "What do you think, Dr. Calloway?" he asked.

"He's suffered quite a bit of trauma to his face, especially the left side. The left shoulder will require some extensive surgery as well," Dee said, taking it all in through his now-experienced perspective. "What happened?"

"Well, it's my understanding that his car was the only one involved. He hit a guardrail and rolled several times, then he was thrown through the windshield. The officer on the scene said that he estimated the car was going ninety to ninety-five miles per hour when he struck the rail. I'll tell you, the guy is lucky to be alive. But that's usually the way it is with those kind."

"*Those kind*? What do you mean?" Dee asked

"Addicts—the guy's arms were covered with tracks. He's been using for a while. It took us forever just to find a vein."

"Man, that's terrible," Dee replied. "Thank you, Dr. Hault."

"Oh yeah, there's one other thing, Dr. Calloway. The guy had no identification on him—police couldn't find anything. No license—nothing. Hopefully, somebody will show up looking for him."

Dee paused for a second and turned to look back at the man. Whoever he was, he was in such bad shape. It reminded Dee of the time that it had once been Tom lying there, trying to hang on to life. He was somebody's child, husband, or brother. It made Dee sad to think that the man was there alone.

Dee walked back out into the hallway and gave the surgical team instructions regarding the patient's operation. He called Dan's room one last time before he went to prep for surgery. The ringing phone broke the silence in room 428. "Hello?" Elizabeth answered.

"Hey, Mama, I'll be downstairs in surgery for the next three hours or so, but I'll be back up there to check on Pop afterwards."

"Okay, Babe. He's restin' fine now. I'll see you then."

Dee made his way down the hall to scrub up for surgery. It was there that he saw Helen Simms rushing through the doors of the emergency room entrance, screaming hysterically. Several nurses and attendants hurried to stop her. "Ma'am! Ma'am! You're going to have to calm down. Who are you looking for?" they asked while leading her to a nearby waiting area.

"My son, he-he was in a wreck. The police just called me. They said he was here. Oh, God—oh, God! Is he here? Is he okay?"

"Ma'am, try to calm yourself. What is your son's name?"

"His name is Jody—Jody Simms! Is he here?" Helen responded, trying with all her might to control her fear.

"Ma'am, just sit right here, and I'll check for you."

The nurse walked back to her station, passing by Dee, who had heard the whole conversation. He was in shock. "The man in the operatin' room . . . he's Jody," Dee said aloud to himself. He hurried into a nearby restroom and locked the door behind him. He leaned over the sink and splashed a handful of cool water on his face. A twinge of nausea shot through his body. His mind raced with a mixture of emotions. A few hours earlier, he had been consumed with hate for the man who had hurt his father. Then, unknowingly, he was moved with compassion for that same man, only minutes before. Dee took a long slow breath, pulling the air in through his nostrils and letting it out through his mouth. He was doing his best to calm his spirit and mind. Somewhere in the middle of a breath, he began to pray, "Oh, Father, I need you now. I don't know what to do. I've got to walk into that operatin' room and do all that's in my power to make him whole again. And, God, I just don't want to. So, I am askin', I am beggin'—control my heart, and control my hands."

Three hours, forty-five minutes, and twenty-two seconds was the official time of surgery. God had answered Dee's prayers. He had controlled his hands and his heart. Jody would make a full recovery, but Dee's struggle with hatred versus compassion in his heart was far from over.

Later, Dee prepared to make his final rounds for the night. Jody's room was the last stop. Dee gently inspected Jody's wounds and prepared to relay the necessary notes to the nursing staff. He paused for a moment and stared down at Jody. He thought to himself, "I hate you. All that you enjoyed with my family—and this is how you thank us. I hate you. There was a time when I would've swapped places with you. I loved you that much, just like a brother. Now, I just hate you. You'll get well, and you'll go right back to the same old way of life . . . and break your mother's heart again. I hate you, Jody."

Pain can make us think irrational thoughts—sometimes with irreparable consequences. Dee thought about how fragile Jody's life was right now and how it would take very little effort to end it. Almost as soon as this horrid thought passed through Dee's mind, a vision of Helen Simms's panicked face from earlier that day flashed through his mind, shaking him to his core. Dee took a long breath, then he turned and walked to the door. He felt ashamed to have even thought of intentionally harming one of his patients—and that was exactly who Jody was: a patient. Dee knew that he had to look at it from that point of view. It was what he had been called to do.

Dee finally made it home. He was so glad to just be able to lay down next to Caroline and be near her. He felt like he could finally breathe.

The next morning was a rush. Dee and Caroline both had full schedules and were running behind, as usual. The kitchen was abuzz with activity. In the middle of it all, Dee called out instructions for everyone as he hurried through the room—one arm in his jacket while trying desperately to not spill the coffee that he was carrying in his other hand. "Mary, I'm goin' to need you to take your mother to work today, please. Joel, let's take out the trash before you leave for school." This moment was followed by a collective *Yes, Dad* from both of the younger Calloways. Dee managed a quick kiss to Caroline and an *I love you all* to the trio as he hurried out the door.

As Dee got into his day, it occurred to him that he and Caroline had not discussed why Dan was in the hospital. "Maybe that's a good thing," he thought to himself. "She had quite a day yesterday, and to know that Jody was the cause of Pop's injuries might upset her a bit. Not to mention, he was here as well—I mean, she grew up with him, just like I did. She wouldn't want to know how bad Jody looked or how desperate he's gotten. I'll tell her later."

It was closing in on lunch time. "A good time to check on Pop," Dee thought as he entered the elevator and pressed four. As Dee felt the movement beneath him of the elevator carrying him up to his father's floor, he took a quick look down at his watch, ever conscious of the time. The elevator dinged, and the doors opened. As he stepped out into the hallway, his cell phone rang. It was Caroline. "Hey, Babe, everythin' alright?" Dee asked.

A panicked Caroline replied, "Dee, somethin's wrong! I started crampin' about half an hour ago, and it's gettin' worse!"

"Caroline, is there somewhere you can sit or lie down?"

"Yes, I'm in the office in the back of the store. Diane's one of my clerks, and she's here with me."

"Okay, just stay calm. I'll get an ambulance on its way to you. I'll meet you downstairs in the ER. Everythin' is goin' to be fine. I'm goin' to stay on the phone with you until they get there."

"Okay . . . Dee?"

"I'm here, Babe."

"I'm bleedin' too . . . I'm so scared, Dee . . ."

Dee's heart sank. He knew this was not a good sign but tried to conceal his concern.

"Okay, Babe, it's okay. The ambulance will be there soon, and we can see what we're up against. It's okay. I love you."

"I love you too," Caroline said as she began to cry.

Dee met the ambulance at the entrance. The EMT's pulled the gurney from the back of the ambulance, and Dee immediately reached for Caroline's hand. He held it tightly and kissed her. He could tell she was still in pain. He held her hand as he walked alongside her.

"Babe, I've contacted Dr. Palmer, and he's on his way. They're goin' to take you to exam room four. It's goin' to be okay. It's probably just stress from the last couple of days," Dee said, trying his best to calm Caroline. Dee stayed by her side as they entered the room. A nurse followed right after, along with the sonographer. A faint glimmer of hope passed through the room as Caroline's pain seemed to ease. After a brief exam, it was determined that the bleeding had stopped as well.

"Dr. Palmer has ordered an ultrasound. So, we're goin' to go ahead and take care of that. He's on his way and should be here soon, Hon," the nurse said to Caroline, trying to give a bit of comfort. The sonographer prepared the ultrasound wand with gel and began to move it around Caroline's abdomen. She and Dee anxiously waited for any signs of movement or the muffled sound of a tiny heart beating. But no sound was to come. Caroline began to cry nervously. The calm, competent pharmacist—wife and mother of two—gave way to a scared, pregnant mother clinging to any hope for her child.

"Are you, you sure that you're not seein' anythin'? Maybe the volume's not up loud enough to hear? Are you sure you have it turned up? Dee, please check it and make sure," Caroline frantically asked. Dee looked over at the tech only for a moment as they both silently acknowledged Caroline's desperation.

"Babe, the machine is workin' fine. Try and calm yourself. Dr. Palmer will be here soon, and he can tell us exactly what's goin' on." Dee said, reassuring her as best he could.

In the rural town of Pelo, Dr. Nathan Palmer was the local "baby doctor." He had been Caroline's ob-gyn for many years and delivered both Mary and Joel. So, it was especially difficult for him to give the news to Dee. After about an hour, he emerged from Caroline's room. Dee was standing directly across from the entry. He had his head down, seemingly in prayer, when Dr. Palmer stepped into the hall. As Dee lifted his head, their eyes met. The two men just stared at one another for a few seconds. Then, Dee gave the slightest shake of his head, not wanting to say the words. Dr. Palmer responded in kind. The news made Dee wince in pain as he raised a hand to his mouth. After a moment, Dee composed himself. He knew that he had to be strong for Caroline. He wiped his eyes and nose with the sleeve of his coat, much the way a child would do. He stepped up to the door, then paused for a second. He needed something to tell Caroline—something that would help make sense of it all. He turned back to Dr. Palmer, "Why?"

"Dee, I wish I had an answer for you. I could give you a hundred plausible reasons. But none of them fit here. Sometimes, these things just happen. I guess she had lived as long as she was supposed to," Dr. Palmer's voice sounded everything short of shaky as he tried to comfort Dee with his answer.

"Yeah, I guess so," Dee replied. He then turned and opened the door and stepped inside. The room was dark and quiet. Dee pulled the small, plastic chair up next to the bed and sat down. Caroline just watched him, without making a sound. Dee reached over and took her hands and held them in his. Caroline pulled him to her and nestled her head in his arms, as if to hide away from it all. They just sat and held each other as they wept in near silence.

When our hearts are broken, tears speak much more eloquently than words. Sadly, there would be more heartache to come. The advanced stage of the pregnancy meant that Caroline would have to deliver the child naturally. So, medications were administered to start her labor. Within hours, she delivered a tiny, but otherwise beautiful and perfect, baby girl named Martha Joy Calloway. The nurse cleaned her, then wrapped her in a blanket and gently placed her in Caroline's arms. Her sweet features and look of peaceful sleep were stark contrasts to the painful reality of the moment.

Over the next few hours, close family came and shared their tears, prayers, and, ultimately, goodbyes. Finally, Mary and Joel came in to say goodbye to their sibling one last time. The brother and sister had decided that they wanted to pick out a gown for Martha. Although the hospital provided one, it had been important to Mary and Joel to do this one, last thing for their sister. Mary stepped over to her mother's bed and pulled the tiny gown from the shopping bag. You could tell that brother and sister had invested some time into their choice of garment. It was soft pink, with seafoam trim at the cuffs and along the drawstring bottom. It was topped with a white, eyelet collar. Mary carefully laid it out across the foot of the bed.

"Oh, Mary, you and Joel did a great job pickin' out Martha's gown. She'll look so sweet in it," Caroline murmured as Mary delicately took her baby sister from her mother's arms. Both mother and daughter dressed Martha in her new outfit. Then, Mary, with ever so much care, lifted her sister up and hugged her, kissing the top of her head where a tiny wisp of blonde hair grew. With eyes full of tears, she whispered, "I love you. I'll see you later." The scene was all too much for Joel. He stood stoic next to the doorway, his hands seemingly cemented into his pockets.

"Joel, do you want to come see Martha before . . . before she has to go?" Dee carefully asked his son.

The youth stood motionless for a moment, then slowly walked to his mother's side. With his eyes fixed on the floor, he quietly spoke, "Bye, Martha. I love you."

Caroline sensed the sadness in her son and reached for his hand, saying, "She would've loved you so much. You would've been the best big brother to her."

Joel, with his gaze still focused down, slowly nodded. Then, he turned and walked out of the room.

All at once, it was just Dee, Caroline, and the baby. Caroline pulled her close to her chest and held her tightly. A mother's love is different from anyone else's in the family. She shares a bond with her children that no one else can. She is the first to feed you, to feel you move, to comfort you, and to communicate with you—and all before you are even born. She has literally shared her life force with you. Among the great loves in your life, her's is a truly unique creation of God. In the midst of her great love mingled with such great loss, Caroline felt like she herself was dying. She knew that when they took Martha, they would be taking a part of her too. That moment came far sooner than Caroline felt ready for.

Dee leaned over and kissed his wife on the cheek and said, "Babe, it's time."

Caroline winced in pain and began to weep. "Oh, please . . . don't take her, please! If they take her, she'll be all alone. Dee, please—please don't let them take her." He could hear the heartbreak in Caroline's voice.

Dee stood for a moment, praying for wisdom—his heart was breaking as much as Caroline's. Finally, he leaned over once more and softly said, "It's time, Honey. She won't be alone . . . she'll never be alone."

Ever so gently, he lifted his baby girl out of Caroline's relinquishing arms. He turned and carefully gave her to the waiting nurse, but not before he gave her one last, tender kiss on her forehead and said, through a choke of tears, "Daddy loves you, Sweetheart."

The nurse took her in her arms and quickly left the room. Dee sat down next to Caroline. With her body and spirit racked with pain, she collapsed in Dee's arms and cried herself to sleep.

Dee and Caroline decided on a small, intimate service with just them, Mary, and Joel. There were no words as they drove away from the cemetery. Joel and Mary watched as their mother cried all the way home.

Dee helped Caroline from the car into the house and to the bed. "Try and rest some, Babe," he said softly. Caroline's body craved rest, though her broken heart would make it hard to find. Dee pulled a blanket over his wife and gently stroked her hair, tucking a few strands behind her ear in the process. Then, he softly kissed her on the forehead. As Dee eased toward the door, a sigh from Caroline noted her inward struggle. It was a sound that would not leave him anytime soon. As he emerged from the bedroom, he found Mary and Joel sitting quietly in the den.

"Hey, you guys hungry?" were the next few words that Dee found himself uttering.

The duo said nothing and just shook their heads.

"Oh, okay . . . well . . . I've got to take care of some paperwork. So, just let me know when you are ready for somethin'."

Dee's request was met with the same kind of response. But it was a slight nod this time. Dee knew that death is a hard thing to process at any age, but it is especially difficult for young people. Dee's mind could not help but flashback to when, as a youth, he once sat on a couch in a funeral home, perplexed and in pain at the unexpected passing of Bobby Ford. He walked over to the sofa and sat down between the two.

"Guys, you wanna talk?"

There was silence for a second, then Mary turned and looked at her father, "Dad, we are really worried about Mom. I mean, we are all so sad, and all of us have cried, even you. But Mom has cried and cried."

"Yeah, she is so, so sad without Martha," Joel added.

"Will she get better?" Mary asked.

Dee wrapped an arm around each of them and pulled them close. "Yeah, Honey, she'll get better. But it'll take time. Let me tell you two somethin' about mothers. Not just your mom, but all mothers . . . a mother's love for her children is so deep and strong . . . the whole time that a baby is growin' inside a mother, she is bondin' with it. She feels every move that it makes. If it's content, she knows. If it's upset, she knows. It feels her too. Its whole world is its mother. So, over those months, the mother is storin' up a lifetime of love to give to her child once it's born. Only mothers get to do that—no one else. So, Mom is so, so sad because she has all of this love stored up and no baby to give it to."

Throughout the evening, Mary and Joel thought long and hard about what their father had told them. They thought about all the things that their mother and sister would never get to do—things that she had shared with them from their childhood but would not be able to share with Martha: no Christmas cookies, no Easter egg hunts, no bandages and words of comfort, no playing in the snow, no last-minute costumes, no words of encouragement to help navigate the awkward stages, no late-night talks, and so much more. But worst of all, no *I love yous*, no hugs, and no kisses.

The night that followed would be a long one, as the house would be awakened more than once by Caroline's sounds of sorrow. She finally found some rest in the early morning hours. She awoke around noon to find a small bouquet of flowers sitting on her nightstand. Along with it was a note written in Mary's handwriting, though it was signed by Joel as well. Caroline pulled the note from beneath the bouquet and began to read the words:

Dear Mom,

Joel and I talked to Dad about your sadness. He told us about the bond that every mother has with her baby, that love is being stored up to give.

And then, when the baby is born, a mother already has all the love she will need to give. But, if her baby passes, her love doesn't. It stays. We love you very, very much and want to help you feel better. So, if you want to give us Martha's love, we will give you her hugs and kisses.

Love,

Mary and Joel

Tears streamed down Caroline's face as she read the words. Her body trembled at such a pure act of love. After a few moments, she folded the note and slid it in between the pages of her Bible, which rested on the nightstand. She made her way to the bathroom and washed her face, then brushed her hair and pulled on a set of light-gray sweats. As she walked out of the bedroom, she could hear Dee and the children talking. She found the trio sitting around the dining table.

Dee, delighted to see his wife up and around, asked, "Hey, Babe, are you hungry? We were just talkin' about lunch. There is some roast in the fridge, and I can make us some cornbread."

Caroline gave a slight smile through her tired eyes and said, "No, Honey, that's fine. I think what we need is ice cream. Mary, Joel—what do you think?" Both lept from their seats and ran to their mother, to hug her and kiss her . . . twice.

Dan's stay in the hospital was short, as he recovered quickly. But the news of the loss of Martha, which he had received while he was still staying at Niobi Baptist, made his homecoming bittersweet.

Elizabeth pulled the truck up to the front of the hospital as the nurse pushed a reluctant Dan out the doors and to the vehicle. "I don't see why I couldn't have just walked—I'm not paralyzed," he complained.

"Dan Calloway, do you think you could appreciate the extra care for just once and quit whinin'?" was Elizabeth's rebuttal.

"Yes, Drill Sergeant!" Dan replied as looked up at the nurse and gave a wink.

The week before Thanksgiving, the Calloway clan was gearing up for the holidays. Elizabeth was busy about the house, preparing for the festivities that the next week would bring. Dan, Frank, and Tom were finishing some last-minute repairs around the farm and house before winter came. Dee and Caroline, after all that they had endured, finally seemed to have found a new normal in a stable routine of the work that they found meaningful. Mary and Joel were enjoying a much-needed break from school. It was a wonderful time of the year.

On one crisp morning, as Dan and Frank were finishing a task before heading to the house for a break, Frank uttered what had become a favorite question for the aging duo, "Hey, Brother, how about a cup of coffee?"

"Sure, that sound's good," Dan said.

The two finished putting away the last of the tools before heading to the house. Tom had decided to go pick up some fertilizer from Kyle's store. The brothers made their way into the kitchen, and each poured himself a cup of coffee. They then walked out onto the front porch, making small talk as they went. The rocking chairs creaked and popped as they sat and talked about the day. Soon, they found the bottoms of their cups. Frank was the first to stand, stretching his arms and placing his cap back on his head. Dan followed and turned his cup up for the last drop. As the two made their way to the old screen door, Frank suddenly noticed, from the corner of his eye, Dan's cup falling. He turned in time to see Dan wince and reach up to touch his face as he stumbled backwards. Before Frank could intervene, Dan fell, striking his head on the railing.

Sometimes you can tell just by a phone's ring that there is bad news on the other end. Such was the case when Dee's phone rang that day. He had worked the night shift and had only been asleep for a few hours when he got the call. With his eyes still closed, he reached for the phone on the nightstand nearby. "Hello? This is Dr. Calloway."

"Dee? Dee, this is Tom . . . I-I-I need to tell you somethin', Brother," Tom's voice crackled through the sniffing and crying. "Dee, Daddy's gone."

"What? What did you say?" Dee instantly sat up in the bed and slid his feet off the side, throwing the covers back. He had hoped that the fog of sleep had caused him to hear something wrong—"What do you mean Pop's gone?"

"He's gone, Dee. They said it was a stroke. He died today, Brother," Tom answered, his voice giving way to crying.

Then, a woman's voice came through, "Dee, this is Hayley. Dee, your father had a stroke earlier today and passed away."

She could hear the disbelief in his voice, "Oh, Hayley—please don't tell me that. Please don't."

"I am so, so sorry Dee."

Dee began to weep uncontrollably as he held the phone in his hands. After a few seconds, he pulled the phone back to his face, "Hayley, how is Mom?"

"She's doing as well as can be expected, Dee."

"Okay, tell her that I'll be there shortly."

"I will."

Dee walked to the kitchen and started the coffee pot. He dialed the number to Caroline's phone and waited for her to answer. When she noticed the familiar number pop up on her cell, she thought it a little odd to hear from Dee when she knew that he should be sleeping. "Hey, Babe, everythin' okay?"

There was a pause, then Dee spoke. "Babe . . ." She could hear him sniffing. "Babe, Daddy died this mornin'. Can you please come home?"

"What? Oh, Dee . . . I'm so very sorry, I'll be right there, Babe."

Dee hung up the phone and laid it on the counter top. He reached into the cabinet and pulled out a small coffee cup. Then, he pulled the pot from the coffee maker and filled the cup. He placed the pot back in its holder and reached for the cup. As he raised it to his lips, his hand shook uncontrollably, spilling droplets on the counter. He sat the cup back down and placed both hands on the counter and lowered his head. It was then that the pain filled in around his heart and began to squeeze. He took three short breaths as he tried to control his emotions. He turned to take a step, leaned over, and put both hands on his knees, trying to catch a breath. He visualized his father's face in his mind. He began to wail uncontrollably. He staggered around the kitchen, screaming like a child. "MY DADDY, MY DADDY. WHERE'S MY DADDY? WHY DID YOU TAKE MY DADDY? WAS MY DAUGHTER NOT ENOUGH? OH, GOD, WHY DID YOU TAKE MY DADDY? WHERE IS MY DADDY?" Dee's pain pressed him all the way to the floor. He sat there on his hands and knees, weeping and wailing uncontrollably until he lay completely on his side and cried himself out.

Caroline finally made it to the house and rushed through the door. She found Dee, who by then had regained himself and was sitting in a chair, staring out of the window. She rushed over and put her arms around him. Dee leaned over and wrapped his arms around her and placed his head on her chest. He began to cry again and said, "He was my friend."

It was the morning of the funeral, and all of the Calloway family had prepared for the day's somber events. Family and friends had traveled, some from long distances, to offer their condolences and share their grief. The tears shed and prayers prayed were innumerable. It had been decided that, along with Pastor O'Neil, Dee would speak at his father's funeral.

After the second song and before the pastor was to speak, Dee stepped up to the podium. "First, just let me say thank you. It would have made my daddy proud to see the amount of love shown for him and for us on this day. The love for a man can be measured by the amount of tears shed at his passin'. So, I thank you for aidin' us as we carry the sadness of my father's passin' and share in the joy of his future. My father was all the typical things to me and my brother that you would expect a good father to be. He was our mentor, our protector, our teacher, and our hero. But, honestly, I think that it was what he was to those around him which inspired me the most and is ultimately what I will miss the most. He had this way of lookin' at someone for who he or she could be, and not necessarily for who they were in that moment. He would always say that if God put that person in your life, then you should do what you could to help them."

Dee paused to regain himself, taking one step away from the podium and standing there silently for a moment. Then, he stepped back to the podium and continued, "I've seen him have compassion for someone who had never known any. I've seen him have patience with a man who had lost his. I've seen him share his strength with a friend who was too weak to stand. And I've seen him give guidance to a boy who didn't know that he needed it. I asked him one time why he did these things—what motivated him to be this way. He said it was because, at one time in his life, he needed all of these things, and they were given to him. And when I asked him, 'By who?' " Dee paused again and stepped back away from the podium. He took his thumb and pushed away a tear from his eye, then stepped back up and continued, "He just smiled and said, 'Jesus.' You see, Pop believed that you had an impact on everyone around you, whether you knew it or not. He said that God had sent so many people into his life when he was in need that he felt like he should return the favor. He believed that we were either a curse or a blessin' to those around us and that we owe it to God to be the latter. I remember he once told me that 'when we listen to God and let Him lead, He always leads to greatness.' " Dee stepped back away from the podium one last time to wipe the gathering tears from his lashes and clear his throat. After a moment, he regained himself and, stepping back to the podium, said. "So, thank you, Daddy, for bein' a great father."

Fourteen

Reckoning

"Gray . . . gray . . . that's the color. It matches the color of my heart," Dee thought to himself as he stared out of the big bay window at the morning sky. It had been months since Dan and the baby had died, and it seemed that every day was still a struggle. He wondered if and when it would get better.

He walked to the kitchen and took the last sip of coffee from his cup, then placed it in the sink. In a trance-like state, he moved to the bedroom, where Caroline still lay asleep. He pulled on his jacket and slid his cell phone into his inside coat pocket. Dee stood for a moment, staring down at his sweet wife. He watched her sleep for a moment and thought about how grateful he was for her. Life would have crushed him long ago had it not been for Caroline. She truly was his better half. But, even so, she could not pull him from this pit of despair. The truth was, she was in pain too. Dee pondered this thought for a few seconds and then quickly shifted to something else, telling himself, "Just keep movin'. Keep my mind movin', keep my body movin'." Maybe the idea was that he could or would outrun his depression.

He leaned over and kissed Caroline on the cheek, paired with a whispered *I love you.* As he did so, he caught a small whiff of her hair—she smelled beautiful. That was the only way that Dee could describe it. Maybe it was because the scent always made him think of her—a small thing, but the small things were what he needed. He needed them to get him through the day. Dee walked to the narrow, wooden table that sat next to the front door. He reached out for the small, clay bowl on it that contained his keys. He thought of the time when Joel was eight and made it for him in vacation Bible school. Joel had scribbled the words *Jesus holds the key to your heart* along the side of it. It was one of many heirlooms that he and Mary Elizabeth had created for their parents over the years. It was one more of those small things that Dee needed.

Dee arrived at the hospital and began his morning rounds. He enjoyed his work. It was a distraction . . . something to occupy his thoughts. It was around 11 a.m. when Dee received a call from the sheriff's department. He had not been expecting a call and immediately thought the worst when he realized who was calling.

"This is Dr. Calloway. Can I help you?" was Dee's dimmed greeting.

"Hello, Dr. Calloway, I'm Deputy Carson with the Stringfellow County Sheriff's Department. I understand that your wife, Caroline Calloway, was in an automobile accident a few months back—one that involved a driver who was on the wrong side of the road and also left the scene."

"Yes, Officer, that's correct." Dee answered, bracing inwardly for the possibility of further news that would bring more pain, "Is there somethin' wrong?"

"No, sir. The sheriff's department is just following up on the incident. We've actually found the car that was involved. It was located at an impound yard just outside of Tremont. We were able to confirm that it was the vehicle from the description that your wife gave the officer at the scene. The same vehicle was involved in several reckless-driving incidents that same day. We also had a couple who managed to get the license plate number. It's definitely the same vehicle. The driver eventually crashed the car and was ejected from the vehicle. Luckily, his was the only vehicle involved."

"Oh, wow . . . did the driver make it?" Dee asked, his curiosity entirely piqued.

"Yes, sir, he did. He was cut up pretty bad and in the hospital for a while I understand. You might have seen him come through there. His name is Jody Simms."

Dee wanted badly to have misheard the officer. "I'm sorry, Deputy, did you say . . . Jody Simms?"

"Yes, sir, that's correct—Jody Simms. Do you know him?"

Dee had fallen silent in shock.

"Dr. Calloway? You still there, Dr. Calloway?"

"Ah . . . yes . . . I'm still here. Yes . . . I think he may have come through the ER."

Dee was not sure why he did not tell the officer that he knew Jody. Perhaps he just wanted to distance himself from him.

"Okay, well, he was charged with DWI and reckless driving. The judge gave him house arrest for whatever reason. I hope he knows how lucky he is. If Mrs. Calloway wishes to press any charges, you'll need to come down and do the necessary paperwork. I would advise you to do that sooner than later."

"Okay. Thank you, Deputy."

Dee hung the phone up in disbelief. "So . . . Jody was the driver," he thought to himself. His mind was now beginning to offer connections that he had never even considered.

The rest of the day was a blur. That night, Dee told Caroline about the phone call that he had received from the sheriff's department. He went on to explain what had happened between Jody and Dan and that he himself was the one who had stitched Jody up when they brought him in. Caroline just sat in disbelief as Dee explained all the events of that day. Through misty eyes, Caroline finally whispered, "I don't know whether to hate Jody or pity him . . . I just can't believe that he would harm your dad like that . . . he always looked up to him like a father figure."

"It wasn't just Pop that he harmed. He ran *you* off the road, Caroline!" An uncharacteristic harshness coated Dee's voice as he spoke. Of all the connections that his mind had made that day, that one felt the most painful to Dee each time that it flashed through his mind.

A heavy pause filled the room as Caroline looked down at the floor, still absorbing it all before continuing, her common sense and her heart of mercy feeling at complete juxtapost, "I understand, Dee . . . but, but he didn't know that it was me . . . or that I was pregnant."

"Maybe not. But if he hadn't been at Mom and Dad's, then he wouldn't have been on the same road that you were on." Dee's soul was still hot as a branding iron—his sadness and sense of loss had finally found a target in the identified culprit whom he had once called a friend, and months of internal bitterness had fully bent his heart into a ready anger. "We opened our home up to him—and our hearts too. All he's ever done was cause this family pain and sufferin'! Now he's cost us Pop and the baby! I should've killed him when I had the chance!"

As grieved and shocked as Caroline felt at the discovery that Dee had shared with her, his last few words were nearly unbelievable to her. It was a side that she had never seen—nor wanted to. "Dee! You can't mean that! You shouldn't even *say* it. That's not who you are! I miss Dan and the baby too. My heart aches when I think about all that we have lost. But . . . but we can't let the pain change who we are or who we belong to."

Caroline's blue eyes begged him to return to something calm, something familiar, something sane in the midst of their emotional storm. Dee's stern expression slowly faded into something softer, though not right away.

A clock ticked in the background—every tick marking the tension of the moment like a sewing needle marking fabric. The dark of the night outside grew darker, but somehow the darkness on the inside did not seem to get any darker. Sensing the moment seemed halfway right, Caroline eventually reached a tender hand out to her one and only, taking his hand with a gentle squeeze, trying to say something that words could not quite capture. "I love you Dee. We'll get through this."

As the weeks went by, Dee's pain slowly changed to a chronic sense of anger. He struggled to understand the purpose in all of his loss, and, as a result of his emotional and spiritual fog, life in the Calloway home began to change. Dee spent more time at work. When he was home, he was mostly distant and brooding. Often, he would have his supper alone. As his self-imposed isolation continued, his soul began to struggle with the lies that came to his mind:

"Keep your distance—you know what happens to those you love."

"If God really loved you, He wouldn't hurt you this way."

"Some doctor you are—you couldn't even save the people that you love.. . but you saved the one that took them, and he's livin' his life with no regard."

A husband or father can set the tone of the home, and Dee's depression began to weigh on the atmosphere of the entire household. Dee had always been so pleasant: first to his family, and then to everyone else, but pleasantries escaped him more and more as his internal world leapt from one unsound emotion or thought to another, his negative flurry feeling akin to a merry-go-round gone bad.

One quiet evening, Caroline slowly opened the bedroom door. She could see Dee lying motionless in the bed. He had the television on, but he was completely oblivious to it. She walked over and sat down next to him. She reached up and gently moved the strand of hair laying at his brow.

Looking at him with a gentle but quizzical pair of eyes, she offered, "Want to talk?"

"Not really."

"Might do you some good."

"Yeah," Dee halfway deflected.

"Dee, we miss you."

"I'm right here."

"Dee," Caroline said, her voice changing slightly from a tone of compassion to accountability, "you know what I mean. You don't have to leave to be gone . . . Your children need you to be present. I need you to be present."

Even in his current state, Dee knew better than to dodge the truth that his wife was speaking. But a proper response seemed to escape him for the next several moments. As his eyes met hers, he could feel them admitting what his heart wanted to say. What he knew that he should say, something like, "I know what you mean, Hon . . . and I'm sorry. I know you're hurtin' too." But the words seemed stillborn in his throat. He broke the gaze, his eyes darting downward with a shake of the head as he slightly shrugged, his body saying what he could not about his feelings of helplessness.

Caroline's wordless response was enough to fill both of their minds and hearts for a moment.

Then, words finally came to Dee, "I'm just so angry."

"I know."

Encouraged by Caroline's undeserved sympathy, Dee forced himself to continue, "Because I don't feel like we lost them." He paused to choke back the forming tears before whispering, "I feel like they were . . . taken."

Tears were forming in both pairs of eyes in that crucial moment. And Dee's honesty with himself led to an unconscious exhale. Caroline herself took a deep breath, or more of a sigh, before pressing on through her own emotions. "Dee, you're right . . . and my heart is broken over it. And it's goin' to take some time for it to mend. But it's broken because of what we've lost. I think that, maybe, yours is broken because somehow you felt you could or should have protected me and the children from it." Caroline paused here, to see how her words would land, to see if there was some resonance with them for Dee. When he gave the smallest of nods, she continued, "But we both know that's not true. I can handle your tears over Martha and Dan. That leads to healin'. But to torture yourself over a lie—over somethin' that not only can we not change it now, but we never could have controlled it—can only hurt us more."

The words of truth burned Dee like a branding iron, searing their mark into him. There was not much for him to say in the moment, and he knew that, so he simply listened.

"Dee, I pray every day for the grace to trust God's will. Some days are pretty hard; and some, a bit easier, and I know He'll see me through it . . . but only if I let Him. I promise you, Dee, He's here with us. I have no answer for the valley we're in. But I know for sure He hasn't abandoned us.

The next day was more of the same for Dee. But he managed to push on to the end of his shift. He made his way through the parking garage and pressed the key fob to unlock his doors. He paused for a second to remove his coat, then opened the back door and reached in for the hanger. A small card fell out at his feet. He reached down and picked it up. It was the card from his aunt and uncle in Natchez, congratulating him and Caroline on the upcoming birth of their third child.

"I thought I'd thrown that away," Dee thought to himself. He crumpled it up in his hand. But he could not manage to toss it. He drove all the way home with it tightly clasped in his hand. It was only when he got to the driveway that he started to cry uncontrollably. He sat in his truck and wept, holding the card until his hand went numb. It was at this point that Dee caved to his anger. The truck revved and spun the tires as Dee backed down the driveway. He sped out into the evening as a golden, setting sun colored the horizon around him in an orange-red glow. The drive took him to an old, double-wide trailer sitting at the end of a dirt road. It was an older home, but it had been neatly kept until recently. Dee's headlight shined across the name and number on the mailbox: HELEN SIMMS, 227 OLD JONES ROAD.

The truck came to a sudden stop—almost a skid—and Dee stepped out and then quickly up to the door. His knocking was hard and determined. Something in his soul demanded a satisfaction, a closing, of sorts, and the day for it to occur had seemingly come. It was several minutes before someone came to the door, then came the tell-tale twisting and popping of locks being undone. Next, the door slowly opened. Jody's gangly frame appeared, half-lit by the fading sun behind Dee, half-dark by the dimness of the house behind him. Both men stood in shock momentarily. Then, Jody spoke first as he stepped out onto the porch, a noticeable timidity hovering in his voice.

"Dee? What are you doin' way out here?"

Though his eyes were steely, Dee's anger gave his voice a quiver as he responded. "I was lookin' for you. I was hopin' your mother would know where I could find you."

"Okay . . . well, here I am. What can I do for you?" Jody's gaze was patchy, if not cowarding.

Dee ignored Jody's question. "You ran Caroline off the road. She was pregnant."

Jody began to tear up as he replied. "I know, Dee. I mean, I know about Caroline. But I didn't know about the pregnancy . . . at least, not at the time." A single sob shook his weathered frame as Jody murmured, "I'm so sorry, Dee."

Dee clenched his jaw and spoke through gritted teeth. "You and I need to take a ride."

"Dee, I know you hate me . . . and whatever you have in mind, I probably deserve it. But I can't leave."

"Can't—or won't?"

"Dee, please—I can't leave. It's not me—it's Momma."

"Your mother? What's this got to do with your mother?"

"It's cancer. She has breast cancer. She's had it for a while. But now she can't leave the bed anymore. Someone has to be with her all the time."

Dee was taken aback by the news. He had not planned on something like that. In his anger, he had only had one thought, and suddenly, his perspective was jerked back into a realization of others, his anger dissolving and vanishing like a tissue in fire. He had gone there looking for Jody. He wanted to make him pay for the pain that he had caused him, but now, suddenly, all that he could think was how much Helen needed Jody right now.

Dee did not say a word. He just turned around, went to his truck, and drove home. He found himself sitting in his own driveway, weeping for the second time that night. But this time, it was out of shame. He was ashamed of what he had become—of how his pain had changed him and caused him to act in ways that had never been a part of his character. The tears cleansed something inside of him as he sat there. Finally, Dee wiped the tears from his face and walked into the house. The house was quiet with sleep. He went to his and Caroline's room. He then made his way around to her side and sat next to Caroline on the bed. The motion of the bed woke her.

"Hey, Babe, I'm glad you're home," she said as she rubbed a hand across his shoulders and back.

"I need to go see Pastor O'Neil tomorrow," Dee said softly, without looking at his wife. There was silence between them for a second. Then, Dee turned and looked at her through the dimness. Caroline had never seen this look from her husband. It was a look of desperation and sadness. She raised herself up in the bed and rested on her elbow. Then, she caressed his face with her hand, saying simply, "I think that's a good idea."

It was around 6 a.m. when Pastor O'Neil's phone rang. His health had forced him to retire from full-time pastoring the year prior. But he had remained a great friend and counselor to many of his former parishioners. "Hello?" was the simple reception of the call.

"Hey, Pastor, this is Dee—Dee Calloway. I'm sorry for callin' so early, but I was wonderin' if you might have some time open that we could talk."

"Hey, Dee, no worries—I've been up for quite some time. I guess it's true what they say about old folks getting up before daylight." A good-natured chuckle indicated the sincerity of the pastor's words.

"Sure, Dee, I would love for us to sit and talk. When would be a good time for you?"

"Well, I've cleared my schedule for the day. Is that too soon?"

"No, no, Dee, today is fine." The chuckle was smaller this time, but still there.

The pastor's study was lined with bookshelves, each one filled with rows of books. Most were about theology, while others dealt with re-lationships—relationships with each other or one's relationship with Christ. The whole room smelt like a library.

"I really appreciate you seein' me today." Dee said, looking around the room. Somehow, in all the years that he had known the man, Dee had never ended up coming to his house.

"Oh, it's my pleasure. Tell me what you have on your mind," the pastor replied.

Dee had never been the kind to take his problems outside of his home. He had always felt that counselors and therapists were for other people, and, if he was being honest, that meant "weak" people, although he would have never allowed himself to believe that as ab-solute. Nevertheless, there he was. It was proof of the weight of his struggle.

Dee began to lay it all out to the pastor. He talked about everything from the pain and confusion of his losses to his relationship with Jody and his deep anger toward him and the subsequent blame that he put on him for the deaths of both his father and his child.

Pastor O'Neil waited and listened to all that Dee had to say. The clock on the north side of the room showed that nearly an hour had passed. Once Dee had finished, the pastor stood and walked over to the window and looked out for a moment, taking notice of the car-dinal hopping around, scratching away in the leaves. Light from the outdoors cascaded over the man's aged features. He thought about all that Dee had just told him. He wanted to settle in his mind what to say to Dee—and how.

"Dee, I've known you and your family for quite some time. I've watched you and your brother grow up. I've seen you become good men of God, and I've seen Him working in your life. I've witnessed Him do some amazing things with you. I want you to understand this, so you'll know where I'm speaking from."

Dee nodded in agreement, as if giving the elder permission to continue.

"Dee, I know it's hard to understand God sometimes. But I'll tell you something that I've learned over the years of watching God work in my life as well as others. He moves with deliberate steps. This is without exception . . . because His motives are always pure and true and right. He never—ever—makes mistakes. The really difficult part is that He never asks for your opinion and He doesn't need your permission. All that He requires of us is faith. You want so badly for Jody to be the cause of your father and child's deaths. You tell yourself that, with this much pain, there has to be someone to blame—someone to punish. So, you've convinced yourself that Jody is that someone. But, in reality, he had nothing to do with their deaths. His proximity makes him guilty in your mind, but life and death are God's business. Your heart, my heart, your father's, your child's—they beat only as long as *He* wants them to. This is where your pain truly comes from.

Dee could feel a lump forming in his throat as the pastor continued. And a decision was opening up before him—he did not *have* to stay angry. He did not *have* to live this way. But part of the problem was, *he had wanted to.*

O'Neil's words continued to extend the invitation to come out of misery and internal prison that Dee so needed, "You've walked most of your life with God. There's been ups and downs—and everything in between—and, along the way, you and God established a rhythm in your relationship . . . an ebb and flow that came to define that relationship. Then, one day, you wake up to find that He's changed that rhythm. He's taken you further out into the deeper waters. When this happened, it wasn't so much the fear of it but rather the heartbreak that troubled you. Because you never thought He would treat you so harshly. When this happens, we can't fall into the mindset that He hates us. He's never hated you. He loves you—and your father, and your daughter. He understands the pain and even the confusion. It's okay to mourn. In fact, He wants you to, because there's a purpose in it. It validates a person's worth in your life. He understands your anger too. But—" a tender, fatherly look overcame the pastor's face, "—you can't let it blind you to His purpose for you. Dee, I've seen God do some remarkable things in your life. Just look at the people that He's put around you. Each life had an influence on you and helped shape you into the man you are now. Do you think that just happened? That was God working on you and in you. Dee, do you know why sometimes we can't see the hands of God in our lives? It's because they're never idle. He's always working for us—even when it seems like He's working against us. I'm not here to beat you up with my words. I just want you to have clarity about your calling. Trusting God can be a very painful thing sometimes."

Dee reached across the small table in front of him and pulled a tissue from the box, then wiped away the tears on his checks.

"You're right, Pastor. You're absolutely right." He paused just for a second, and then continued, "What do I do with this anger?"

"Dee, son, you've got to give that to God. If you don't, it'll always be a barrier between you and God's full purpose. I promise: if you ask, He'll take it."

Dee gave a quick nod, acknowledging the pastor's words before he wiped his face once more, "I have a lot of doubt . . . my journey has never been a conventional one."

"Ha, Dee, it's never conventional when you're following Christ. I think that's the way He wants it. Think about Moses, Jonah, David, or Paul. I wouldn't exactly say that their journeys were very conventional. Understand something, Dee—they all suffered for their calling, some more than others. But yet here we are, thousands of years later, and we are still studying and talking about them. That proves one thing, Dee. Before He used them greatly, He allowed them to be hurt deeply—remember that."

Dee stood and wiped his face one last time, then reached out to hug his friend. "Thank you, Pastor."

"You're very welcome. You can come see me anytime."

"Can we pray before I leave?" Dee asked.

"Absolutely."

The two men knelt on the library floor and prayed. As they did so, the pastor could not help but notice how the light streaming through the window at full force now rested across Dee's shoulder, as if it was a symbol of how God was taking possession of him upon Dee's refreshed invitation.

A month had passed since Dee's visit to the pastor when they got the news about Jody's mother. She had finally lost her battle with cancer. The rumor mill spun a dozen stories about what happened on the night that she died. The most popular one was that Jody had gotten tired of waiting on her to pass, so he smothered with a pillow. The second wildfire tale was that he and some of his friends got high there in the house while she lay dead in the next room.

Unfortunately, sometimes a cruel lie is more readily accepted than the truth. The truth was that Jody had been clean and sober since the wreck. He had waited on his mother hand and foot during her illness, and, when her time drew near, held her in his arms and sang to her as she passed. Afterward, she laid in the funeral home for seven days while Jody tried to raise money for her funeral. In the end, Elizabeth Calloway paid for everything. It was a small, graveside service with only a handful of people, most of which were Calloways. As the small crowd began to leave after the service, Dee stood for a while from afar and watched Jody. Long after the last person had left, Jody stayed by his mother's coffin, his hands resting on top, between a spray of flowers. It was not until his legs started to give way that he finally lifted his hands and slowly walked away.

In the days that followed the funeral, Dee struggled to reconcile his anger toward Jody. He had questions, and he needed answers. He wanted to hear Jody apologize for what he had done. He needed to see the sorrow of regret and remorse in Jody's face—something, anything, to say that he understood how horrifically he had impacted Dee and his family.

The phone at Helen Simms's house rang for several seconds before someone picked up the receiver. Finally, a voice came through on the other end.

"Hello?" It was a quiet voice, much like Helen's.

"Jody, is that you?" Dee asked.

"Yes, it's me, Dee."

"You and I still have some things to talk about," Dee retorted, with a sternness in his voice.

"I understand, Dee. I'll wait for you here."

Dee hung the phone up and climbed into his truck. The drive to Jody's seemed longer today. As Dee drove, he passed by so many places where he and Jody had played as children.

The memories they offered flooded his mind. He thought about their first camping trip and when his parents had met Jody's mother for the first time. "What happened?" Dee thought to himself. "When did things get off track? Could I have been a better friend?"

Dee pulled to the side of the road and killed the engine. It was the first time that he had questioned himself in their relationship. It was enough to make him stop and listen, and what he heard was God speaking to his heart. Dee closed his eyes and began to pray, "Father, I need Your help. I'm about to go in that house and say some things. Please, God, help me to . . . to . . . be a blessin' and not curse." After a few minutes of stillness, with his thoughts slipping back and forth between earnest prayer and honest emotions, Dee started the engine and pulled back onto the road. Soon, he found himself turning into the driveway.

Dee killed the engine once more, opened the door, and stepped out. He wrestled with his emotions as walked up to the front door. He was not sure what would be waiting for him on the other side. Jody had sounded calm earlier on the phone. But it was not a peaceful calm. It had sounded more like a hopeless calm—the way a person sounds when all is lost. Surely, Jody would not try something crazy.

Dee finally made it to the door and knocked. There was silence for a moment, followed by a small voice, "Come in, Dee."

Dee opened the door and stepped inside. The house was dark, but not so dark that you could not see. Jody was sitting in a chair to the left of the front door. His hands were fastened to his knees, as if to brace himself somehow. Although he was not looking down, he was more or less looking into the distance, across the room, seemingly unable to look at Dee as he entered. Dee stared at the human before him for a moment. Neither one had any idea of the battle raging in the other's heart and mind.

Dee was the first to move. He took a deep breath and stepped over to Jody. Jody slowly looked up at Dee's face. He could see the anger through his former friend's furrowed brow and clenched jaw. A clock in the background counted off the seconds as Dee decided what to do next. Suddenly, Dee reached down and placed a hand on each of Jody's bony shoulders. Then, he stood Jody up with one swift jerk. Jody had fully prepared himself for whatever was to come next. He had taken from the people in his life for far too long, and now it was all about to come home to him. Instinctively, he turned his face away and winced in preparation.

"Jody, look at me—look at me!" Dee exclaimed. His hands were still firmly attached to Jody's shoulders. Jody was not a small man, but the emotion surrounding the moment made him feel that Dee could crush him with the slightest provocation. The two men stood facing each other. Both struggled to control their bodies, which were now beginning to slightly tremble from the adrenaline. Jody wanted to shout at the top of his lungs, "I'm sorry! So, so sorry!" But he knew that words were too little, too late.

Dee shook with anger as he stared at Jody. All he felt for him was hate. He wanted to tear him open and pour some of his own pain and hurt into him. Dee wanted to look into Jody's eyes and see the loss in them that he himself had felt over his own father and child. He wanted to see Jody writhe in pain as it twisted his heart and spirit. For a moment, Dee felt himself about to lose control. It was in that moment that Dee heard these words, "He does feel what you are feeling, Dee, and he has lost too."

The truth of the words shook Dee to the core—for a second, his eyes averted from the guilty party as he tried to grasp what he had just heard. Then, he looked back at Jody and spoke the exact opposite of what his heart was screaming. "I DON'T BLAME YOU FOR WHAT HAPPENED TO DAD AND THE BABY," he said with plain, concise words. He wanted Jody to hear each one clearly. They were way too difficult to utter more than once. Dee's expression never changed as he stared into Jody's eyes. He searched intently for the young boy in worn-out clothes—the one who had loved life and been so determined to not let the mistakes of his father define the man that he would become . . . but that boy was gone.

Jody's body melted back into his chair as Dee released him. He felt like his spirit had momentarily left him. He was astonished and relieved by Dee's words. Soon, a loud and heartfelt sobbing, like the sound of waters rushing from a broken dam, could be heard coming from the ragged wingback while Jody's shoulders seemed to periodically vibrate from the emotion. Dee stood in perfect silence, taking in the sound of remorse—teary eyes and heavier breathing characterizing his own person as he did so. It was not the sound that Dee's soul had been demanding for so long, but it was the sound that his spirit needed to hear.

Neither man had wanted to see the other on that day. But God had worked a miracle. Jody had wanted forgiveness and acceptance from

Dee more than anything else. But to ask his friend for such a pardon after all that had happened seemed selfish, if not obscene. The last thing that Dee had wanted was to excuse all of the sorrow that he felt his friend had brought into his life.

Dee's freshly pressed shirt was damp from sweat. The circles around his collar and under his arms were plainly visible through the white cotton. The stress of the meeting had been nearly too much for him. All he wanted now was to go home and fall into Caroline's arms. The room seemed so much smaller now. The dark, paneled walls were riddled with nail holes from random pictures and paintings. The wall opposite the big window bore a faded outline from years of unhindered sunlight. The worn linoleum gave off a dank smell—its Southwestern patterns were nearly invisible: the pale brown and green colors of it could only be seen near the base of the walls, where no traffic had been. The structure's moldy smell, along with hints of spilt beer and cigarettes, gave Dee a twinge of nausea.

"I've got to go." Dee said, turning and reaching for the door.

"Please, wait!" Jody blurted, "I know you don't want to listen to anythin' I have to say, but I need for you to hear this. Then, if you want, we never have to speak again."

Dee paused for a second and drew a long, slow breath. The miracle that God had worked a few minutes before seemed incredibly delicate to him—Dee was afraid that if he didn't leave now, something else would break from the strain of it all. With his back still turned to Jody, he replied in a low, exhausted voice, "Say what you have to say."

Jody began, stumbling a little at first, "I, I know what, what you did for me, and . . . and I can't express how much I appreciate it." As he said it, despite the fact that Dee could not see him, Jody motioned his hand toward the scars on his face and shoulder. "People like you and your family are uncommon. You don't find compassion and kindness like y'all's every day, and, believe me, I know. I, I took advantage of that compassion and kindness—and I am so, so very sorry."

Dee still could not look at Jody, but he turned his head slightly, trying to catch the words as they tumbled out.

"I thought about this while I was lyin' on the side of the road after the wreck. I thought about this for a while actually—then, somethin' happened. I don't know if I died or I just passed out and was dreamin'. But I found myself in hell—or, at least, that's the only way I know to describe it." Jody's eyes widened at the recall of it, "There were rows and rows of people. They were all marchin' in one direction—like you see in the army movies. As I looked closer at their faces, I could see they were all cryin' and wailin' as they marched on toward this pit. And this pit . . . it was on fire." Jody began to struggle even more as he described his vision, his voice becoming thicker with emotion. "They would . . . all march right up . . . right up to the edge . . . and then fall in—screamin' and pleadin'. But it was like they couldn't stop. I ran up to them and tried to help . . . I tried to stop them. But . . . it was like they couldn't see me." Jody paused to wipe his face, fresh tears having started to run over his cheekbones. "That's when it hit me, Dee. That's when I got a good look at their faces. These were people I knew, some we even went to school with. I can't describe the horror in their eyes. Then . . . then, I saw him. It was my father. As they marched on by, I could see him. Then, suddenly, they stopped—and he looked straight at me. I . . . I was completely frozen. He turned to the empty space beside him and then back to me. In a split second, they all began to march again. That's when I knew, Dee—that's when I knew that spot was for . . . for *me*. The next thing I remember was comin' to as I heard the siren from the ambulance. I laid there in that ditch, covered in dirt, blood, and glass. It was the most grateful I'd ever been in my life. It was in that moment I gave it all to God . . . I could hear the EMTs makin' their way down to me. I knew I was in bad shape. But I wasn't afraid like I was before. If I didn't make it, that was fine. He had already saved me . . . I've been clean and sober since then. And . . . in a way, I'm grateful for these scars it gave me. They're reminders of the damage I did and the different person I am now."

Dee had no words. He had wished nothing but hate and destruction on Jody since the day that he was brought into the hospital—to leave now, without saying a word, would not result in a complete reconciliation. A brief prayer for wisdom led him to his next words.

"Jody, I have somethin' to say as well . . ." Dee's head dropped a little, his eyes focusing on the door handle as he made his utterance, "I have harbored a terrible amount of hate toward you. I was consumed with your destructive ways and disregard for your mother and my family. And I wished some bad things on you, and comin' here today to forgive you was not my intent . . . and . . . for those things . . . I . . . I ask for *your* forgiveness."

Jody stood to his feet, the idea of being asked *to forgive* astounded him. Finally, he said, "I understand, Dee. But you didn't take Momma from me, and I can't give you back your baby or your dad that I took from you. And I don't know what to say other than as long as you can forgive me, then it's all in the past."

Dee turned to face his friend and, with a tearful nod, opened his arms, simultaneously giving full surrender to God in that moment as well as offering proof of his position toward Jody. Jody accepted the invitation and stepped into a brief but meaningful hug. As they let go, Jody, overwhelmed with gratitude, said, "You know what, Dee? God sure is good."

Dee just looked back and, finally calm on the inside himself, said, "All the time."

Not long after that day in Simms home, Jody sold the property and moved away. No one really knew where he went or what for. And, as far as Dee and his family were concerned, it did not really matter. He and Jody had parted ways not only as friends on the road to restoration but also as brothers in Christ—a bond that runs deeper than friendship itself. Life around the Calloway home slowly returned to normal, as the release of Dee's anger meant in turn personal freedom from the despair and depression that had hung over his household like a lingering cloud. As time progressed, there was work and school and much love.

It was close to a year before Dee heard any word from Jody. It came in a letter. He had been living in a little town just outside Jackson, the capitol. He had decided to go to school. Intrigue swayed Dee's features as he absorbed the message:

Dear Dee,

It's been awhile. I hope everyone is doing well. I meant to write sooner. But I've been quite busy. I decided to go back to school and get my counseling degree. I know you're probably in shock. Ha! But I think I have something to offer. I want to specialize in young people with substance abuse. They need people that can identify. I want to give them some hope. If I can.

You told the story once about the thin, pink line on your father's arm. There's something I've learned, Dee. There are an awful lot of us that have that thin, pink line on the inside, and it takes a whole lot longer to heal when it is on the inside.

Dee, I wrote this letter for two reasons. First, I need y'all's prayers. College is not easy, in case you didn't know. Second, I need to share something with you about the day you came to see me after Momma's funeral. Because it's a big part of why I'm here.

I had been up most of the night before. I just couldn't sleep. I was so depressed and lonely. At one point I went and bought a bottle of whiskey. I came home, sat that bottle on the table and went and got Momma's pistol. I just sat there, trying to decide which one to use. That's when I began to talk to God. I asked Him if I was now "a new creation," as the preacher called it, then why am I sitting here with this gun in my hand? If I had known then what I know now. The fact that I hadn't broken the seal on that bottle meant that I wasn't the same.

But I continued to talk to Him. I pleaded for a sign. I kept asking Him, over and over, for some kind of reassurance that I wasn't on my own in this and that what had happened to me was real. That's when the phone rang. It was you. My friend coming to my rescue one more time. You've saved my life more than once, Dee. You and your family truly have been the hands and feet of God in my life, and I still come to tears when I stop and think about it all. We never know what struggles the other person is going through and they don't know yours. Only God knows these things. That's why we just have to trust Him and let Him lead us, so He can use us for His purpose. So, thank you, Dee, for letting Him use you. I'm truly a different person now, and you helped me find His purpose for me.

Your friend,

Jody Simms

Dee sat for a while, holding the letter in his hands. Then, he walked into the kitchen and extended it toward Caroline.

"You need to read this. It's from Jody."

She gave Dee a slight look of concern as she took the paper from his hands and began to read. He watched her intently, wanting to know her thoughts as they came to her. As she neared the end, her eyes began to feel with tears.

"Oh, Dee, I don't know what to say. This is the most beautiful letter I've ever read. What are you goin' to do?"

"What do you mean?" Dee replied.

"We need to do more than just pray."

The next morning, Dee drove out to his mother and father's. There, he made the walk across his parents' yard to the flower garden. He walked up and down the rows, clearing his mind and opening his heart. He prayed for Jody, for Caroline, for the children, and for his family. Then, he asked one simple question, hoping for a clear answer, "What's next? What's next, God?"

Fifteen

Legacies

It had already been five years since Dan passed. Seasons change, and they keep on moving. One day, we are enjoying the summer's warmth; and the next, feeling the bite of winter's chill. God designed it this way—life moves between experiencing the mountain tops and the valleys. Hopefully, as we experience the variety, we learn to trust Him to carry us through it all.

Tom and Hayley were running the farm now, along with their two teenage sons, Tom Jr. and William Davis. But everybody called William Davis "Dee."

Uncle Frank still helped as much as he could with the farm, but he spent a good deal of his time with Frank Jr., who had retired from the U.S. Army and moved home to help take care of his aging father.

Jody had finished his degree and started counseling young men who were suffering from substance abuse.

Joel Calloway had become a football star like his dad and eventually played for the Ole Miss Rebels. He then graduated from the university with a degree in history and started teaching at Pelo High School. Mary Elizabeth had gone on to get her license as a nurse practitioner, after which she began working in the hospice unit at Niobi Baptist. Both had married and, in time, would bless their grandmother, Mamaw Bett, with a total of four great-grandchildren.

Elizabeth still lived in the same house that she and Dan had built, spending her summers taking care of her great-grandchildren and tending her flower garden.

Dee and Caroline had continued their careers in medicine, establishing themselves in their community through their professions.

Simon F. Catlet Construction were the words on the sign on the door. "Dee and Caroline, are you sure that you want to do this? It will be quite expensive." The word *quite* was given a particularly meaningful emphasis as the architect said it.

"Simon, are you tryin' to talk yourself out of work?" Dee asked with a slight grin. "Caroline and I have seen your estimate and are confident in God's resources. The family has already donated the land; so, yes, we absolutely want to do this."

Three months passed before the next meeting occurred. When it did, Mr. Catlet presented the blueprints for Dee and Caroline's approval.

"Okay, here are the plans. You will notice that we added all the details to your specifications."

Dee and Caroline inspected the blueprints, being careful to take note of all the important additions.

"It looks good to me, Honey. What do you think?" Dee asked Caroline.

"I think it looks wonderful, Babe. Everythin' is exactly the way we want it, even down to the design on the front of the buildin'. See it here?" Caroline's finger traced the section that she was the most pleased with.

"Speaking of the design, Dee," started in Mr. Catlet, curiosity finally getting the better of him, "Where did you come up with that? A cross with three eagle feathers at the base of it—that's kinda unusual. What was your inspiration?"

"Well, the inspiration came from a good friend of mine. Those three feathers represent him, and the cross represents Him," Dee said, motioning toward the heavens in the latter part of the sentence. He then added, "All healin' begins at the cross." Dee knew that the highly educated architect was far from being a believer, and Dee was not going to waste an opportunity to point him on the right path.

"So, Simon, when can we get started?" Caroline's gentle voice broke in.

"Well, we can start pouring the foundation the first of next week, if the rain holds off."

Dee and Caroline smiled at one another, then they stood and shook Mr. Catlet's hand and thanked him.

Six months had passed since the construction company had broken ground on Dee and Caroline's dream. The day had come for the dedication. All of the special invitations had been sent, and the guests had arrived. They walked around the lobby of the new building, in awe of its beauty.

"Dee, I cannot believe you and Caroline are doing this. It's an absolutely phenomenal place. You two will do a lot of good . . . a lot of lives will be changed here," Dr. Hault murmured admiringly, smiling as he shook Dee's hand and gave Caroline a slight hug.

"Thanks, Bob. That's what we're hopin' for. We're really excited—and humbled—to be able to give this to the community."

The time came for the dedication, and all the guests found a seat in the commons area of the new structure. Dee stood up from his chair and walked to the podium. He could see his mother, children, and grandchildren, all sitting on the front row. He took note of all the familiar faces—people he had worked with, family friends, and relatives. Today was the culmination of a life of trying to follow. He paused for a moment and looked back at Caroline, who was sitting in the chair adjacent to his. He smiled and gave her a wink. She just smiled back. He turned and began to speak. "Let me say first that I appreciate everyone showin' up today. It is such a blessin' to Caroline and to me. What you see around you is a culmination of five years of prayer and work. I want to share with you how this dream came about, and hopefully, along the way, you will be inspired. If there is one thing that I have learned in life, it's that you have to have patience. You can't rush things. Especially when you're tryin' to follow God. You see, He has His own timetable, and He does things exactly—and I do mean *exactly*—the way that they are supposed to be done. The problem is, we struggle to wait on Him when, in reality, we should never wait on God. We should learn to wait with Him. When you learn to wait with Him, you accept His will. That means, when you turn thirty-four and He suddenly decides that you need to go back to medical school and become a doctor, you just need to say, 'Alright, then!' "

A wave of laughter rolled over the crowd in response to Dee's humor.

As it faded, Dee continued. "When you accept God's will and begin to wait with Him, you accept that—wherever He takes you, however long He asks you to stay, and whatever the job may be—it's the right thing. But it will require a certain amount of waitin'. You see, *waitin'* is a word I am now well acquainted with. It seems that most of my life I have been waitin' on somethin' or someone. It is a word that, although you may become acquainted with it, you never get used to. But I think it is the attitude in which we wait that makes the difference. They say good things come to those who wait. I'm inclined to agree. But always remember that, most of the time, the size of the 'good thing' is in direct proportion to the amount of time you will wait; therein lies the attitude. I would like to share a poem with you about waitin', if I may:

In life, I waited to be born.
In Mother's arms, I waited to walk.
In night's darkness, I waited for the morn.
In Father's love, I waited to talk.
In learning, I waited to be smart.
In play, I waited for my friend.
In fighting, I waited for the start.
In school, I waited for the end.

In Christ, I waited for His call.

In my youth, I waited for manhood to arrive.

In disappointment, I waited to be tall.

In faith, I waited for the blessings of life.

In work, I waited for the pay.

In love, I waited for her heart.

In marriage, *I do* I waited for her to say.

In fatherhood, I waited to do my part.

In my old age, I waited for rest.

In the end, I waited for the cost.

It was with all the great things that I had been blessed,

and all the sacrifices were not lost.

In life, we must be patient and wait with God. He has great things to do for those who are willin' to work. He has great blessin's for those who are willin' to receive, and He has great places to take those who are willin' to follow. That, my friends, is patience's perfect work. I tell the story often of seein' our family doctor tend to a horrific cut on my father's arm when I was a child. He took such care, and, in no time, all that remained was a thin, pink line. I was amazed. It was actually the first real-life event that made me want to be a doctor. A few years back, a really good friend of mine opened my mind and heart up to the fact that there are a host of people around us—every day—that carry their thin, pink line on the inside. Those wounds take the longest to heal. I have spent the last decade helpin' to heal the wounds on the outside. The ones we could see. Today, we start to help those whose wounds are on the inside. I would like to present to you The John Tuleeves' Foundation for Alcohol and Substance Abuse."

The guests rose to their feet and applauded.

Dee smiled and nodded toward the crowd, thanking them again for their attendance. "I'd like for everyone to stay. There are refreshments provided. Feel free to tour the facility."

The guests began to move around, continuing to take note of the facility's beauty and state-of-the-art accommodations. One of the faces in the crowd belonged to a much-restored and significantly healthier Jody Simms. Dee made his way through a wave of handshakes and congratulations until he found Jody. He smiled and gave him a great, big hug and said, "Jody, I'm so glad that you made it today. It's really good to see you."

"Dee, I'm glad to be here," Jody uttered, pausing for a moment to take in Dee's face—the rekindling of their connection had been no small feat, "You and Caroline are doin' a wonderful thing here."

"Well, thank you—God has really blessed us. I have somethin' special that I'd like to show you," Dee said. He then led Jody down the main hall. They walked until they came to the door that noted, "Facility Chapel," with a gold plaque underneath that read, "In honor of Helen Simms." Below those words was a portion of scripture, from Proverbs 31:28, that read, "Her children rise up and call her blessed . . ."

Jody reached up and brushed his fingers across the plaque and began to cry. Dee placed his hand on his friend's shoulder. For Dee, watching his childhood friend's moving reaction was almost a holy moment.

After his tears calmed, Jody regained himself and turned to Dee and said, "Let's go in and have a seat."

The two entered the chapel and took a seat up front. Jody soaked in all of its beauty; the artwork, the architecture, the whole feeling of being at peace.

"Jody, there is one more thing I need to say," Dee said as he looked over at him, "I want you to come here and work. I want you to be head counselor. You need to share your story and give hope to those who are hurtin'. Will you do that for me?"

Jody's face winced as he was overcome with emotion. He simply nodded yes as the words would not come. After a moment, Jody regained himself and reached over and hugged his friend. The two men sat for a moment, staring up at the lighted cross that was hanging on the wall at the front of the room.

Dee was the first to break the silence. He first looked over at Jody, whose gaze was still fixed on the cross, then back to the cross and said, "God is good."

Jody just smiled, something in his heart being sealed and settled at last, his gaze still latched on his very hope and Savior as he replied, "All the time."

Acknowledgement

I have to start by thanking my Heavenly Father from whom all blessings flow.

My profound gratitude goes to my amazing grandmother and favorite author, Opal Sanderford. She was a small lady with a large presence, raising three children in a time when that was uncommon. Although she has been gone from this earth for many years, her creativity and love for the written word continues to inspire me.

I am humbled by the love and dedication of our children and grandchildren. I am deeply grateful to Austin, for being my long-suffering "scribe", and to Blake, Bethany, Hanna, Daniel, Simon, Ashley and Samuel for being a never ending source of inspiration.

I am forever thankful to my parents, Richard and Carol, for a lifetime of love and to my in-laws, Martha and Snap, who loved me like their own.

Special thanks to the Sanderford clan, the Lucius clan, and all of my brothers by blood or bond, for bringing the characters to life.

Lastly, I would like to thank my editor, Emma Hatcher, for her valuable suggestions, insightful comments, skillful editing, and patience.

"Remember"